PENGUIN CRIME FICTION

THINK ON DEATH

David Willis McCullough compiled two collections of detective stories, *Great Detectives* and *City Sleuths and Tough Guys*, before writing his first mystery starring Ziza Todd. He is a Member of the Editorial Board of the Book-of-the-Month Club. He lives in Hastings-on-Hudson, New York. His second mystery is *Point No-Point*.

Think on Death

A HUDSON VALLEY MYSTERY

**DAVID WILLIS
McCULLOUGH**

PENGUIN BOOKS

PENGUIN BOOKS
Published by the Penguin Group
Viking Penguin, a division of Penguin Books USA Inc.,
375 Hudson Street, New York, New York 10014, U.S.A.
Penguin Books Ltd, 27 Wrights Lane,
London W8 5TZ, England
Penguin Books Australia Ltd, Ringwood,
Victoria, Australia
Penguin Books Canada Ltd, 10 Alcorn Avenue, Suite 300,
Toronto, Ontario, Canada M4V 3B2
Penguin Books (N.Z.) Ltd, 182–190 Wairau Road,
Auckland 10, New Zealand

Penguin Books Ltd, Registered Offices:
Harmondsworth, Middlesex, England

First published in the United States of America by Viking Penguin,
a division of Penguin Books USA Inc., 1991
Published in Penguin Books 1992

1 3 5 7 9 10 8 6 4 2

PUBLISHER'S NOTE
This is a work of fiction. Names characters, places and incidents
either are the product of the author's imagination or are used
fictitiously, and any resemblance to actual persons, living or
dead, events, or locales is entirely coincidental.

THE LIBRARY OF CONGRESS HAS CATALOGUED THE HARDCOVER AS FOLLOWS:
McCullough, David W.
Think on death : a Hudson Valley mystery / David Willis McCullough
p. cm.
ISBN 0-670-83493-9 (hc.)
ISBN 0 14 01.3942 7 (pbk.)
I. Title.
PS3563.C35293T48 1991
813'.54—dc20   90–50322

Printed in the United States of America
Set in Garamond #3

FOR KATY AND BEN AND THE OTHERS
WHO WERE ONCE CHILDREN
OF THE HIGH FALLS HOLDING COMPANY

I range the fields with pensive tread,
And pace the hollow rooms.
And feel (companion of the dead)
I'm living in the tombs.

ABRAHAM LINCOLN, 1846

Think on Death

1

⌬

The *e* on *olde* was new, "Olde Smyrna Road," and so was the street sign, larger than any proper street sign should be, Colonial gray, black and white, shaped like the top of a Chippendale highboy, with a golden crown in the center of the curve on top. If she had made the turn more slowly, Naomi was sure she would have seen little lines drawn around the crown, rays of light. Nothing new about that.

She was expecting changes. She had prepared herself for them. More than twenty-five years had passed since she had been back to the old place. More than a quarter century, a quarter of a century. So far, the changes had been more a matter of housekeeping, wear and tear. The Thruway was beginning to look a bit shabby, too many blacktop patches on the long concrete road that had been clean and new the last time she had seen it, too many Day-Glo plastic cones and temporary signs warning of single-lane traffic ahead. At the exit, the toll taker had wished her a good day and a happy weekend, more cheer than she would have expected from a civil-service employee. Or was he just letting her know that he belonged there and she was just passing through?

A Taco Frankie's that must have closed as soon as it opened was just beyond the exit, its shiny new plastic burros grazing in a parking lot choked with weeds. Beyond that was an old stone farmhouse—Dutch-built and low to the ground—so close to the road that Naomi could remember when she and Lew had only to slow down the pickup truck to throw empty beer cans through its glassless windows. Now there was glass and crowded flower boxes, a freshly painted flagpole and a sign that said "Antiques." Just "Antiques," no cute name. Naomi approved of that. The old yellow wooden firehouse farther down the road had been replaced by a cinder-block affair with a blue neon sign that blinked RESCUE SQUAD even at four o'clock in the afternoon. Then came the turnoff to the Old—no, *Olde*—Smyrna Road. She braked hard and heard something roll across the trunk.

Before Lew's family had the name changed to guide that first wave of tourists to Smyrna so long ago, it had been the Old King's Road, before that the Old Kingston Road and before that, with no name at all, it was just the road that led to Kingston, then a good day's ride away. Running north and south along the last stretch of flatland in the valley below the great blue wall of the Catskill Mountains to the west, it had been built to connect farms, and some of them were still there. But there were now more trailers than Naomi remembered, well-established trailers with picket fences and wishing wells and deer antlers mounted over the doors, so many identical antlers over so many identical doorways that Naomi wondered if they were plastic, bought at Sears along with the aluminum screen- and storm-door sets.

Lew's family—if you could call them that—were the Quicks. In Naomi's purse on the front seat next to her were two carefully folded pieces of paper. One was a letter addressed to her. It was only a sentence long, typewritten, but it mentioned Lew, calling him Llewelyn, just as everyone else did. The other was a newspaper clipping, the obituary of Aunt Nan, "Anna May Quick, 93, Commune Survivor." It had appeared yesterday, two days after Naomi had received the unsigned letter. The *Times* did not have much to say about Aunt Nan, a few words about her being the last direct family survivor of one of America's most financially successful nineteenth-century utopian communities. Then there was a brief rundown of the history of Smyrna, how it had gone from being just another crackpot—the *Times* didn't actually use that word, but Naomi could read between the lines—upstate religious commune to an important manufacturing concern, still in business but without the ideological tenets of the original enterprise. Funeral service to be held at the Smyrna complex near Catskill, New York, Saturday. Tomorrow. No survivors. That we know of, Naomi thought.

Dead ahead was the stunted tower of the Dutch Reformed Church. When you come to the church, they used to tell visitors to Smyrna, slow down and get ready to turn left. Its needlelike steeple had blown off in a hurricane decades ago, but when Naomi and Lew used to wander around the church's cemetery, the steeple had still been maintained, a fallen soldier given a fresh coat of white paint every few years, lying next to the cemetery gate as though in hope that Judgment Day would bring not only the resurrection of the dead but the reerection of the steeple.

The ugliness of the place was what had appealed to Naomi and Lew—its ugliness, its privacy and the fact that it seemed to interest no one else at Smyrna. From a distance the graveyard had looked like one of those autumnal New England cemeteries that photograph so well, crooked rows of thin, stately slabs, a few ornamental urns, each gravestone carved with the face of a winged angel and, no doubt, inscribed with a suitably mournful verse. Up close, these angels became smug, smirking, petulant, a congregation of Cinderella's stepsisters, clearly the work of a self-taught nineteenth-century stone carver who had been so fortunate in finding willing customers that he had never moved on to try his luck elsewhere. Maybe he was the preacher's brother-in-law, maybe the preacher himself moonlighting. As for the inscriptions, there had been some scattered attempts at verse or Biblical quotation, a few were in Dutch (*Hier lycht begraven . . .*), but most simply read: *Think on Death.*

Naomi was so busy looking back through her rearview mirror, trying to catch a glimpse of the cemetery, that she forgot to slow down and almost missed the turnoff—a newer, wider one than before. She slammed on the brakes. The car slipped sideways on the fresh gravel and just missed a dark-green pickup truck that had been waiting for her to pass. As her car rocked to a stop, something rolled again across the trunk and smashed into the tire iron, and the car filled with the smoky smell of scotch. Her lungs filled with it. She could taste it on her tongue. Shit, thought Naomi, totting up how much a fifth—let alone a quart—cost these days. Plus the bother of an extra trip into town. She rested her head momentarily against the steering wheel, caught her breath and looked back, trying to reconstruct what had happened. The truck had not moved, but the driver was leaning out of the window and looking back at her. After a few seconds, a few seconds longer than necessary, he waved with exaggerated slowness. It wasn't a greeting but a dismissal, and as he pulled away, spinning his tires and throwing gravel back so that it splattered against her car, she noticed the golden crown painted on the green door. No writing, but a crown large enough so you could see the lines of light radiating from it.

The driveway was, indeed, a new one, she could see that now. A huge signboard, still wrapped in canvas, was at the intersection she had skidded through. She drove on carefully, as though she did not quite believe the blacktop was dry. The road curved through a well-ordered pine forest, all the trees in perfect line whichever way you looked, just like tombstones in a military cemetery, the dead lower limbs—always called "brash" at Smyrna—removed to the height of six feet. Naomi remembered hearing about the summer they planted those trees. Putting the seedlings in the ground had been the easy part; planning where each tree would go was a pain in the ass, committee meetings deep into the night, until Young Father Quick (Lew said he must have been in his eighties then) lost patience and put a stop to the whole process. The old man laid it out himself, Lew said, walking the land, poking his stick where he wanted the trees to be planted. Which, after all, was how all problems had always been solved at Smyrna.

The forest, which cut the community off from the road, became known as the plantation. The trees grew quickly, and by the time Smyrna's summer camp was in operation—when Naomi came to know the place—one of the daily work details was the Brash Patrol, squads of campers who kept the plantation tidy and the wood boxes well supplied with kindling. When she and Lew ran through the plantation to get to the Dutch Reformed cemetery he had to stoop just a little bit, and when he forgot he got a mouthful of pine needles.

The new road did not cut straight through the woods but curved to give the impression that the plantation was bigger than it was. Along the way were several more signs, wrapped like the first in dark canvas. They reminded Naomi of the time her senior class in high school went to New York City during Easter vacation. She had ducked into St. Patrick's to see what a Catholic church looked like, but all the statues were shrouded in purple cloth for Holy Week, wrapped up and bagged like silverware in a chest, like the new signs at Smyrna. When the road came out into the bright, open fields again, Mansion House was directly ahead, and for a moment it seemed as though nothing had changed at all: the brick pillars, the yellow wood trim, the round window over the huge front door, open as always, the tall chimneys, the ivy that seemed about to reclaim the whole structure, the sense that except for the front door and the pillars and the window there was no order to the building, simply a maze of wings running in all directions.

In front of Mansion House was a huge circular driveway surrounding a grassy lawn called the Heart. It was not heart-shaped, nothing so obvious as that, but it was where Old Father Quick, Smyrna's founder, had held his first outdoor meetings, years before Mansion House was built, and it was supposed to be the spiritual and physical heart of Smyrna. At least, Naomi remembered, it was the only patch of grass on the place that was watered, rolled and taken care of as a proper lawn should be. No flowers, of course.

The driveway was parked solid with cars, a fine turnout for a funeral, and off to the side, where there had once been a gazebo and a stand of mountain laurel, was a new parking lot with more cars, even a few yellow school buses. Had all of them, Naomi wondered, really come to say goodbye to dear old Aunt Nan? Great-aunt Nan, the last of the Quicks, unless, of course, Lew was still around somewhere? Of course not, even if her name rated six inches on the crowded *Times* obituary page. No one had given Aunt Nan a thought in twenty years; the old girl had been gaga for at least that long, cooped up in her suite in a back wing of Mansion House, cared for by nurses paid for by the corporation. By the stock-holders, most of whose cars were now parked around the Heart. No, Naomi thought, there might be a last-minute funeral on the program for tomorrow, but this had the ear-marks of business, a gathering of stockholders, the salesmen brought in from around the country (school-bused from the Hudson train station or the Albany airport). It was the annual meeting of Olde Smyrna Community, and the final plans were being made for the days when they would unwrap the canvas from those new signs.

And had Naomi herself returned to Smyrna just for a funeral? Not likely, she thought, not bloody likely.

She did not turn into the circular driveway but kept on, down a steep slope until she was driving parallel to a stream more swollen with water than usual for this late in the spring. The water would be freezing cold. It was as chilling as the Maine ocean even in August, fresh from the Catskills, having tumbled down one waterfall to another over a length of nearly twenty miles. At one time she could have named them all ("The Falls" was a camp cheer shouted faster and faster as it went along): Kaaterskill, Bastion, Fawn's Leap, Bridge Falls, something, something, Dog's Hole, Niobe, Fern Wood, something, something, Little Falls, High Falls and then—drawn out until it sounded like a train conductor calling—*Schmeer-naaaaaaa!*

At the foot of Smyrna Falls was a jumble of brick buildings, the old wooden-box factory, the first of the community's business enterprises and as successful in its time as all the rest would be. Work had recently been done on them, Naomi could see that. Fresh glass, still with PPG stickers, was in many of the windows. The old waterwheel was again turning, and there was another new parking lot, this one with a freshly peeled log fence around it. But there was no disguising the hideous brightness of the brick, redder than any red-brick building ought to be, even after a hundred years. The bricks had been fired locally, over along the river near the town of Catskill, and they had been a bargain. When Old Father Quick built Mansion House, he sent up to Albany to a quality kiln and got bricks the color that bricks were meant to be.

Farther downstream, just before the creek went around a bend, was the dam—only its uprights now remained above water—that formed the camp's swimming area. It had a grand name, everything at Smyrna did, but at some point the kids started calling it the Frog Pond, and the name caught on. Except in the slick brochures the Quicks published to advertise the camp. There, photographed so you could see the Falls and the rustic swimming pavilion but not the box factory, it was called Lake Smyrna.

The old pavilion still stood, a place where parents could get out of the sun or, more often, rain during visiting-day swim meets, and from the look of it, it had a new roof. Naomi drove around a log that blocked the dirt road at the far end of the new parking lot and headed back through a ragged forest not planned or planted by a member of the Quick family, toward *her* Smyrna, the place she had first come to as a camp counselor thirty years before, the place where she met Llewelyn Quick, fell in love and married, married him right there in the mess hall, with every boy in the camp as their best man. And where she lost him. She was not being euphemistic. She abhorred euphemisms. One day, not long after their second anniversary, Lew was simply no longer there. She had lost him, and no one had been able to find him.

The road was bumpy but seemed well used. The woods thinned out into what looked like abandoned farmland, but the place had not been allowed to grow wild. In the center of the clearing was the old mess hall, a high-peaked frame farmhouse with one absurdly out-of-proportion wing tacked onto the side. It ran toward the creek and was dominated by an off-kilter stone fireplace that looked in danger of pulling the whole place down. Close by was a tiny Dutch stone house, a miniature of the antique shop near the Thruway. The cutout sign nailed over its weathered front door identified it as the Gnomes' House. The youngest campers stayed there, and because she was the camp's only female counselor, that was Naomi's home her first summer at Smyrna. The other buildings were hidden in the trees.

She pulled her car around behind the mess hall. With luck the old coach house would still be standing and she could tuck the car away in there. It was, and although its wooden floorboards groaned alarmingly when she drove inside and the sliding doors would not slide, the car was out of sight. She was not hiding, Naomi told herself, but there was no need to advertise her presence. She was not looking forward to opening the trunk, and when she did, the mess from the broken scotch bottle was worse than she had feared. Who would have thought the old man had so much blood in him? (A little Macbeth, she thought, is better than crying over spilt scotch.) The bottle had shattered, and there were bits of glass everywhere. The fumes were enough to take your breath away. Worse yet, the vinyl carryall was soaked, and in there were all her clothes. (Does waterproof mean scotchproof?)

She picked out the larger pieces of glass and dumped them into an empty oil drum, and she mopped up what she could with copies of the *Weekly Eagle* that had been stacked in a corner. Some were only a month old. Perhaps the place had not been abandoned after all.

She threw the carryall over her shoulder, closed the trunk and crossed the overgrown lawn to the back door. Covering the back wall of the building was a metal spiderweb of scaffolding, and at the top a stiff canvas drop cloth moved gently in the breeze. Like all good Smyrna buildings, the mess hall was unlocked. Inside, the kitchen was as cool as a root cellar and as long and narrow as the Brooklyn brownstone apartment she had rented for the past few years. The stove was where the stove used to be. The refrigerator, too was in the same old place. In fact, they seemed to be the same old stove and refrigerator.

The wooden shelves were still full of heavy crockery cups and plates (each decorated with a blue ring around its edge). A familiar green-painted table sat in the center of the room, littered with dead petals from wildflowers that someone had left in a now-dried-out milk bottle, wildflowers and mouse droppings. There was a slight hint of damp rot in the air and the cat-pee smell of bottled cooking gas. All in all, the kitchen was just as it always was when Naomi entered it for the first time after a long winter.

She took her carryall with her as she went up the stairs to the mess hall itself, the Big Room, as they always called it. One end was taken up with the huge stone fireplace, framed on each side by matching Gothic-style dumbwaiters, the fanciest bit of woodworking in the place. Fresh-cooked meals came up from the kitchen on the right, and dirty dishes were sent down to the washroom on the left. Mornings in the valley were so cool that beginning on August first there was a fire every morning for breakfast. The boys would line up outside in a circle around the flag every morning. After a prayer, they checked the head count, but no one was ever missing, at least not until Lew. Then they would march in to eat, the fire already burning away.

The old sign still hung over the hearth: carved out of wood was a golden crown and under it the words "(but thou art rich)," which was the only Biblical quotation Naomi had ever seen that included a parenthesis. She and Lew had been married in front of that fireplace and its twin dumbwaiters, with a congregation of campers, everyone from Mansion House willing to make the trip through the woods and a few of her friends from the city. The kids had been too full of giggles for their own good. The Mansion House people were painfully polite. Naomi's city friends acted as though she were institutionalized and they were there on visiting hours. Which meant they all laughed too much. But the music was wonderful. The Mansion House people could all sing hymns with a passion, and so many were doing harmony it was often impossible to pick out the melody. Aunt Nan had played the upright piano, her back straight as a board, raising her hands—fingers dramatically arched just as she had been taught as a young girl—a good foot and a half from the keyboard and letting them fall. Every verse ended with a chromatic flourish. No one watched the bride.

The piano was still there. Naomi raised the lid and struck a chord, a metallic harpsichord clank followed by a scurrying of tiny feet deep inside. The sheet music on top—a piece by Erik Satie, *The Rodgers and Hart Song Book*, a coverless hymn book—was all water-stained, and the floorboards around it billowed like farrows in a cornfield. The mystery of the leaking roof had obviously remained unsolved. The old dining tables were gone, but a number of green wooden chairs were still scattered around. Someone had brought in an oversized Ping-Pong table from the games shed and an undersized pool table from a local garage sale, the price tag still on one of the legs.

Naomi went through the door into what had been the living

room of the original farmhouse. When the camp offices had
been there, the walls were covered with group photographs
of year after year of campers. Now they were gone, replaced
by stuffed deer heads, more tag-sale items. Upstairs were
bedrooms for special visitors and one that had been hers and
Lew's, the old master bedroom at the front where on quiet
nights they could hear the waterfall and, after especially heavy
downpours, smell the fresh mud in the stream. She climbed
the paint-chipped stairs. The old green wallpaper was still
there, some 1930s version of William Morris chrysanthemums and ivy broken only now and then with rips and a
surprisingly white flash of plaster. She left her carryall on
the torn quilt that covered the bare mattress on the bed (not,
she thought, the one that used to be there) and went back
downstairs.

It was getting dark, but she did not turn on the lights. She
did not even check to see if the electricity was connected.
She opened the front door and pulled over a rocking chair
so she could sit and look out through the oval screen door
(patched, but patched neatly and recently). She was careful
to sit back far enough in the hall so that no one going by—
if by any chance someone should go by—could see her.

Think on Death, those old gravestones had warned over
and over again. Think about the Dead. Aunt Nan. Lew, if he
was dead. Being back made her realize how little she actually
thought about Lew, how little she could actually remember
him. That body that had once seemed so important to her,
what had it actually looked like? When she remembered his
face, it was old photographs she recalled. She remembered
one of his knees, with a broad scar from some boyhood
accident that had healed as clear as mica. His right knee or
his left? She remembered that when they were first married
he stood on the bed while getting dressed in the morning
(why?) but soon got over that. (If you grew up in a place as
cold and drafty as Mansion House, he said, you would stay
off the cold floor, too.)

Think on death. A winter caretaker had once died in this house, down in the kitchen, next to his bottle. He had hemorrhaged with the bottle all but empty. It had been a terrible mess. Think on death. Her father had died hooked up to the most modern machines medicine could provide in the best hospital money could buy. And that was a terrible mess. Lew—by just disappearing—had been terribly tidy.

After she lost him she left Smyrna and never came back. She found writing jobs here and there—in an advertising agency, a radio station, finally on a small newspaper whose publisher refused to admit he served an all-black city. There were enough white suburbs (where the publisher actually lived) to get away with it, for a time. She did neighborhood news, social events, school-board meetings, every morning checking the overnight police reports to see if there had been any crimes involving whites, white criminals, white victims. If so, she wrote them up. But if you were black you could murder or be murdered and it wouldn't be news. Black news was when a retired postal worker and his wife celebrated their seventy-fifth wedding anniversary, surrounded by their five children, all Howard University graduates.

Think on death.

All those corpses, all unreported amid the news of the Lions and Kiwanis and Rotary and the Rainbow Girls and the battle over the new school-board budget. There had been drinks after work with friends, then drinks after work and, finally, just drinks. Just drunks. Time somehow slipped by, and now she was back at Smyrna, sitting in a familiar rocking chair, feeling the breeze through the screen door, listening to the waterfall.

Along the Olde Smyrna Road, just before getting to the church, she had seen a boy alone in a field, walking along, kicking a battered cardboard box in front of him, a boy too far from town for baseball. It was the sort of thing Lew would have done at nine or ten, a country boy making up his own games, not needing anyone else.

Would he show up for Aunt Nan's funeral tomorrow? He would if he was alive.

Naomi could see lights coming on through the trees. Someone was living in the old camp cabins. Music was playing, country and western, a band she did not recognize. She listened for voices. In the dark hallway, she rocked and waited and watched.

2

𝒆

The horn on the UPS truck had blown almost a dozen times before Ziza Todd came out onto the front porch of Mansion House to see what was going on. Everyone else was at breakfast, and she was late. The driver gave one last blast after she appeared, and then he slowly slid out of the open cab door. He was carrying an eight-inch-square silver cardboard cube.

"Harry Van Schoonhoven?" he asked, reading from a label on the box.

"Obviously not," she said.

"Know him?"

"He's probably inside having breakfast."

"Sign," he said. "Special overnight personalized service."

The label had a black border. The gray typeface was clearly chosen to be in the best possible taste. But flowing across the bottom, in understated Art Deco lettering that didn't call attention to itself, were the words CONTENTS: HUMAN REMAINS.

"Sign," he said, holding out a wad of multicolored pages thick with carbon paper. "If you please." She suspected he had just noticed her clerical collar.

She signed. He held on to the package and searched through the carbons for the right page to give her. Ziza now suspected he was actually looking at her feet. Nothing looks newer than new running shoes, she thought, and hers were still as bright and shiny as baby bootees.

He handed her the package—which seemed almost weightless—along with an unreadably smudged receipt and headed for his brown van with the rolling stride of a sea captain returning to his ship. "Have a nice day," he said, slamming the truck into gear.

As he raced around the circular driveway, Ziza shook the package once—not a sound—and headed for the dining room.

The sign-in book for breakfast was crowded with signatures, two long ledger-pages full, the largest turnout anyone in the kitchen could remember. There was a Leffler, a Miracle, two Van Zandts, a Siler, a Hazzard, a Vly. There were Vanvalkenburgs, de Vissers, a Todd, a Mills, a Benedikt, several Van Schoonhovens, but not a single Quick. In the huge old house that one Quick had built almost a century ago and that had been dominated by Quicks for decades, there was not a Quick to be seen. There were cousins, nieces and nephews, but they all had other names. They were there—the family, the corporation officials, the salesmen—for the community's annual meeting, the annual meeting to end all annual meetings, as one of the salesmen put it.

"The old girl had more flair than I would have thought," said Hagadorn Mills. "She waited for the biggest possible audience, then kicked the bucket."

"Cashed in her checks," added Sherman Benedikt, "if I may keep with the spirit of the occasion."

Mills and Benedikt were not seated at one of the round tables (each with a lazy Susan of condiments and a crock of wildflowers in the center) but at the end of a long, otherwise empty refectory table that ran along one side of the room. By tradition, it was where people sat when they came by themselves. There were no tables for one—or two—at Smyrna. On most days, the long table was the only one in use, and indeed they were both sitting in what others would have called their usual places. But today, as company employees, although indeed very special ones, they had not sat there out of habit. They were making a point of not joining the others.

Both men were dressed as though they were off to an English country-house weekend or perhaps Saturday lunch at the faculty club. And although they were about the same age, their late forties, Benedikt might have been taken at first glance for a successful professor—perhaps with an independent income—while Mills seemed to be an intent and aging graduate student.

Benedikt's pale-blue tie was decorated with Smyrna crowns so tiny you had to get very close to see what they were. Mills wore a white turtleneck pullover under his patched tweed jacket. Benedikt's trousers were sharp-edged military twill, Mills's unpressed corduroy.

"The holy mother, I see, is bringing the Good News to the salesmen," said Sherman Benedikt. He nodded toward one of the jollier, more colorfully dressed tables, all men except for one young red-haired woman wearing a clerical collar and an unusually large pectoral cross.

"And sporting her habit," added Mills. "Interesting, although hardly my idea of a priest."

"With those freckles she's more like a jailbait altar boy. She was asked to do the funeral only because she was handy."

"Always ready to be helpful, our Ziza."

Both men looked at the Reverend Ziza Todd, who seemed—to their delight—ill at ease at a tableful of arguing salesmen. In the few days she had been at Smyrna, she had become their favorite topic of conversation and speculation.

For Hagadorn Mills (he asked his friends to call him Andy), she was a possible rival. Mills was on an extended leave from Wesleyan University (the Connecticut Wesleyan, a distinction he liked to make clear) to serve as the company's official historian. His contract said he was to produce an illustrated history of the community and company to be published by his regular New York publisher with the approval of Olde

Smyrna Community, Inc., and that he was given complete access—"within reason"—to all Quick family and company papers.

He had been a find for Smyrna and probably a bargain as well. Hagadorn Mills's study of spiritualism in nineteenth-century New York—which he and all his colleagues had assumed would be a proper scholarly affair, unread except by a few experts "in the field"—had through some fluke (perhaps it had been an especially dull month) been selected as the Book-of-the-Month. For February. Then *Silver Trumpets in the Valley* won the Pulitzer prize (but not the Bancroft, Beveridge or any of the more respectable historical prizes), was sold to a popular paperback reprint house (not one of the classy "quality" outfits) and appeared, over the course of eighteen months, on both the *New York Times* hardcover and softcover best-seller lists. As a result, Mills considered himself ruined. There was all that money to deal with. Complete strangers were calling him Andy after the *People* magazine piece came out ("Prof Finds Spooks in the Ivy Halls"). The Wesleyan history faculty, or so it seemed to him, cut him dead. Even Mills heard the rumors about Big Bucks and a possible movie adaptation with Shirley MacLaine. This was not the way things were supposed to be. He contacted the MLA convention and told them he would not, after all, be able to present the scholarly paper on Victorian-American thanatology he had promised them. He never even showed up for the convention. The thought of all those knowing stares, those hidden smirks, was too much to bear. His wife left him—although that might have been in the works anyway—for a minimalist composer, a youthful—and utterly unsuccessful—disciple of Philip Glass, who composed epic oratorios based on American Indian legends using an eighteen-key electronic keyboard. So Mills called his agent (for now, indeed, he had an agent) to find him a writing job—anything—that would get him out of Connecticut. The agent found Smyrna, which was looking for an in-house historian, and Hagadorn Mills looked more than respectable to them. It may have been slumming, but he took the job.

His secret plan was to write the book Smyrna had in mind and then use the same material to produce a volume— volumes, maybe—of monumental dullness that could be published by a university press. No paperback outfit would want it. Book clubs would run the other way. With any luck at all, it would save his self-esteem. But his research had dragged on for more than two years, the company was getting restless for its book (especially with all the new plans) and now on the scene appeared Ms. Aimee Semple McTodd, Presbyterian minister, who was looking up a few things for her graduate thesis on the libraries of homegrown American religious communities. Or so she claimed. Hagadorn Mills had his doubts about her, and so did Sherman Benedikt.

Benedikt called himself "the flack with tact." He had done publicity for a top-of-the-line book publisher, discreet charities (no diseases), the New York Public Library and a couple of foundations (the kind that prefer *not* to have publicity in newspapers other than the *Times* and *The Washington Post*) before becoming "spokesman" (as they now called it) for Olde Smyrna. That was almost five years ago, another new beginning. He had grown up in Sacketville, North Carolina, and had spent his high-school days being everyone's "nice Jewish friend." Then came Columbia University, where he discovered that being Jewish didn't mean he had to be the class mascot, but where he was a different kind of exotic, a Southerner named Sherman. At Smyrna, he found for the first time that a public-relations officer with access to the right kind of boss could have unexpected power. In a woman with the unbelievable name of Melody Horn he had found that boss. He had hired Hagadorn Mills, but he had not approved Ziza Todd's research visit, and he wondered who had.

Ziza had taken the empty seat at the salesmen's table, hoping to find a change of pace, anything to avoid another meal of ironic questioning from that pair at the long table. Instead she sat in silence—the silver cardboard cube at her feet—while the men talked around her about monthly quotas, diversification and Disneyland. A month ago she had been taking graduate classes at the seminary and working with children in an outreach program in a downtown church. They talked around her there, too.

Her last afternoon in the church basement had been typical. She had been assigned a group of nine-year-olds she was supposed to lead in a discussion about the dangers of drugs and alcohol. JUST SAY NO, the bright red letters on the teacher's guide said. The guide suggested getting the kids to make a list, two lists, of reasons to drink and dope up and reasons not to. This, the book said, would lead naturally to just saying no.

Why shouldn't you drink? she asked her little circle of boys and girls. They were having paper cups of milk and blocks of government-surplus American cheese on day-old bread. The first answer got right to the point. You shouldn't drink when you gamble, said a bright young face. Or when the welfare lady's coming. Or when you have to make a delivery. Delivery? asked Ziza. Sure, they all said. And there were lots of reasons to celebrate. New babies, one said. You should have a drink to celebrate a new baby. Or Friday night. Weddings. A new job. Birthdays. Cousins coming to visit. What about getting sick? Ziza asked, hoping to lead the discussion the way the book said to. Yeah, gettin' sick is a good reason to get high. Gettin' better was a better one. And they were off again, leaving Ziza behind.

"Your name's Zorro, like the cowboy?" one of the salesmen said. She realized that the whole table was looking at her.

"Ziza," she said. "Rhymes with Liza," and she found herself falling into the safety of a familiar routine. "My mother said I got my name because the cat ran away. While she was pregnant with me, my father became interested in family history and started going through all kinds of genealogy books. In one of them he discovered that his great-grandmother's name was Ziza and kept going around saying what a great name it was. So my mother said, 'Good Lord, if we have a daughter he's going to want to name that poor thing Ziza.' She went to the Humane Society, picked out a kitten and brought it home and said, 'Frank, Ziza's too good a name to waste. The kitten's a female. Let's call her Ziza,' and he went along with that. Then, the week I was born, in all the confusion and what not, the cat took off and never came back. So my father said, 'Ellen, Ziza's too good a name to waste, so that's what we'll call the baby.' And what could she say?"

They laughed. People usually did. The trick was to guess how real the laughter was. "And then when I got to Oberlin, I came across one of those All-the-people-in-the-Bible reference books, so I looked up Ziza and found out there were two of them—ready for this?—both men. One gets mentioned just in passing. He begat someone or something. The other grabbed someone else's land. Now, why do you suppose a parent would want to name a little girl after him?"

They laughed again (this time it did not sound like a real laugh) and got back to business. Business was good. Smyrna was the country's biggest producer and seller of high-school class rings. But changes were in the works, and change might be bad.

"They're going to fuck it up and fuck it up good, excuse the French, Father," said one, addressing the last few words to Ziza's collar. "They got a good thing going. It's worked for, what, sixty-five, seventy years and now they want to open some sort of Disneyland."

"Diversification . . ."

"Low-rent Disneyland, Jim and Tammy Bakker stuff . . ."

"Look at the Universal Studio Tour in Hollywood, the Hershey circus down in Pennsylvania, the Amanas in Iowa— people love it. We'll be able to offer free trips to Smyrna as sales bonuses to the high-school kids. Rumor is that there's going to be all kinds of profit-sharing coming out of this."

"Yeah, well, rumor this, friend. We sell rings and we sell lots of rings by hitting the line and hitting the line hard, not by pushing some sort of u-toe-pee-ah playland. Less said about the old stuff, the better."

"Look, all those old cults are big these days. Shakers? All the Yuppies want Shaker furniture. Amish? Busloads of people from Queens go off to Lancaster to stare at bearded old guys who ride buggies to the A&P and don't have buttons or electric milking machines. What do they do? They stare, buy some scented candles or junk hex signs that were probably made in Taiwan, eat an expensive lunch of greasy slop they could get at their local diner at home and get back in their buses a little poorer. And then they fart their way back to Queens." This salesman seemed considerably younger than the rest and better dressed. "They have all the old stuff up here, the old factory, the buggies in the barn, this crazy old building, maybe even some of the old Smyrna believers for guides. Put it to work, what's the problem? Anyway, Melody Horn says it will pay."

"Melody fuckin' Horn, give me a break. Madame MBA who has the old Schooner by the balls." He gestured with his head toward a corner table where a middle-aged man with an unnaturally red face was sitting with a young woman whose hair and knitted dress were the color of vintage champagne. "The problem is that we're going to get fucked and we're going to get fucked good." Another dip of the head toward Ziza.

"What *I* don't like," said the oldest man at the table, the one who asked Ziza about her name, "is that they've dragged us in here for their annual meeting, given us each a room in Mansion House and laid on some fancy meals. They've never done that before. I'm afraid they're up to something more than announcing the establishment of Ye Olde Smyrna Village or whatever its name is. I'm afraid Mr. Van Schoonhoven is going to tell us something we're not going to want to hear, and it's going to be more than saying we're all expected to attend the old girl's funeral."

"Which reminds me," Ziza said, getting up from the table. "I've got to earn my keep. The service is at eleven-thirty in the Meeting Room." She took the package and headed toward a red-faced man at the corner table, Harry Van Schoonhoven, president of Olde Smyrna Community, Inc.

"I believe this is yours," she said.

"Take it, Melody," he said.

Melody Horn ignored him. "Ziza, we're so happy you're here," she said, "so relieved that someone with experience will be handling the service." Melody Horn's title was general sales manager. Before that it had been regional sales manager, the region being the Midwest—Ohio, Indiana, Illinois, Iowa—Smyrna's most lucrative territory. The word was that she had been discovered at the Harvard Business School by an executive recruiter.

"Indeed," said Mr. Van Schoonhoven, "indeed."

"You'll be saying a few words," Ziza said. It was not a question.

"Oh? I suppose I'll have to. But I want you to say a little something about family history. The last of the Quicks, that sort of thing. Not much. Just local color."

"Maybe the official historian should. . . ."

"No. He'd just bring up the doll business, and I've heard enough about that."

Aunt Nan's best-known contribution to family history was an interview she had given back in the 1950s to some journalist, all about the time her father, Old Father Quick, had made the little girls at Smyrna throw away their dolls because they had developed "special attachments" for them. It was a story that seemed to pop up every time someone wrote about the old days.

"And another thing," he said, "one of the workmen told me Llewelyn's widow is lurking around. Almost ran him over yesterday, drunk as a skunk from the sound of it. Apparently she's hiding out at the old camp mess hall. Probably thinks she's invisible. Car's in the shed. The workman said he checked it out, and it smells to high heaven of booze. We'll try to keep an eye out for her, but if some lunatic makes an appearance, you've been warned."

"I feel warned, but I think Hagadorn Mills should—"

"Forget Mills, got it?"

"Got it." She waited for more, but Mr. Van Schoonhoven had turned his attention back to his eggs. "What's in the box, Melody?"

She studied the receipt for a moment and then said, "Aunt Nan."

Ziza headed for the door. Harry Van Schoonhoven wasn't a real Quick, she knew, just an in-law, but she wasn't sure how his wife was related to Aunt Nan. Great-niece. Some sort of second or third cousin, Lord knows how many times removed. He had worked his way up through the company, beginning in the ring factory, which was now located down the road in Palenville and not on the original Smyrna land, then out selling on the high-school circuit, pushing the rings (with birthstone and without, with individual monogram or without, with all kinds of wonderful options, including— for only a slightly extra charge—logos depicting one's favorite extracurricular activity). Apparently he had done well enough, but he excelled as a manager, and it was when he came back to Smyrna to reorganize operations that he came into his own, and the presidency had become his almost by inheritance.

Except for those few years on the road, he had lived in Mansion House all his adult life, almost forty years, lived there still with his wife, the authentic Quick.

The dining room at Mansion House was to the right of the open front door. The Meeting Room was straight ahead, down a wide, uneven hallway paved with small identical cobblestones set in fan-shaped patterns, and beyond a Y-shaped double flight of stairs that led to the second floor. The sunlight from the huge round window over the door blazed a bright circle on the stones. Ziza walked through the door and opened the double doors leading into the Assembly Room. It was a musty-smelling auditorium, wider than it was deep, ringed on three sides by a balcony open to the upstairs hall-ways. The front of the stage was painted so that it looked like the marbled endpapers of a leather-bound book. The walls continued the same design up to shoulder height. Above that appeared to be darkened wainscoting, but the plaster was chipped enough for Ziza to see that it was another painted illusion. The effect was heavy and somber, the only light coming from tall, thin windows that ran along one wall, slashes of brightness that looked like the spaces between prison bars.

At the center of the narrow stage was an attached oak pulpit. There, every night, once stood Old Father Quick and then Young Father Quick, speaking to the assembled pop-ulation of Smyrna, lecturing them, setting up the critical dis-cussion groups that Smyrna's modern defenders liked to compare to group therapy sessions. Because of the open de-sign of the balconies, the sick and the frail could stay in their rooms and, by keeping open their doors, hear everything their leaders had to say. Behind the pulpit, painted on a trompe l'oeil scroll, was the familiar crown and the words from Revelation: "(but thou art rich)."

Ziza climbed the steps to the stage. She always liked to stand in a strange pulpit once before she faced the congre-gation. She liked to grasp the wooden sides, check the light to see if it worked and get over the urge to say something utterly outrageous or obscene. Instead she said those old words from the book of Revelation addressed to the early church at Smyrna: "Be thou faithful until death and I will give thee a crown of life." She spoke louder than she ex-pected. She could hear the echo of her voice down many empty hallways. She heard a door bang open and then footsteps, running footsteps and feet clattering down a distant, uncarpeted stairway.

Something was wrong. In the short time she had been there, Ziza had never heard or seen anyone run at Smyrna. She left the pulpit and climbed the open oak staircase to the balcony and then down the hall where she thought she had heard the running. The hallway was not straight but made several turns, went up two steps and then down three. All the white doors on the yellow-painted hall were closed until, almost at the end, she came to an open one. Inside was a narrow iron bed that had been stripped to its mattress. There were no curtains on the pair of windows. The shelves were crammed with books and papers, but the white walls were bare except for one large, framed sepia photograph of a carefully arranged group of people standing in front of Mansion House. The frame looked homemade, an intricate weaving of twigs and white birch bark.

The closet door stood open, and inside hung four or five dark cotton dresses, one with white polka dots. On the shelf was one large, floppy straw sun hat. On the floor were two perfectly aligned pairs of shoes, one highly polished, one scuffed. There was a sweet, overripe fruit smell of old age and settled dust. It must have been Aunt Nan's room.

Balancing the closet door, on the other side of a white-painted chest of drawers, was another door. It, too, stood open, but it had obviously been wrenched open violently. Nails that had been pounded through to keep it shut protruded through the door itself. Ziza ran her hand along the jagged frame, avoiding the splinters. The door had clearly been painted shut for years.

She looked inside the dark room but could see nothing except a thin line of light at the window. She made her way over and pulled back the heavy plush drapes. The walls were covered with pictures clear up to the ceiling, long, thin *Last Supper*-style photographs of young men in T-shirts seated at tables, crowded shots of baseball teams, what looked like a swim team, a group—a barbershop quartet, perhaps—posed in an exaggerated out-of-date position in front of a huge stone fireplace. Another group of teenage boys with musical instruments, a 1950s high-school dance band with QUICK AND THE DEADS painted on the drum set. A blue felt pennant proclaiming SMYRNA was hung with caterpillars of dust. There was a geodetic survey map with a small American flag stuck along the meandering blue line of a creek.

Below the map was a camp cot on which a mummy-style sleeping bag had been unrolled, the kind of tight-fitting winter sleeping bag that has only a small, face-size hole at the top, room for the eyes, nose and mouth and not much extra space for cold to get in.

For a moment Ziza thought she saw a face looking up at her. She must have been wrong. She moved closer, kicking the dust in front of her as though it had been a thin layer of fresh snow. She caught her breath. There *was* a face looking out of the opening of the mummy bag. It was a clownish yellow-orange, with rosy cheeks, lips as red and as perfectly shaped as the wax chewing-gum lips she used to buy at the candy store after school, painted-on black eyebrows that Groucho would have been proud of. Without thinking she reached toward it and, bending closer, saw that it was one of those papier-mâché masks that kids might make on a rainy day at camp. But this one was unusually well done. There even seemed to be a tear painted beneath one of the holes where the eyes were supposed to be.

She touched its nose, and the mask slipped sideways. Before she knew that it was a jawbone that had fallen into her hand, she breathed the stale, rubbery smell of death, the smell of air escaping from an inner tube that had lain too many summers at the back of a garage. The eyeholes in the mask were replaced with the empty eye sockets of a skull.

She did not scream. (Later, she was proud of that.) She said simply, "Oh, my God." It was a prayer, not a curse.

She left the room, carefully closed the hall door so that no one else would see what she had seen and went down the back, uncarpeted stairs. She would report what she had found to Mr. Van Schoonhoven. They would call the police. She would conduct Anna May Quick's services at 11:30. She would tell some anecdote about Olde Smyrna but not mention the dolls. She would remain very, very calm. She did not yet realize that she was still holding a human jawbone.

3

*

"Now we all get to play detective," said Hagadorn Mills.

"Oh, for the love of God, no," said Sherman Benedikt.

They were in the second-floor library, a bright room with the largest windows in Mansion House, one of Old Father Quick's architectural innovations. Benedikt sat at a table but was using his metal clipboard as a desk. He wrote quickly, making what seemed to be lists. Mills sat in one of the leather chairs in front of the fireplace. Ziza was in the other. Both of them had empty glasses. A bottle of Black Label was within Mills's reach.

"Freshen that up?" he asked, already adding a splash to his own glass.

"Why not? I fear the old parson's going to tie one on tonight."

It was something she had said before. Before the previous drink, for instance, and the one before that. The police had already talked to Ziza. That had happened down in Mr. Van Schoonhoven's office—first a man in a state trooper's uniform (who took notes) and then a man in a gray business suit (who didn't). Their questions didn't seem as pointed as she thought they should have been. They weren't at all curious about whoever it was she had heard leaving Aunt Nan's room. They never seemed to grasp the importance of the fact that the person was running. What they were interested in was time.

When she found the body. How long she was in the room. What time she made her report to Mr. Van Schoonhoven. How long they waited to call the police. How you spelled Ziza, one *d* or two in Todd, capital *V* or not in Van Schoonhoven. Why she touched the mask. Why she carried the jawbone to Mr. Van Schoonhoven's office.

The bone had rested on a paper towel in the center of Mr. Van Schoonhoven's desk blotter all through the interview, a suspiciously neat and tidy bone. All the teeth of the lower jaw were in place. Ziza couldn't help but notice that whoever it was had very few fillings. It had that licked-clean look of a leftover soup bone that had been given to a dog to finish off. Mr. Van Schoonhoven had refused to touch it.

"I couldn't believe it," Ziza told Hagadorn Mills. "I was calmly telling Mr. Van Schoonhoven what had happened upstairs and how we had to notify the authorities, and he just kept pointing at what I had in my hand, demanding that I put it down and then having a fit when I tried to hand it to him."

"Not the old Schooner's finest hour."

"Started calling for his secretary but got Ms. Horn instead and sent her off for the paper towel."

"Is it long-lost Llewelyn or not?"

Ziza shrugged and looked toward Benedikt. "Is it?"

"We are awaiting the medical examiner's findings," he said, sounding like one of his press briefings.

He had already talked with a TV crew from Albany and some local newspaper reporters. More were probably on their way.

"Mr. Van Schoonhoven's instructions," he said, "are to maximize—his word—the positive publicity for Olde Smyrna—that means lots of picturesque shots of the Falls and the waterwheel at the old box factory—and minimize what he calls the scandal. He honestly believes that I can convince a bunch of guys and gals"—he nodded toward Ziza, as though he were making an important concession—"on deadline that there's not much of a story in the fact that some ninety-year-old old maid kept a corpse in her closet. Wait until the New York papers get here and start asking if she was the murderer. Was the corpse her love slave? And don't forget that old favorite: What kind of a cult is this Smyrna, anyway? Do they really believe in free love? Oh, Lord above!"

"I'll be happy to handle any briefings on the historical aspects," Hagadorn Mills said.

"Van Schoonhoven has already thought of that, but he would like the Reverend Todd to join you, providing, of course, that she wears her clerical outfit and not her running shorts and Virginia Slims T-shirt."

Ziza snorted and drained her glass. Mills watched her suspiciously and then glanced over at Benedikt, who studiously continued to work on his lists. "How well," Mills asked her, carefully swirling the last of his drink, "do you know the old Schooner?" Benedikt stopped writing, waiting for her answer.

"Not well enough to remember his first name."

"But well enough to get invited to Smyrna?"

"Well enough to know that it's not going to be long before he remembers that we didn't have a funeral this morning."

"But not well enough to know that he has already covered that," Benedikt said. "No funeral for the duration of the 'scandal.' Private scattering of the ashes at the waterfall tonight at sunset. Family only. Memorial service perhaps sometime in the future."

"Family *only*?" asked Hagadorn Mills.

"*Only,*" said Sherman Benedikt. "Not us. Except, of course, for the reverend."

Ziza reached for the bottle. Hagadorn Mills polished off his drink and headed for the door.

❧   ❧   ❧

Harry Van Schoonhoven seemed to be alone in his office on the first floor of Mansion House. He carefully arranged a stack of papers, tapping down the short side of the pages on his desk, then the long side, getting the stack perfectly straight. He placed it next to the telephone and weighed it down with a piece of black basalt he had picked up years ago in the stream. He then fanned out a playing card–size deck of pink telephone memos (WHILE YOU WERE OUT, read the printed heading, although he had been in the office all day), and he checked to make sure his secretary had arranged them in chronological order. Most were from the media, although one was from a medium, an old-fashioned medium who claimed she could contact the owner of the bones "on the other side" and find out how they got into Aunt Nan's spare room. He threw it away. He could forget about that one. One was from his contact at GB&H. He tore that one up before throwing it away. He would remember that one. He put the memos in a small wooden box—one of the original products of the old box factory—on the other side of the telephone. He carefully patted them into a corner, so that that pile, too, was perfectly straight. He picked up an accordion-fold computer printout sheet and tried to figure out which end was the beginning.

"Are you trying to drive me stark raving bats?" said the woman sitting in the corner.

Harry Van Schoonhoven jumped.

"Gwen! Forgot you were there. You've been as quiet as a mouse."

"I've been waiting for an answer. She was *my* aunt, after all."

Gwen Quick Van Schoonhoven was physically the opposite of her husband, small, compact, dark, not a touch of gray in her hair. Even in her early sixties she maintained the edgy calm of a schoolgirl athlete. "His name?"

"Story. Mr. Nicholas Story, not inspector or lieutenant or anything like that. Apparently the new state police policy is that uniformed men are called by their titles, plainclothes are simply mister. Better community relations. But I don't see that calling him—"

"At the Leeds Barracks?"

"Leeds. But he's just going to tell you what he told me. They won't know anything for days."

"He's going to have to tell me to my face that that old lady is a murder suspect. Thank God she didn't live to see the day."

"There aren't suspects until they know there has been a crime. Melody Horn says—"

"I sometimes wonder how that woman escaped becoming a really first-rate secretary."

"Gwen, this is an important time for this company. Everything is about to boom. Don't make waves."

"Company," she said, standing and walking slowly toward the desk. The room was not wood-paneled, as it may have looked at first glance, but skillfully painted, like the Meeting Room, to look like wood. On the walls were elaborately framed pictures of class rings. "Company? At Smyrna we never say 'company.' We say 'community.' Some of us can even say 'family.' After all these years, you should know that." She leaned forward and tapped, ever so gently, the side of the wooden box, just hard enough for the neat stack of pink messages to fall sideways.

≈   ≈   ≈

The Parlor had not been so full in years. Located just across the cobblestone hall from the Dining Room, it looked like the lobby of a prosperous but unfashionable summer hotel. Most of the furniture was dark-green wicker, with heavy, darker-green cushions. There were rustic twig end tables and wicker plant stands thickly planted with ferns. The wrought-iron floor lamps had been made at the old blacksmith shop down at the box factory, with twisted tripod legs and dark parchment shades held in place by iron beasts—dragons, maybe, or griffins—the work of long-dead apprentices.

The chairs and couches were full of middle-aged and older people. They were dressed more for a country weekend than a funeral, and a number of them were clutching stacks of color photographs, which they seemed to be trying to show to their neighbors. No one more than glanced at anyone else's pictures. Afternoon tea had been promised. The scattering of the ashes would come later.

One of Smyrna's traditions was that anyone who had been a member of the community was always welcome at Mansion House. "In my father's house are many mansions," Young Father Quick had liked to say. "The big front door is always open. There is always room at our hearthside." And room upstairs in the bedrooms and in the Dining Room. Only simple tasks were required in return. In the old days many took advantage of Mansion House's open door, especially those who were down on their luck. But over the years luck—and the community's quarterly stock dividends—seemed to have turned better, or perhaps the unlucky ones simply died off, and now there were only two full-time "resident guests," the Butler brothers, Charley and Frank.

Instead, it became popular for the old-timers who had once been Smyrna's children to use the place as a country inn, dropping by once a year or so for long weekends, usually in the fall when the leaves were changing. They frequently would arrive with photographs of their grandchildren (visiting privileges were not inheritable) but more often with photographs of their travels, snapshots of Asolo and Machu Picchu, Disneyland (the new one in Japan) and Milford Sound. They were enthusiastic travelers but liked to think of themselves as explorers, always ready to extend their deepest sympathy to the less-dedicated tourist (a word they would never use to describe themselves) who may have visited Brittany, say, but somehow failed to see the particularly well-preserved *Dance of Death* fresco in the ducal chapel at Isquit.

This unusually large turnout in late spring (always Smyrna's most unattractive season) was not an accident. Invitations had been sent out. Signed by Melody Horn.

Melody was eager to look at everyone's photographs, praising their color, their composition, their invention ("Why I've never seen Luxor photographed at quite that angle before," she was heard to say several times, substituting Newgrange, Petra or the excavations at Xi'an when necessary). She worked the room, introducing herself (she was new to everyone), laughing at jokes, throwing her head back when she laughed, the way Californians do, and then brushing her long blond hair back into place with a single stroke of her hand and a shake of her head.

"She doesn't even have to touch it," Frank Butler said.

"Touch it?" said Charley.

"Her hair."

"Touch it?"

"It goes back into place just by shaking her head."

"Her hair?"

"She has it trained."

The Butler brothers were watching Melody Horn over fresh copies of the *Mountain Weekly*. Charley had the first section, with the accident news and police reports (DWIs mostly), Frank the second section, with the obituaries and the agriculture roundup. As full-time residents they were making a point of avoiding the "day-trippers," as Charley called them.

"See any of the other salesmen?" he asked, knowing full well that Frank had not.

The brothers were not thought to look alike. Charley was larger, heavier, messier. He had the look of a man who enjoys a good cold beer. In his sixties he had come down with diabetes (which he called sugar diabetes or just "the sugar") and claimed he watched his diet. He had the sort of face that appears in newspapers on the sports page under a headline that reads GOVERNOR NAMES BROTHER TO HEAD RACING COMMISSION. Frank was smaller, more compact. He always wore a tie and always seemed to have just patted his lips dry with a freshly pressed handkerchief. But both had the same clear blue eyes that, even in their late seventies, did not need glasses. Both had small noses and large ears and mouths that

smiled but did not laugh. In fact, their faces were identical.
The differences were simply a matter of exposure.

They had been born at Smyrna. Their parents were among
the original believers who had followed Old Father Quick
from Massachusetts. Once the boys were toilet trained they
left their parents and lived in the Children's House, which
was actually a wing of Mansion House, with dormitories,
schoolrooms, a library and—most important, so Young Father Quick claimed—a laboratory where the children could
experiment in scientific Christianity. Charley and Frank
(Charley was older but not enough to matter) apprenticed in
the box factory and then went on the road as ring salesmen,
a daring thing at the time. Salesmen had always been outsiders
working on commission. The Butlers were the first of the
community children to go on the road.

When they arrived at a high school—and they specialized
in country schools—Charley headed for the boys' locker
room; Frank charmed the girls. Together—and they always
worked together—they broke all sales records. And they in-
vented the bank. Frank always claimed it was Charley's idea.
Charley gave Frank the credit, but either way, the bank became the gimmick that made Smyrna the most successful
high-school-ring supplier east of the Rockies. The idea was
simple enough. For ten cents—which was counted as part of
the down payment—a student would get a metal dime bank
as black and as shiny as a Model T Ford and with a lock that
was all but foolproof. With each new dime deposit, the total
would appear at the top, and when five dollars was reached—
that was the price of a ring back then—a golden Smyrna crown
would pop up and the bank could be turned in for an Authentic Smyrna-Styled Smyrna-Crafted Class Ring.

The sales went through the roof, but Young Father Quick
began to worry that the boys might be becoming too worldly
and called them home. Together they took charge of the
company offices as treasurers, bookkeepers, office managers.
Charley coached the community's athletic teams; Frank di-

rected the band and the choir and even had a hand in organizing young Llewelyn Quick's jazz band. When Harry Van
Schoonhoven took over, the boys, as they were still called,
were named honorary comptrollers and, as Charley called it,
put out to pasture. But they did not leave.

"She's either trying to get money out of them or she's going
to put them to work somehow in this new scheme," Frank
said. "Maybe dress them up in costumes and pass them off
to the tourists as old believers." Frank was careful not to
move his lips or look at Charley.

"Stock proxies," said Charley.

"She isn't mentioning the company stock at all."

"Exactly my point."

As though she knew she was being talked about, Melody
Horn turned to look at the brothers, and although they
seemed to be intent on their newspaper, she waved. Charley
waved back. Frank bowed from the waist. She turned quickly;
her hair danced wildly, but with a flick of her head it fell
back into place.

"Exactly *my* point," said Frank.

ﮊ   ﮊ   ﮊ

If ever a procession could be called furtive, Ziza Todd
thought, this one was. Mr. Van Schoonhoven's instructions
had been clear enough. At 7:30 she was to take her Bible or
prayer book or whatever she needed ("No cross or crucifix,
of course." "Of course, Mr. Van Schoonhoven") and head
out—those were his words, *head out*—toward the top of the
Falls. He would follow, unobtrusively—again, his word—with
the ashes. Mrs. Van Schoonhoven would, of course, be ac-
companying him ("Of course, Mr. Van Schoonhoven"), and
perhaps some of the other family members might tag along,
but he suspected most would wait and say goodbye to Aunt
Nan at the memorial service, whenever that was rescheduled.

At 7:29, Ziza came down the cobbled hallway and paused
before going out onto the front porch. She was dressed, she

thought, sensibly, with clerical collar but without the large cross she wore at breakfast, low shoes (for scrambling across the rocks at the top of the Falls) and no hat. Mrs. Van Schoonhoven, standing in front of the Parlor door as though she were blocking an exit, was wearing a hat, a large floppy rain hat, designed, perhaps, for drizzly garden parties. She was also wearing what looked like a knit poncho. Her husband stood just behind her in the doorway, and Ziza tried to catch his eye. Mr. Van Schoonhoven, however, was intent on studying the pattern of the fading light on the cobblestones. He had the silver UPS package with him, tucked up under his arm as though it were a football.

Ziza was just about to say something when, without ever looking up from his cobblestone reverie, he motioned toward the front door with his head, one sharp move as though he had a severe tic. She remained where she was. He had another seizure, and Mrs. Van Schoonhoven, addressing no one in particular, simply said, "Move." Ziza moved, and as she passed through the open front door she heard two pairs of feet falling into step behind her.

The hallway had been empty, but the front porch with its tall columns was crowded with salesmen and family members—separate groups, of course. Ziza found herself being reminded of the opening scene of *Gone With the Wind*, without the crinolines, the red-haired Tarleton twins (she always noticed other redheads) or the dazzling Georgia sunlight. Instead it was downright cool (she coveted Mrs. Van Schoonhoven's poncho), and the light was "the lovely golden light of evening," another useless literary hangover from childhood reading, *Winnie-the-Pooh* surely. She must have paused at the top of the steps leading down to the driveway. She sensed that although there had been no obvious lull in the conversations, there was a slackening in the rhythm. She was being watched, not directly but out of the corners of dozens of pairs of eyes.

"Move." The word came from behind her, through

clenched teeth. She moved. No, remembering her instructions, she headed out. Down the stone steps toward the curve in the circular driveway, and then, before she came to a parked police car, just for the hell of it she cut straight onto the Heart, the spiritual center of Smyrna. She did not look back as she crossed the carefully tended lawn, but she could sense what was happening. Directly behind her were the Van Schoonhovens, and for a while there were only the Van Schoonhovens. But by the time she was halfway across the Heart others began to come down the steps. Not in any organized way and not as though they had planned to, but in groups of twos and fours (no one came back to Smyrna alone) the furtive procession was formed, walking toward the creek and the long orange lines of a smudged Hudson Valley sunset, the sort of thing, Ziza thought, that Thomas Cole might have whipped off on a slow day.

Beyond the Heart, Ziza led them down the road, past one of the canvas-covered signboards, across an open field to the rock bed of the creek. In the distance she could hear the roar of the Falls, but the creek itself flowed on silently and undisturbed by rapids as it sped toward the drop-off.

This spot on the Kaaterskill Creek played an important role in Old Father Quick's homegrown educational system. It was something Ziza had learned while snooping around the library. The old man claimed he was following the example of Gideon, who, obeying the Lord's instructions, winnowed out the misfits in his army by leading them to a creek and observing how they drank from the stream. Quick's test involved the children, but drinking had nothing to do with it. It was how they played. Boys, Old Father believed, had a natural instinct for throwing things into water. The bigger the object, the more masculine the boy. The natural girl wouldn't throw anything. She would play along the shore, and the most feminine of all would build small protective harbors out of pebbles in which they could float leaves or pieces of bark. The most masculine boys would bomb the harbors, splashing the girls as much as possible.

Each child, at the age of five, was taken to the stream and allowed to play with the other children. They were observed and detailed records kept, some of which were still in the library closet. Future leaders of the community were spotted, the potential of mothers-to-be duly noted. There seemed to be some difference of opinion (the notes were in several hands) as to what it meant if a boy chose to throw a tree trunk (something that splashed and floated) rather than a rock (something that splashed and sank), but Ziza had noticed that it usually all came down to being a matter of size.

Had the notes survived on little Nan? Ziza wondered. Was that old maid once a maker of harbors, a floater of leaves? She would have to make a return visit to the library closet. And what about the mysterious Llewelyn, whose name she had been hearing all too often since she had discovered the corpse? Were they still giving the test when he was a boy?

The creek sped along a bed of solid rock, and when Ziza reached it, she turned and looked back. Her furtive procession was not as tidy as she had imagined. The Van Schoonhovens had kept up with her pace, but the others were scattered back as far as she could see. She turned downstream and headed for the roar of the unseen Falls. For the first time she noticed that there were some people waiting for her, two of them, men, standing next to a giant pile of sticks, twigs and logs that looked like a misplaced beaver dam. As she got closer she could see in the deepening twilight that they were the Butler boys, Frank and Charley. Both had taken off their suit jackets, although they still wore their vests, and when they saw Ziza they began waving.

"We decided to have a birthday brash fire for Aunt Nan," Charley called out as Ziza got closer. "It's a tradition."

"For birthdays," said Frank.

"Summer birthdays," said Charley. "A big fire at the top of the Falls with lots of brash from the pine plantation and all the driftwood you could drag over."

"Providing it was dry wood," said Frank.

"That goes without saying," said Charley.

"Not necessarily," said Frank. "I distinctly remember a birthday brash fire that was nothing but foul smoke and more than enough of that."

"That was an unusually wet summer. Rain began in April and didn't stop till it turned to snow."

"Nevertheless," said Frank.

"Nevertheless," said an out-of-breath and puffing Mr. Van Schoonhoven, "this is *not* a birthday. It's a funeral. . . ."

"A scattering of ashes," said Mrs. Van Schoonhoven, who was not the least bit out of breath.

"A bonfire on such an occasion smacks of heathenism," her husband insisted. "Tom-toms. Gourd rattles."

"I think it's a lovely thought," said Mrs. Van Schoonhoven, reaching out to pat Frank's hand.

"It's not a thought," said Charley. "It's a fire. There's a birthday brash fire sitting right here ready to light."

"And sit there it will remain," said Mr. Van Schoonhoven. Beads of sweat were running down the sides of his face.

"Actually," said Ziza, deciding to add a practical touch, "I think we're going to need the light. We don't want anyone falling down on these rocks. It's going to be pitch black in a few minutes."

"And it gets cold this time of year once the sun goes down," said Mrs. Van Schoonhoven. "A fire is just what Aunt Nan would have wanted."

Charley took that as a go-ahead, and he struck a match. Within seconds the dry pine brash caught fire and the whole creek was bathed in a harsh but flickering light that revealed dozens of would-be mourners carefully helping one another cross the rocks. When everyone seemed to be in place, Ziza began.

"Our help is in the name of the Lord," she began. It was not her first funeral or scattering or whatever it was. Although she had not yet been ordained or given a church of her own,

as a student pastor she had filled in more than once. She had
officiated when there was not a damp eye in the house and
when the widow had to be led away from the grave after she
inexplicably attacked a funeral wreath. She had done it
enough to be familiar with the nervous sadness of most fu-
nerals, of the social unease of people knowing that something
terribly important was happening but not knowing quite what
to do. This service was nothing like what she had done before,
the heat from the roaring fire, the cool night wind, the rumbling of the Falls, the shuffling of feet on the rock. There
was something heathen here, if heathen meant older than
Christ. Indeed, she found herself listening for tom-toms and
gourd rattles.

She then read a few psalms: "God is our refuge and
strength . . . ," "I lift up mine eyes unto the hills . . . ," "Lord,
Thou hast been our dwelling place in all generations. . . ." It
was, she could see, a family service. None of the salesmen
was there. Melody Horn, Hagadorn Mills and the others had
stayed away. In the distance she could see some flashlights
heading from the direction of Mansion House. She then
turned to Old Father Quick's favorite passage from Revelation, the one she was reciting in the Assembly Hall when she
heard the running footsteps:

And unto the angel of the church in Smyrna write:
These things saith the first and the last, which was dead
and is alive:
I know thy works, and tribulation, and poverty, (but
thou art rich) and I know the blasphemy of them which
say they are Jews, and are not, but are the synagogue of
Satan.

Fear none of those things which thou shalt suffer: be-
hold the devil shall cast some of you into prison, that ye
may be tried; and ye shall have tribulation ten days: be
thou faithful until death and I will give thee a crown of life.

When she looked up she saw that the flashlights had reached the group, Sherman Benedikt and the state policeman who wore civilian clothes. She also saw that a woman was standing just out of the range of the firelight. She couldn't make out any features, just some flashes of white in her hair. Ziza nodded toward Mr. Van Schoonhoven.

"Unto the mercy of Almighty God, we commend the soul of our sister departed . . . ," she read from the prayer book, and he dumped, as though emptying grounds from a coffee maker, Aunt Nan's ashes into the stream. There was an uneasy silence, a sense that someone was about to begin singing a hymn, but no one did, and Ziza said the Benediction.

Flashlights came on all through the group as people turned away from the boys' slowly subsiding fire and headed unsteadily back toward Mansion House, like tipsy Christmas carolers making their rounds. Benedikt and Nicholas Story came up to Mr. Van Schoonhoven. "We have a report on the corpse," Benedikt said.

"Preliminary report only," said Story, addressing Mr. Van Schoonhoven after nodding toward Mrs. Van Schoonhoven and Ziza. "No identification as yet. We expect more information tomorrow, but the body hadn't been in that sleeping bag long, which means that someone had only recently placed it in the old lady's room."

The Van Schoonhovens and Ziza thought about that. It meant that Aunt Nan could not have been involved.

"And," prompted Benedikt.

"And the skeleton's not complete," Story continued. "It seems that a number of bones are missing."

"An incomplete set," said Mrs. Van Schoonhoven, staring off across the stream toward the shadowy figure Ziza had seen before. The woman was waving but not at them. Ziza glanced over to the Butler boys, who were still tending their blaze. She saw Frank raise his arm as though he were going to wave back, and she saw Charley reach out and stop him.

4

❧

Everyone in the room was looking at the brown package next to Naomi's folding chair. When she set it down on the linoleum floor it made a clunk, a not-quite-so-solid thunk, that everyone there recognized: the sound of a glass bottle coming down—not as carefully as intended—on something solid, a full bottle from the sound of it.

The chairs were arranged in a semicircle around a plain wooden table and chair, still empty, so that everyone had a good view of Naomi and the brown bag tightly twisted around the clearly defined silhouette of a bottle—a fifth, more than likely, too small for a quart, not the right shape for wine.

Naomi had been to a liquor store for the first time in more years than she would care to remember, although she knew the exact number. First she had browsed around, ignoring the solicitous interest of the kindly-looking gentleman (he was wearing a tie and jacket) at the cash register: "Need any help, just call," he said. She didn't need any help, but the store was empty, so the man watched her. He didn't bother watching in the convex mirror rigged up in the corner. He watched her straight out: "We're having our annual spring white sale on your gins and your vodkas and some of your Chablis," he said, waiting for a laugh he didn't get. "It's traditional," he said.

Naomi remembered when the store was indeed traditional,

when the selection amounted to different price ranges of bourbon and rye, Canadian, some scotch, some of your gins and just about none of your vodkas. The word "Chablis" would never have been mentioned. There was Gallo Brothers red and white and for variety a few bottles from the Finger Lakes, Hammondsport, something sweet and greenish called Lake Niagara. Now there was a whole wall of wine bottles racked up on their sides under trellises of plastic vines bearing plastic grapes. An imported section, a California section (even the Gallos, she noticed, had become fancy), an Our Vintner's Pick-of-the-Month section. Off in the hard stuff, the options available were staggering, and so were the prices. The fifth of Dewar's she picked up seemed twice the price of the last one she had bought. Could that be right?

"Traditional," she told the clerk. Behind him on a shelf were a few limited-edition bottles in the shape of Rip Van Winkle, some with Rip asleep, some awake, one with his dog. A hand-lettered sign said PRIVATE COLLECTION: NOT FOR SALE. What was the dog's name? It was one of the stories she used to tell the younger campers. She felt like old Rip himself when she was given the wrapped bottle and less change than she thought she deserved. The clerk told her to take it easy, assured her that she would have a nice day and hoped he would see her again.

"Wolf," she said, remembering Rip's dog.

He looked shocked, but Naomi, heading for the door, feeling the familiar weight in her hand, didn't notice.

She did not go back to her car on Main Street but walked up a flight of cement steps that led past a veterans' honor roll from some war or another to the next block, a narrow street crowded with bulky buildings that seemed to have been planned for a much grander location, two white wooden churches and a tall Masonic lodge that looked as though it should have been a church. She checked the address she had been given when she called the number in the Yellow Pages and went up the walk of a plain Presbyterian church laden with a row of oversized Corinthian columns that easily could have been pillaged from a bank or a particularly successful nineteenth-century resort hotel. In the basement she found the room she was looking for, with its circle of folding chairs and its brown linoleum floor.

No one looked at her. They just eyed her package. And no one spoke. Every time Naomi read about AA meetings they always sounded like jolly affairs, full of camaraderie and Rotary Club conviviality. Over the twelve and a half years she had been coming to meetings in one church basement or another, she had never found them particularly friendly. They were useful, maybe lifesaving, certainly sobering, sometimes funny (intentionally so), often deep in bullshit (they were, after all, nothing but a bunch of drunks), but they were not friendly, not at the beginning. She felt accepted at meetings but never especially welcome. In fact, she suspected many people came to meetings just a little late because they couldn't stand the lull during those minutes before the chairman called the group to order, a time that reminded Naomi of a stage full of actors waiting for the curtain to go up.

The chairman, who looked curiously like the clerk at the liquor store, stood in front of the empty table and said that Jerry had called him at the store—it was the clerk, she was sure of it—just a few minutes ago to say he couldn't make it tonight. Would anybody like to volunteer to be speaker? Naomi avoided looking at him but carefully studied the posters on the wall behind him: TAKE IT EASY, said one; FIRST THINGS FIRST; an IBM THINK sign hung upside down, something she had never seen before. What was that supposed to mean?

She had always been amused by the program's fondness for slogans and acronyms. "Take the cotton out of your ears and put it in your mouth" was one of the few good ones. "Strength Through Boredom" was one she made up herself but found that it wasn't very popular. Then there was the danger signal "HALT" for Hungry, Angry, L-something and

Tired—for what to avoid. What did *L* stand for? Hungry-Angry-Lonely . . . How could she have forgotten that?

"I see we have a newcomer," said the chairman, who if he wasn't the clerk was surely his twin. "Maybe she'll say a few words." Naomi felt the eyes in the room move toward her and her package. So she picked it up, walked to the table, sat on it and put the bottle down next to her, making no effort to do it noiselessly.

"Hello," she said. "My name's Naomi, and I'm an alcoholic." ("Hi, Naomi," said the group, just as though they were in an old Susan Hayward movie. Naomi's regular group in Manhattan never did that, and it always surprised her that just about everyplace else did.) "And this is my bottle."

She hadn't meant to say that, but she did, and seeing the familiar row of faces in front of her (it was the row that was familiar, not the individual faces; the feeling in the room rather than the room itself), she felt strangely at home. And she began to tell her story—edited of course, always edited. How she had come back to the area for the first time in years (although not exactly why), about a death in the family (but not exactly who), about her drinking habits over the years. She talked frankly about her fondness for driving after a few drinks (that seemed to get their attention), how she turned to AA after she had failed to stop drinking by going to a medical doctor and taking Antabuse, how she always kept a bottle in the trunk of her car because the familiar rolling sound it made was somehow comforting. "I broke my old bottle and had to get a new one." The chairman smiled at her like an old friend. ("My name is Paul," he had said at the beginning of the meeting. "Hi, Paul.") As she spoke, the door at the back of the room opened and then after a few seconds closed. Several people turned to see who had come in, but there was no one there. Naomi ended with another slogan she had once heard at a meeting: "Anybody can meet a crisis. It's everyday living that kills you."

Nice applause. Quick smiles. Paul asked Janet to pass the

plate for donations, and one by one the others raised their hands to speak. Some of them thanked her. A few talked about drunk driving and accidents they had been in. Most mentioned everyday living killing you. She listened and nodded, and her mind drifted back to the night before and the brash fire at the top of the Falls. The shadows and the flickering light, hearing those old Biblical words about Smyrna—it all brought back the old days. Although hearing the words read quietly by a pretty young woman was strange ("but thou art rich" was always said in thunder), and there should have been a hymn. There had always been singing at Smyrna. She had stayed in the shadows, but there had been no sign of Lew. And what if there had been? What played on her mind did not have to do so much with Lew as with herself, with the way she remembered feeling when she was with him.

The group was joining hands. They closed with the Lord's Prayer, another difference from Naomi's Manhattan meeting. While everyone else was still on the Amen and the squeezing of hands, Paul said, "Keep coming back," and darted for the door. The others drifted away more slowly, breaking naturally into twos and threes.

"Everyone knows everyone here," said a middle-aged man with a conspicuously new haircut. He had remained in his chair, and unlike everyone else except Paul, he wore a suit, gray suit, gray tie. The local undertaker was Naomi's guess. "So you were a nice breath of fresh air. My name's Nick."

"Hi, Nick," she said as though the meeting were still in progress. Local undertaker trying for a pickup, thought Naomi.

"Walk you to your car?"

"It's on Main."

"Good place for it."

He held the door for her, walked on the outside along the curb, talked about the unusually wet spring—all things she might expect from a man of his age with slightly out-of-date manners. Naomi didn't say much of anything. They turned down the cement steps. "You staying in the Mansion at Smyrna? Must be crowded there right now." She almost stopped walking.

"I didn't say where I was staying."

"But I've seen you at Smyrna. Last night, in fact."

They had reached Main Street, and this time she did stop.

"At the Falls," he said. "The bonfire," as though more hints would help remind her. "Why don't we go and have some coffee?" He pronounced it like a New Yorker. Caw- (like a crow, rhymes with "paw") fee. Two distinct syllables. "Coffee" was one of those words that gave New Yorkers away, like a Canadian saying "about." You could always spot them. So he wasn't a local, at least not originally. "There's a place just down the block."

Before she could brush him off, a male voice behind her said, "Inspector Story, what a surprise." She turned to see Harry Van Schoonhoven and his wife. "And Naomi, a double surprise." The surprise, she sensed, was not in seeing either one of them but in seeing them together. "We're just off for a bit of light supper. Join us, please."

"Do," said Mrs. Van Schoonhoven, smiling with a broadness that could hardly be real.

"We were just off for coffee," said Nick. Or was he Inspector now?

"Supper comes with coffee. It's a wonderful place, the old soda fountain next to the movie theater. You probably remember it, Naomi. From before. Still has the original stamped-tin ceiling and fixtures. Has been taken over by a young kid just out of the CIA—"

"The Culinary Institute of America," offered Mrs. Van Schoonhoven, her smile unchanged, "over at Hyde Park."

"—and he is doing wonders. Wonders. Even managed to get a liquor license." As they talked, the Van Schoonhovens ushered them past the old movie theater (now a Cinema Duplex) to the front of Ben's Sodas and Newspapers. Naomi indeed remembered. "We have a lot of catching up to do, Naomi. And we have, I believe, some other things to talk about. New things. Right, Inspector? Developments."

"Nick, not Inspector."

"I'll take that to mean yes," and he pushed open the front door of the empty restaurant. "They know us here."

The kid from the CIA was nowhere in sight, but the waitress certainly knew the Van Schoonhovens. "My regulars," she said in a tone that sounded a bit ominous to Naomi. "Anywhere you want," she said, gesturing at the vacant room. They slid into a booth under a 1940s-ish poster of a convertible full of teenagers waving Nehi bottles. "I know what they want," she said, addressing Nick and Naomi's side of the table. "Anything from the bar for you?"

"Now we'll find out whether or not the inspector is on duty," said Mrs. Van Schoonhoven.

"Coffee," he said.

"Watch out, Naomi," said Mrs. Van Schoonhoven, "anything you say may be taken down and used against you."

"And the lady?" the waitress interrupted, eyeing the wrapped bottle Naomi had placed on the table. "We're not still BYO, you know. The license came through."

"Diet Coke."

"I can sell you Diet Pepsi."

"Sold."

"An evening of moderation," said Mr. Van Schoonhoven.

There was no bar. The drinks came out of the kitchen. The Van Schoonhovens' first round—scotch and a martini—was placed not in front of them but in the middle of the table. The four sat in silence as the waitress went back to the kitchen and returned with a full coffee cup and a frosty old-fashioned Coke glass, which she placed in front of Naomi and Nick, getting the order right.

"You two ready for refills?"

"Not *quite* yet, thank you," said Mrs. Van Schoonhoven.

"We'll be having dinner, then, tonight," said the waitress, bringing menus from another table. "I'll be back for your order."

"We'll be having leisurely drinks with our friends first," said Mrs. Van Schoonhoven.

"You bet."

"I think, Harry, that we have been seeing altogether too much of what's-her-name," said Mrs. Van Schoonhoven, following the waitress back to the kitchen with her eyes.

"With Naomi back with us again, let's not talk about waitresses," said Mr. Van Schoonhoven. "You have, my dear, our deepest sympathies."

"Although," his wife added, "after all these years it must be a relief to be an official widow at last."

Naomi looked at Nick.

"A body has turned up," he said, twisting sideways in the booth so he could face her. "Remains from long ago. They have been identified by dental records. Llewelyn Quick." He put his hand not on her hand but on her forearm, gently, as though he were making a kindly arrest.

"Surely you knew," said Mrs. Van Schoonhoven.

"I should have told you back at the church," Nick said. "I should have gotten right to the point." His hand was still on her arm. Oddly enough, Naomi thought, Gwen Van Schoonhoven was right. It was a relief. She felt a calm that was almost frightening. It was finally over.

"Where?" Naomi asked, and Story told her about Ziza's discovery.

"Where is he now?"

"Still at the forensic lab in Albany. The skeletal material will have to remain there for a while."

"Until the rest turns up, I suppose," said Mrs. Van Schoonhoven. Her smile was not as sweet as she probably supposed it was.

"The skeleton was incomplete," said Nick.

"Phalanges, metatarsus, tarsus," said Mrs. Van Schoonhoven. "Fibula, tibia, patella, femur." It suddenly occurred to Naomi that Gwen Van Schoonhoven wasn't perfectly sober, that the scotch she had just finished had not been her first of the day. "Phalanges, metacarpus, carpus, ulna, radius, humerus."

"Does that mean he had been hacked up? That pieces of his body were taken away? Stolen?"

"No, no, my dear," said Harry Van Schoonhoven, the comforter. "He died and rotted away, and then someone messed around with his bones and lost some of them. Something like that, isn't it, Nick?"

"Something, yes. Stray bones from all over the body are missing, not a complete foot or finger or anything. . . . I think maybe we should drop this for now."

"Fibula, tibia, patella, femur," Mrs. Van Schoonhoven repeated. "Isn't it curious that the leg is so much more musical than the arm? Although humerus has a nice sound."

Naomi slowly eased herself out of the booth. "I have to be going," she said. Nick followed, picking up her package for her.

The waitress came back with her pad. "We're skipping dinner, right? Another round?"

"Just for the Van Schoonhovens, I believe," said Mr. Van Schoonhoven.

"I guess my instinct was correct, after all," Naomi said. "Lew did return for Aunt Nan's funeral."

5

❧

Melody Horn opened with a smile, a radiant smile, a welcoming, warm and loving smile that was not directed to the room in general but to individuals. At each table there was at least one pair of eyes she seemed to pick out and acknowledge before she moved on. The Mansion House Dining Room was full of people who felt that they were the ones she had chosen for a special nod or a knowing look. At each table there was at least one who would have sworn she greeted him and no one else.

It was the sales conference brunch, the last get-together before everyone went off again. Over the past two days there had been other meetings and seminars. Samples of the new catalog had been discussed; the new videotaped sales presentations had been screened and debated (they must have cost a fortune to produce); new members of the enlarged staff had been introduced; sales territories had been reorganized. There had been a good deal of surprise and only a little grumbling. But this had been billed as a special event. The stockholders were there. Big news was expected.

The Long Table had been rigged up as a dais with a podium at the center. The podium, where Melody Horn stood, had a seal, just like a presidential press conference: the Smyrna golden crown. The Van Schoonhovens sat on the dais. Ziza

Todd was there (she had said the blessing before the wait-resses—high-school kids from town—brought out the scrambled eggs, stewed tomatoes and bacon); so were Hagadorn Mills and Sherman Benedikt, who were as surprised to find themselves sitting on either side of the supposedly mysterious Naomi Quick as she was to have received an invitation. The Butler brothers, separated, sat at each end of the table, silent as bookends.

"Smyrna," said Melody Horn, "is going to be fun. Fun! And profitable." She smiled again across the room as though she expected applause, and she got it. Mr. Van Schoonhoven beamed. Mrs. Van Schoonhoven seemed to be studying the setting in her ring, and Mills and Benedikt exchanged glances across Naomi. "Olde Smyrna Community, I can now assure you, *will* open on Memorial Day with a major publicity and advertising campaign." She gestured graciously toward Sherman Benedikt. "Our historic home *will* be one of the major tourist attractions of the Hudson Valley. Dinner at Mansion House *will* be a regional gourmet must. The old buildings a living museum. Playland, with kiddie rides, in the old orchard. A petting zoo at the farm. It's all going to raise our profile and make your jobs easier, and that's only the beginning. As the man said, You ain't seen nothin' yet."

This time Mr. Van Schoonhoven led the applause. When Melody Horn took the podium to speak, everyone assumed she was there to introduce the old Schooner, but clearly she was the main act. "Smyrna has always, historically, had innovation as its hallmark. We even, at this very table today, have the men whose salesmanship and creative point-of-purchase merchandising put Smyrna on the map. I mean the Butler brothers, of course, and their wonderful bank. Let's give them a big hand." She gestured for Frank and Charley to stand, and after they exchanged a glance along the Long Table, they rose and, with a dignity that would not have been out of place in the Japanese imperial court, bowed to the two corners of the room. The salesmen, eager as high-school students taking advantage of an excuse to make noise, cheered and gave the boys a standing ovation.

"In the spirit of Frank and Charley," Melody Horn shouted over the noise, "Smyrna innovation will break new bounds." She went on to announce Smyrna's new communications division, a publishing wing to produce high-school yearbooks ("a natural market we've somehow overlooked all these years") and the "coming thing," videotaped yearbooks ("memories that move and speak"). Then, hailing everyone in the room, salesmen and stockholders, as members of the Smyrna "family," she recalled that they were a community blessed with a prophet as a founder. "He told us, 'Thou art rich,' and, friends, he didn't know the half of it."

"Oh, Melody, Melody," said Mr. Van Schoonhoven as he took her place behind the podium. "I hadn't planned to say this, but as I stood, the words of an old hymn came to me: 'In my heart there rings a melody / of Heaven's harmony.' If our beloved Aunt Nan were with us, she could play it on the piano.

"When you mentioned the Smyrna banks I also couldn't help but remember how we decided to discontinue using them. They had become quarter banks by then and were a lot jazzier than the old black models. But—I'm sure you remember this, Frank, Charley, it's something we can look back on now and laugh—we had a whole shipment that didn't add correctly, and, I'll tell you, we had to eat a pretty hefty loss that fall. But enough of memories. Now it's time for my contribution to the program, and this brief announcement will send us on our parting way. It will be news to all but Melody herself, but effective immediately I will be stepping aside as president of Smyrna to assume the new role of chairman of the board. I will also soon be appointing a board to be chairman of. And without further ado, I am pleased to introduce—and will you stand to welcome her—our new president, the innovative and talented (and dare I say, lovely?) Miss Melody Horn."

The silence before the applause lasted a second too long, and most of the people in the room made up for it by clapping louder and longer than they would have normally.

"It sounds like a bloody talk-show intro," said Mrs. Van Schoonhoven to no one in particular.

"It's the first person totally outside the family to head the community," said Frank Butler to the person on his left.

"It's the first person totally outside the family to head the community," said Charley Butler to the person on his right.

A woman to run Smyrna, thought Ziza Todd.

"Benedikt," said Mr. Van Schoonhoven, easing down the table toward him, "I want you to get a press release out on this to the *Times* and *The Wall Street Journal* right away."

"Getting set to take the stock public?" asked Benedikt, knowing immediately, from the look on Mr. Van Schoonhoven's face, that he shouldn't have.

Naomi, who had never paid much attention to the business side of Smyrna, heard the word "stock" and began to wonder how many shares were in fact still in Lew's name (it was a limited-stock company, she did know that, all shares held privately by family members), and what, now that he was about to be declared legally dead, would become of them?

The crowd coming to the Long Table divided naturally into two groups, the salesmen bursting with congratulations surrounding Melody Horn, and the stockholders more warily approaching Mr. Van Schoonhoven. Melody caught Benedikt's eye and elaborately mouthed the words "You and Mills wait here" and pointed to the table. They sat and waited, Naomi still between them, and were joined by Ziza, who looked as though she had questions to ask.

"Mrs. Quick, I'm Ziza Todd."

"The Reverend Miss Ziza," said Hagadorn Mills.

"Not officially," Ziza said. "I haven't been ordained."

"I saw you at the service for Aunt Nan," Naomi said. "It was lovely, the fire and all. Maybe you can do something for Lew, Llewelyn, my husband, late husband. . . . That is, of course, when we get him back from Albany."

"Of course," said Ziza, "and maybe we could have a talk about the old days at the boys' camp. It's a time no one around here seems to say much about."

"Later, I think, on that," said Sherman Benedikt, firmly enough to put an end to all conversation. The four sat in silence, listening to Mr. Van Schoonhoven assure the crowd around him that all was well with the company and that he was indeed not headed for pasture, while Melody Horn was telling those hanging on her every word that it was still good old Smyrna ("Olde with an *e*," someone interrupted and got a laugh) but now it was going to be a good, olde (this time she said *oldey*) Smyrna that was catching up with the times and maybe getting a little bit ahead.

"Harry had his facts wrong on that bank story," Charley said to Frank.

"As per usual," said Frank.

"Dead wrong," said Charley.

The Dining Room was emptying out, and high-school girls began clearing the tables. There were no carts, so they had to pile the dirty plates on trays and carry them to the kitchen. Naomi had been telling Hagadorn Mills about Young Father Quick's Food Utility Theory—that you shouldn't eat food produced more than a day's travel from where you lived, that the human body was biologically attuned to digest only local food, that trying to cope with food from distant places caused cancer. He made a note on a 3 × 5 card. Earlier in the meal she had tried to tell Sherman Benedikt about it, but the public-relations man immediately began to quibble over what constituted a day's travel ("What about jet planes, the Concorde?"), and she changed the subject. It was not a theory she was much interested in explaining. Like so much about Smyrna, it was curious but not defensible.

Melody Horn came back to their end of the Long Table and gave them a look that made them know what a relief it was for her to get away from the others and be with them.

"Sherman," she said, "Andy. We have to make plans. Naomi, Ziza, you don't mind?" They might have, but they got up and wandered away from the table.

"Sherman, you've got to get to the *Journal* and the *Times* ASAP and give them the whole schmear. Small, independent, private company. Best year in its history. Historic past. Bold new leadership. Limited diversification. Blah-blah-blah. Everything we've been talking about. I also want you to get on the art scene—American Folk Art Museum, Hirschl Adler Gallery, MOMA, someone, whoever it was that wanted to do a show of Aunt Nan's collages or whatever they are. Now that the old lady is gone, we can get moving on that. . . ."

"We'll no longer be respecting her wishes?"

"The dear simply didn't understand, old as she was. She was an unknown primitive master who deserves recognition. There are hundreds of her things around here, and I want them cataloged. The art business takes years to do anything, but I think we have a possible star on our hands. Think of a good name for her. Aunt Nan sounds too much like Grandma Moses. Something that includes the name Smyrna. This is going to be fun.

"And Andy, I want you to set aside lots and lots of time for me. We've got to get your Smyrna history ready as soon as possible. I also have some plans for you in the communications division. Think local history. Every town in the country has a historical society, and they all think their collections of photographs are priceless. Since we're setting up to do high-school yearbooks it will be no problem to do local histories. They send us the stuff. We do everything. And they get a handsome book to sell to their members, complete with an introduction by a Pulitzer Prize–winning historian—you. I think it has gold mine written all over it. Think about it. Smyrna is moving, and we are going to have fun."

And she was gone, out the door, down the hall.

"What. A. Woman," said Mr. Van Schoonhoven, who had strolled over while Melody was talking. "A mold breaker. Shall we follow her example, gentlemen? Today, after all, is the first working day of an all-new Smyrna."

Naomi and Ziza watched Mr. Van Schoonhoven elaborately usher Benedikt and Mills out of the Dining Room. "I don't think gentlemen really call each other gentlemen," said Naomi. "I think it's a word used by admen and city editors and people who write television soap operas about high-powered businessmen. But I don't think it's a word used by real gentlemen."

"You are assuming there are real gentlemen, of course," Ziza said.

There was still a full pot of coffee on the table, and the two women had decided to have another cup. Naomi had tried out Quick's cancer theory on Ziza, and Ziza found herself talking—for no reason she could think of other than a desire to make some contact with this nervous woman—about a street kid she had been counseling who told her how hard it was to pull a knife out of someone once you stabbed them all the way up to the hilt.

"Actually, I think I recently met one," Naomi said, getting back to the subject of gentlemen.

"Not at Smyrna," Ziza said.

Naomi did not answer. They continued to watch the waitresses, who were just about finished. There seemed to be some problem. The three girls who had been filling the trays were talking together excitedly, first looking at something on one of the tables and then something on another. Then another.

"Something wrong, girls?" asked Ziza.

"It just doesn't make sense."

"What?"

"Bones."

"Bones?"

"Little bones on the tables, all picked very clean. You don't usually get bones with bacon and eggs."

Ziza went to look. Naomi didn't. The bones were small and very white and dry, and just about every one of the circular tables had one or two, tucked up in the center on the white paper doily, under the potted plant.

"Leave them there," Ziza said. "Don't touch them." They looked like pieces of fingers or toes or maybe something from the backbone. "And don't throw out anything from the kitchen until the police get here." All activity in the Dining Room came to a halt.

"I'll call," said Naomi. "I know who to call."

She walked quickly out of the room, and the girls began to look frightened.

"It's all right," said Ziza. "Don't be afraid. It's just someone's idea of a joke, a silly prank."

Two days before, she had run down a hallway carrying a bleached bone. Later she had made a joke about playing detective. The time had come, she thought, to begin in earnest.

6

❧

"It's been a busy day for company," Naomi said as she led Ziza down the stairs into the old camp kitchen. Two empty coffee cups still sat on the long table near the stove. It was a table from the mess hall that someone had once tried to strip down to its natural wood. Uneven layers of green paint had been removed, and in places the original pine, now darkened with age, shone through so that the broad plank top now looked like a sheet of weathered bronze.

"Nice effect," said Ziza.

"By accident. That took four gallons of paint remover twenty years ago. Then I gave up. The Quicks gave every stick of mess-hall furniture a new coat of green enamel every spring. It would take an archaeologist to get to the bottom of it." She put the dirty cups in the sink. "How about some tea?"

"Fine," said Ziza.

She had come to find out something, anything about Llewelyn Quick. The trick, she decided, was simply to get Naomi to talk about herself and him. The one thing she had learned as a minister was that everyone wanted to talk about himself. They might not tell you the truth, but even lies are clues, and if you kept quiet they would talk. She had spent hours at the youth project in the Baden-Ormond section of Rochester listening, letting the kids talk (if only to tell the plot of some TV show). At first she thought she should be giving advice—surely she was being paid to do something—but soon learned that if she talked, the kids wouldn't.

"So," she said, "something brought you back to Smyrna after all these years."

"Something." Naomi filled a kettle and put it on the stove.

"The camp looks as though it had been quite an operation."

"Oh, it was."

"Successful."

"Very."

"Just boys."

"Boys."

"From all over."

"The City, mostly."

"New York?"

"New York City, yes."

"For all summer?"

"Six weeks, yes."

"Rich boys."

"Oh, yes."

Silence.

"Swimming, crafts, hiking, sports?"

"It was a boys' summer camp, yes. But no team sports."

"Oh?"

"Young Father Quick didn't hold much for team sports."

"Oh?"

"He had his reasons, as usual."

"Oh?"

Silence.

"Lots of singing around the campfire, I suppose."

"Some."

Silence.

"Much homesickness?"

"With the little ones, but only at first—the gnomes, we called them. They were my job. We never sent a boy home early unless he was sick or had a broken leg. Even the ones with broken bones—not that there were that many, although the Quicks were big on rock climbing—even they usually asked to stay. It was a happy camp. The boys would come back year after year, and then they would try to get jobs here."

The water boiled.

"You don't mind tea bags." It wasn't a question.

"Young Father Quick was the camp director?"

"Oh, no, he had died years before. But His Spirit Lived On, if you know what I mean. No, the director, at least on paper, was Harry Van Schoonhoven. But he and Gwen stayed up at Mansion House and didn't have much to do with things except on opening day and parents' weekend, although they tried to make a point of attending the evening meal. No, it was Lew's show, at least during my time here. And after he . . . left, the camp went out of business."

"A lot of responsibility for someone that young."

"Twenty-three when I came here, not all that young for someone raised to be a prince."

"He had a way about him, then?"

"Oh, nothing slick or polished, no. Some people at that age are all finished, completed. You know what they'll be like for the rest of their lives. Not Lew. He was still growing. He even looked like he was still growing, as though he wasn't yet all put together. But he was one of those people other people keep their eyes on. You were always aware that he was there."

"Handsome?"

"No. Yes, in a tousled sort of way. Unfashionable. He wore his hair parted in the middle when no one did that outside of an Archie Andrews comic book. His clothes never seemed to fit, but he always looked right in them. And to watch him climb was a wonder. He would be up the face of a cliff while everyone else was looking for the first handhold. His climbing classes were the most popular activity in camp. We have a lot of cliffs in this valley."

"You climbed, too?"

"Good Lord, no," Naomi said with a laugh. "I'm not that crazy."

The two women sipped their tea in silence. Ziza could see that the room had recently been cleaned. A chipped Dundee marmalade jar full of fresh wildflowers was sitting on top of a Spanish tile on the table.

"From this morning's gentleman caller," Naomi said, noticing Ziza's interest in the flowers. "A gentleman from the police. Mr. Nick Story. He led me through all the questions you just asked, and he got just about the same information. He also asked me about the night Lew dropped out of sight. Are you about to get to that?"

There was a pause. Ziza looked at Naomi. Naomi looked back. Neither attempted to make a joke.

"Yes," Ziza said, "I was. Perhaps with the second cup of tea, maybe after telling you a bit about myself. To gain your confidence. Just as they tell us to do in human relations class."

"You have my confidence," Naomi said. "You're a seminary graduate student with not much church experience but with a little social work under your belt. Right? I'd be glad to hear about your life sometime but not as an interview ploy. There's absolutely nothing I can tell you about Lew's disappearance. One morning he was gone. That's it. On our second cup of tea I'll tell you why I'm here. That's something Mr. Story, using all his professional charm, never got out of me."

Ziza was puzzled. Was Naomi simply putting her on, or were they having a friendly girl-to-girl chat? For the moment, she suspected, neither answer was correct. Naomi, too, had a mystery to solve, and perhaps she saw Ziza helping her solve it. With the second cup of tea came Oreo cookies.

"I received a letter. Unsigned. 'Llewelyn returns home on the weekend of the twentieth.' How could I have passed that up?"

"Do you have it?"

Without answering, Naomi stood and picked a yellowed

piece of paper from the top of the refrigerator and handed it to Ziza. It was a single sheet of paper with a Smyrna crown as its letterhead. There was no date. No salutation. Just the words Naomi had said, typed with a ribbon that should have been changed a thousand words ago. No signature.

"No envelope?"

"I threw it away before I thought better of it. I always open my mail, stack up the letters and throw away the envelopes. It had a Catskill postmark, I remember that."

"This paper's so old you can smell the dust on it. 'Llewelyn returns home on the weekend of the twentieth.' Who called him Llewelyn instead of Lew?"

"Everyone but me. Lew's the only name I ever used."

They both continued looking at the letter as though there were something they had missed.

"Now you know what brought me back to Smyrna." She took the paper and carefully placed it in front of her on the table.

"What got you here in the first place?"

"I think it's my turn to ask you questions. I answered a classified ad in the *Times,* if you want to know the truth. How did *you* get here?"

So Ziza fell into her own trap and began talking about herself—about the divinity school in Rochester, with its tradition of preaching the social gospel ("considered revolutionary, circa 1917"), about her boredom with homiletic nitpicking, about the social work she felt totally unqualified for and about her adviser, who came up with a research project for her thesis. A change of pace. Smyrna, he said, was one of the few nineteenth-century Christian utopian communities still in operation (however different it was from its origins). Unlike Oneida and the Shakers it hadn't been researched to death, and most of its records still seemed to be intact. So she wrote to Mr. Van Schoonhoven, and he said, "Come ahead."

"You like the idea of being a minister?"

"I like the idea of being bad."

"And getting away with it?"

"No, of knowing better."

Naomi thought about that for a minute, then picked up the dirty cups and put them into the sink with the others.

"It was you who found him," she finally said.

"I found the sleeping bag, yes."

"It must have been a terrible experience, the shock and all."

"Yes."

"I'm so sorry."

"No, no, it's you who've had the shock. And the bones on the table at breakfast yesterday . . ."

"Those bones were just silly, a bad joke. A shock would have been Lew walking into the room and asking where I'd been all these years. Come on," she said, "I have something to show you. Bring the letter."

They went upstairs, through the shadows the scaffolding on the back of the house threw across the empty mess-hall annex and back into the original farmhouse. "One more flight and then we go up into the attic," said Naomi, now out of breath. Ziza could feel Naomi's excitement and was uneasy about it.

The door to the attic stairs had once been padlocked, Ziza noticed, but the hasp was pulled away. "I'll go first," said Naomi. "I know where the light pull is. It might be dark up there." The stairs were steep, but the small dormer windows let in enough light to see. By the time they got to the top, Naomi was panting.

"We can rest a minute," Ziza said.

Except at its center, under the peak of the steep roof, the single attic room was low-ceilinged and close. The flooring, which was only loose sheets of plywood, did not reach to the edges, where open rafters exposed lathing and the plaster ceilings of the rooms below. In one corner was a heap of broken green chairs from the mess hall. There were stacks of mattresses still musty with the smell of bed-wettings from decades before. There was a tangle of old floor lamps and a pile of molding canvas. The air was thick with the drowsy sound of buzzing flies battering themselves against the grimy windows.

"I didn't tell Nick Story about this," Naomi said, "but I've been doing some detective work of my own. Over here, look."

Ziza stooped and followed Naomi toward a far corner, pausing on the way to force open a window. The trapped flies escaped and cool fresh air rushed in, scattering the dried husks of hundreds of dead insects that had piled up on the rotted sill.

"No, over here," said Naomi, impatient to show off her discovery. "Here. I found it yesterday."

It was an old Royal portable typewriter. Next to it was a box half filled with yellowed stationery bearing crowned letterheads. "Look." She rolled a sheet of paper into the machine and typed quickly and expertly: *Llewelyn returns home on the weekend of the twentieth*. "Compare."

Ziza didn't need to. The faint gray writing on the dingy paper was unmistakable.

"It was done here," said Naomi.

Yes, thought Ziza, but done when and—noticing that there were no envelopes in the box—by whom?

7

It was called the library closet, but it was really a small, windowless room. Sherman Benedikt had shown Ziza where to find the light switch, then went back out to his usual place at a table in the main alcove of the library. "I won't close the door all the way," he said. "I don't think you have all that much air in there."

Ziza had learned that she had a better chance of finding Benedikt in the library than in his assigned office downstairs, a room the size of the library closet next to Mr. Van Schoonhoven's suite. In fact, she noticed, Benedikt seemed to have moved most of his equipment into the library—his IBM Selectric, a telephone extension, a double-wheeled Rolodex, an oversized Mexican coffee cup full of perfectly sharpened number two pencils and a two-drawer wood-grained metal filing cabinet on wheels (locked, she noticed when she had just happened to tug on the top drawer handle). Everything, she thought, but a Plexiglas photo cube of family snapshots, and there wasn't one of those in the downstairs office either.

The library closet was a mess. The wooden shelves that lined it from floor to ceiling were a jumble of yellow file boxes, ledger-size journals, papers tied up in hemp string and loose sheets spilling out of open folders. She could taste the dust in the air. In one corner was a large cardboard box brittle with age and filled to the top with identical copies—maroon binding with bright gold lettering embossed on the cover— of *The Social, Mercantile and Ecclesiastical History of the Smyrna Community of Greene County, New York,* by Idris Quick. Of course it would be a Quick, Ziza thought. Curiously, it was not a book she had come across on the community history shelf in the library. The publisher was a Catskill printing company, and the copyright date was 1939. She blew dust off the copy she was looking at and slipped it into her purse.

"My father's magnum opus," said Mrs. Van Schoonhoven. "Do take a copy."

Ziza jumped. She may even have cried out in surprise. Mrs. Van Schoonhoven was full of apologies.

"Oh, dear," she said, "I had no intention of startling you. Sherman told me you were deepening your research, so I thought I would drop by to offer a helpful hand. Or word. Or what I could. As the daughter of the first official historian, late though he is, I might be of some assistance. Of course, I made the same offer to Mr. Mills, Andy, whatever. But he seems in control of things."

"He's been through all this?"

"I suppose so. It would be the place to start, once you've done the obvious." She motioned vaguely toward the half-open door.

"These papers don't look as though they've been touched in years."

"I suspect Andy's touch is very light indeed. He has been working away like a little beaver down in the old children's wing. Excuse me, the new Publications Center. *Pace,* Miss Melody Horn."

"I hadn't been aware of your father's book. It's something I'll want to get into right away. It looks, well, hefty."

"Overlooked is what it is. Ignored."

"Why?"

"Why, indeed. That's a question you must put one day to Mr. Van Schoonhoven. And get back to me with his answer.

I'd love to hear it." She ran her hand across a file folder ("Maturity Tables, Development of Secondary Pubic Hair: 1908–1911") and carefully studied her smeared fingertips.

The door suddenly swung completely open, and Mr. Van Schoonhoven's head appeared around the corner. Then came a shoulder, an arm, a leg, then—with a sideways leap—the rest of him. His face was sweating. He was panting. "Aha," he said. It was an entrance right out of summer stock or, perhaps, Punch and Judy.

"My dear," he said, apparently addressing his wife, "Mr. Story has been about. *Again.* There seems to be no end to his questions about poor Llewelyn. I've been telling him that was a subject you were far more qualified than I to discuss." He paused significantly and nodded rather formally toward Ziza. "My wife and poor Llewelyn were once quite the two-some—before, that is, her wandering eyes met mine."

"Or the arrival of Naomi?"

"That, too," said Mr. Van Schoonhoven.

"Be serious, Harry. Ziza, he's talking schoolgirl crush. It's nothing to bring up with a detective."

"He's downstairs, getting no information at all out of Melody. Come."

He guided her into the library and then out the doorway. She protested as she went, protested until they reached the hall ("He was practically my brother, for crying out loud." "Not really." "Cousin, then." "Not really." "Really enough"), and then there was silence, only the sounds of footsteps heading for the staircase.

Ziza had followed them into the library. "Sometimes," Sherman Benedikt said to her, "I suspect that they never speak when they're alone. Only when there's an audience."

"Witnesses," said Ziza.

"Nick Story's been here this morning, too. The state troopers probably don't have top-of-the-line detectives, but I suppose he knows what he's doing, asking a question here, a question there, whatever pops into his head. It seems to me he's straying pretty far from solving the Mystery of the Ancient Bones in Auntie's Mummy Bag."

"Oh?"

"It's his silences that can drive you nuts. He asks a question. You do your damnedest to answer it the best you can, and then there's an endless pause before he can think up something else. Some of them were even about you. A lot of them, actually."

"Such as?"

"What you are doing at Smyrna."

"And you said?"

" 'Not my department' is what I said. He seemed to think you've been asking a lot of questions yourself."

"Research."

"Wanted to know if you had talked with me about Llewelyn, or the Schooner and the missus, or the Butler boys or even Naomi. He seemed especially interested in *your* interest in Naomi."

"Nothing special."

"Really? But he seems to think that Naomi has told you things she hasn't told him. Apparently he's seen quite a bit of her, and lately she's been hinting about something she knows—and you know—that he doesn't. It sounds as though she's become quite the little flirt."

"Naomi has been through a lot. I suspect she's lonely and needs someone to talk to. Talk with."

"More likely to drink with, from what I've heard."

"Just what have you heard?"

Benedikt did not answer. He stared, his brown eyes focusing on something just over Ziza's left shoulder. She refused to turn her head to see if anything was there. Instead she stared back, trying to look him straight in the eye. He was older than he seemed at first glance, more wrinkles, more tiny blotches on the skin. His haircut was too expensive-looking to have been done locally, his jacket a touch too tweedy, his William Morris tie too casually knotted. In the middle of Greene County, he was still dressed for midtown Manhattan.

"We could always pass the time with knock-knock jokes. You first."

His smile was thin, but Ziza suspected it was genuine. He stretched his arms backward and sighed the kind of painful groan people usually save for occasions when they have to show they recognize a terrible pun. "What I hear are questions—'What's Ziza Todd up to?' Mostly from Andy Mills. 'What's old Naomi doing here, and isn't it odd that she turns up just when poor'—he's always poor—'Llewelyn surfaces?' Mostly from the Schooners. 'When's Mills going to finish his Smyrna book?' From Melody Horn. Also, 'Why doesn't the *Times* financial page give us more space on the expansion plans?' From the Schooner himself. 'Thank God, but why have the papers, even the local papers, paid so little attention to the bones?'

"We've been lucky there," Benedikt continued. "One day on the first page of the second section and nothing more. Thank God for a mass murderer loose in the emergency room of the Troy hospital—small children the victims of choice. He's captured the ghouls' attention. In fact, the only person who seems in the least bit curious about the bones is dogged old Nick Story."

"What was all that about poor Llewelyn and Mrs. Van Schoonhoven?"

"Ancient history isn't my game."

"Don't know or won't say?"

Benedikt paused long enough to make Ziza suspect he was being coy again. "Don't really know, except that Llewelyn wasn't really the grandson of Young Father Quick. But that's no secret. It's part of the local theology. Just like Young Father wasn't really the son of Old Father. It seems as though a pillar of Smyrna dogma was that the heir to the community must be chosen as a baby through some sort of ritual. Leadership couldn't be inherited."

"Like choosing the Dalai Lama?"

"Knowing this bunch, it was probably not as simple as that. They believed that God would make His choice known, and then he would be adopted into the Quick family."

"By heir, do you mean that Llewelyn actually owned Smyrna?"

"Oh, no. It's a joint stock company. All the heirs of the original members of the community own shares—which they supposedly must not sell—and since the company has done very well over the years they're all pretty well off. The Quicks, though, have the biggest share. Had, I guess. Aunt Nan, Llewelyn, Mrs. Van Schoonhoven."

"But they couldn't sell?"

"Individual shares can only be inherited, and I heard Melody Horn say that Aunt Nan's stock, since she died without an heir, would simply revert to the block controlled by management."

"And management is Mr. Van Schoonhoven."

"More or less."

"And Llewelyn's shares, did Naomi inherit them?"

"You've got me."

Was he being coy? "You must hear a lot about what goes on in the office," she said.

"Actually, I left the fax machine downstairs and moved up here so I wouldn't."

"Maybe we could work as a team. You, Mr. Inside. Me, Ms. Outside. Together we could crack this case."

"What case?"

"The Mystery of the Ancient Bones in Auntie's Mummy Bag, as a starter."

"Listen, Ziza. I'm an adult. I have an adult's job. Perhaps not a grown man's job, but an adult's job. I'm to get the right kind of news about Olde Smyrna in the right kind of publications. I'm supposed to get financial writers to take all these changes seriously, to get travel editors to plan big stories about the opening, even to get fashion magazines to shoot layouts on our grounds. Now Melody has some wild idea about promoting Aunt Nan's crazy collages as Great American Folk Art. I'm supposedly the flack with tact, and I'm not paid to play Nancy Drew or Father Brown or whoever your role model might be."

"But you answer Nick Story's questions."

"As a law-abiding citizen I cooperate with the authorities."

This time the long pause was Ziza's. "I *do* know something Story doesn't know." It was her turn to play hard to get. Now she looked over Benedikt's shoulder and studied one of Aunt Nan's contructions on the far wall, a giant collage of bark, scraps of yarn, fabric and painted wood that indeed looked more than a little like the Smyrna waterfall.

He didn't seem to be taking her bait. Then, "What?"

"Why Naomi's here."

"Why?"

"A letter. It said 'Llewelyn returns home on the weekend of the twentieth.' "

"From?"

"Someone here."

"Are you sure?"

"Almost."

He carefully threaded a sandwich of paper and carbons into his typewriter. It had been years since Ziza had seen anyone use carbon paper. Either Sherman Benedikt was hopelessly out of date or he had something against using the Xerox machine downstairs. Without looking up, he said, "Great Bear and Highfield."

"What's that?"

"Check them out in *The Wall Street Journal*. Just about any issue will do. The old Schooner gets all uptight when he has to return their calls, which seems fairly often. And I heard Andy Mills mention it once. Only once."

"Does Story know?"

"The real question is, Does Mrs. Van Schoonhoven know? Or Melody Horn?"

"Do they?"

"Don't you have a closet to clean?"

Instead she went over to the couch and began looking through Idris Quick's history, the pictures first, mostly steel engravings of various buildings and a few portraits. She was studying the faces in a group portrait of students in the Children's House when Charley and Frank Butler came in.

"Gwen Van Schoonhoven said you were both here," said Frank.

"She said Ziza was working in the closet," said Charley.

"The closet in the library," said Frank.

"We're all invited to dinner tomorrow night," said Charley. "All of us, *en famille,* says Gwen. Eight o'clock. No latecomers, in the Dining Room."

"How nice," said Ziza, "I suppose." She held up the book she was reading. "Are either of you familiar with this?"

"Where did you find that?" asked Frank.

"There's a whole boxful of them in the closet," said Charley.

"I haven't seen one in years," said Frank.

"There's been a boxful of them in the closet for years," said Charley.

"Is it any good?" Ziza asked.

"I don't know about good," said Frank, "but it was written to be the official, authorized history."

"But never was," said Charley.

"What happened?"

Charley looked to Frank, who looked to Charley. "Things change," said Charley.

"Does that invitation include me?" Sherman Benedikt asked.

"You bet," said Frank.

"I was afraid of that," Benedikt said.

"History doesn't change," said Ziza, riffling through the pages.

"Historians do," said Benedikt.

Her fingers stopped about two thirds of the way through. "There are some pages missing," she said.

"We have to go," said Frank.

"It's in a chapter called 'Well On With The Work,' pages 303 to 306. They've been very neatly torn out."

"We'll see you at dinner," said Frank. "Naomi's coming, too. And Mr. Mills, I believe. Maybe even Miss Horn."

"At least there are a lot more copies. I'll try another," said Ziza.

"Don't bother," said Charley, following Frank out the door. "They're all that way."

8

❧

Hagadorn Mills parked a Smyrna pickup in front of the camp mess hall. He left the headlights on and walked up the over-grown flagstones to the front door. There was no bell. The iron door knocker, a woman's daintily curved fist, was rusted into place, and a trail of oxidation the color of faded blood discolored the door below. So he banged his knuckles on the sill twice, waited a while and banged once more, as though it were a code. He was dressed like an overage college stu-dent, loafers, gray slacks, a blue oxford-cloth shirt and rep tie hidden underneath a plain gray crewneck sweater (all pur-chased from a preppy mail-order outfit somewhere in the Midwest). No answer, so he banged twice more, this time openhanded, louder than before. Mrs. Van Schoonhoven's orders were that they weren't to be late.

The light came on in the hall, and the door opened. "Ah, Mr. Mills, my blind date," said Naomi. She was dressed in a gray skirt and sweater with a circle pin, high heels and stock-ings. Together, she thought, they looked like a black-and-white photograph from a 1959 issue of *Life*.

"Call me Andy."

"No flowers?" she asked, teasing.

"You might have been allergic," he answered seriously.

"No chocolates?"

"You might have been diabetic."

"Or on a diet."

They eyed each other, she wondering how serious he could really be about all of this, wondering, also, what this evening was all about. She closed up the house, followed him down the walk and was all set to jump into the pickup when she realized he was positioning himself to open the door for her. She waited; he pulled the handle. She was all set to jump up into the truck when he took her arm, more ceremonially than practically, and helped her in. She sat up straight and looked dead ahead, toward the old stone Gnomes' House. Someone had recently been in it, she noticed, or at least the screen door had been opened and not pulled shut. Andy Mills closed her door slowly, not banging it, walked around the hood and slipped into the driver's seat. It was all done so solemnly that Naomi suspected his whole performance was a put-on. She waited for the bad joke, something like, What time do your folks expect you home?

"You're someone I never thought I would get a chance to interview," he said, talking slowly and with a measured cadence, as though speaking to someone very old and possibly very distinguished. Surely, Naomi thought, we must be about the same age.

"You were there," he said, as they started down the dirt road.

She did not ask where. Or when.

"You must have heard people talking when they were still young enough to be indiscreet. I got to talk to Aunt Nan just before she died, but that was like talking to the bedpost. She just sat in her room all day gluing pieces of junk together. Talking to the Butler boys is like playing Ping-Pong with a doubles team. And Mrs. Van Schoonhoven, well, she's either cagey or just plain silly. Sometimes she sets traps. But you must remember the way things really were."

"What I remember, only vaguely, is what it was like to be twenty-one or twenty-two. I remember more about myself than about them."

"Pencil me in."

"What?" She half expected him to say "ma'am."

"For sometime tomorrow morning or afternoon, a good two-hour block. Let's make a firm appointment. My office is in the old Children's House, and we can let our hair down. You haven't filled in the Reverend Todd, have you?"

"We've had a nice talk or two."

"Oh, God. Please save it for me. We can even work out some sort of contract, maybe even a royalty payment of some kind. Melody Horn has been talking made-for-TV series, cassette rights, you name it."

He pulled around the curve of the Heart and parked next to the front steps of Mansion House. Before he had turned off the ignition and unbuckled his seat belt she was out of her door and on his side of the truck opening his. He looked appalled.

"Please, Mrs. Quick."

She did not answer until they reached the Dining Room, and she kept ahead of him so he couldn't help her up the steps.

In the doorway she paused long enough to say, "Ten o'clock. No tape. No notes. Just talk, and the name, Andy, is Naomi." He reached out to take her hand in both of his, but she evaded him.

The room was completely dark except for a circle of light in front of the fireplace, where a round table had been set for nine. There were lighted candles and an old wooden trencher full of pinecones as the centerpiece. The silver was real, the plates were china, there were linen napkins. An impression was being made. Mrs. Van Schoonhoven confirmed it by giving Naomi a big welcoming kiss.

"It's past eight," she said, "but we can hardly call you late, Andy, since our host has yet to appear." She laughed as though she were kidding. "There are drinks on the trolley. Have something, and freshen mine."

Everyone else was there. The Butlers were talking with

Ziza Todd, who was wearing a red velour jumpsuit and an elaborate silk scarf that looked, to Naomi, like a Palio flag from Siena. What I did on my summer vacation. The brothers wore their identical dark-blue three-piece suits and official Olde Smyrna neckties decorated with golden crowns large enough to be seen in the light given off by the fireplace. Sherman Benedikt was deep in conversation with Melody Horn, who held on to his arm. She talked; he nodded his agreement. They were both dressed for a fashionable cocktail party. Everyone seems to be in costume tonight, Naomi thought, even Gwen Van Schoonhoven in her long black dress decorated with oversized silver sequins that looked like fragments of armor. Dress-up night at Smyrna, rainy-day-at-camp activities.

Ziza had watched Naomi race Hagadorn Mills across the room to the fireplace, saw Mrs. Van Schoonhoven's warm embrace of her new guest (What was she, cousin-in-law? Step-cousin-in-law?) and found it very hard to pay attention to Frank and Charley, who were telling her about the time Young Father Quick told them they were going to go out into the world as salesmen. She had hoped to use the evening picking their brains about poor Llewelyn and how he was chosen to be the heir, but she could not deflect them from retelling a story she had heard before, a story they had told so often they were not even listening themselves. As they talked on about Young Father and his advice to teenagers about to leave home ("Never, never accept free lodging . . ."), the Butlers themselves were also watching Gwen and Naomi and, from time to time, stole a glance at Melody Horn.

Hagadorn Mills approached the two women with an amber-colored drink in each hand, sniffed them, and handed the scotch to Mrs. Van Schoonhoven, the ginger ale to Naomi. Before he went for his own drink, he insisted that both women taste theirs to make sure they had the right ones and that there was enough—but not too much—ice. (Naomi could have told the drinks apart from their color, and she suspected

Gwen could, too.) Before the women could begin a conversation, Andy had returned with his own drink (scotch, no ice, no water, by the look of it), a tiny silver bowl of peanuts and a handful of cocktail napkins. "*Mangia, mangia,*" he said. "*Ess, ess, mein Kind*" and smiled a painfully crooked grin, grotesquely boyish as all get-out. Was he, Naomi wondered, someone who had absolutely no sense of his own age, fifty if he was a day, or was this all simply an inept display of what Andy Mills considered charm and company manners?

Gwen Van Schoonhoven completely ignored him. She glanced over to Melody Horn and seemed to exchange the slightest of nods with her, an exchange everyone in the room noticed and assumed no one else had. With one swallow, she polished off her drink, handed the glass back to Andy without actually acknowledging his presence and said "Friends" loud enough to bring all conversation to a stop. "Why don't we sit down? We have some things we can get started on while we're waiting for Mr. Van Schoonhoven."

There was some polite fumbling around the table as they all chose their seats ("Boy-girl, boy-girl," said Charley Butler), and Naomi found her chair being held for her by Andy Mills, who sat down on her right side. The chair on her left was empty, reserved for the host. Ziza sat surrounded by Butlers.

A Smyrna employee came out of the kitchen, filled their wineglasses and left. They waited, some looking at Mrs. Van Schoonhoven, some at Melody Horn, most glancing back and forth between them. Melody carefully rearranged her silverware. Mrs. Van Schoonhoven spoke: "I suppose you can call this an information session. As you all know very well, we have been having repeated visits by that very nice state policeman. What's the name of your friend, Naomi?"

"Are you referring to Nick Story?" asked Naomi, an unwilling straight man.

"Of course I am. He keeps asking about the day, or night, that poor Llewelyn disappeared. It was so long ago, who can remember? But Harry, or maybe it was Melody, had the suggestion that if we all got together maybe we could reconstruct that time and refresh memories all round. And then all of us, even our new friends, would have a clearer idea of what happened."

And we'll all have identical stories, Ziza thought.

"I remember as though it were yesterday," said Charley.

"Mr. Story should have just come and seen us," said Frank.

"It was the night of the birthday bonfire, which was always at the end of August, just before camp closing—"

"A huge fire," interrupted Frank, "bigger than any before or since. There had been a lot of storms that spring, and the creek banks were holding more dried-out driftwood than I'd ever seen. The boys had a wonderful time building that fire. They kept piling up the logs, and Llewelyn kept sending more crews back to the plantation for brash so there would be enough kindling to get the bigger logs going. He needn't have worried. The whole thing lit up like a Polish church and—"

"Llewelyn was there for the fire?" asked Ziza.

"Of course he was, it was his show," said Charley, "always was, lots of singing and a lion hunt—"

"A lion hunt?" asked Hagadorn Mills.

"It's a story with sound effects," said Naomi. "We'd sit around the fire, and the leader, Lew, would say 'Let's all go on a lion hunt,' and everyone would slap their thighs in the rhythm of someone walking, and there would be different noises for swimming rivers, going through swamps and high grass, jumping streams and so on. At the end, of course, they meet a lion, and the whole thing, with all the noises, is repeated as fast as possible in reverse order as though at a dead run."

"The boys always loved a lion hunt," said Frank.

"Actually," said Naomi, "I always felt they didn't enjoy it that much. They thought it was kind of silly, but Lew clearly enjoyed doing it so much they all went along with it. They were always asking for the lion hunt, but their real fun was watching Lew make a fool of himself."

"You're saying that they were just humoring him?" asked Mills.

"Children spend a great deal of their time humoring adults," said Ziza.

"What they did like—honestly like," Naomi said, "was the ghost story."

"Bonfires always ended with a ghost story," said Frank.

"Usually the same one," said Charley.

" 'Black Isobel and the Evil Judge,' " said Frank.

"Black Isobel was a slave," said Naomi. "This was set back about the time of the Revolution, and she was owned by an evil judge in the village of Catskill. One day she escaped and ran off and eventually found a hiding place on the old farm that used to be here. The only thing that's left of it is the Gnomes' House over at the camp. Well, the judge tracked her down—this part can be dragged on for a long time as the fire gets lower and lower—to the waterfall, caught her, tied a rope around her neck, jumped up on his horse and rode back to Catskill, making her run along behind, never stopping once. By the time he got home, Black Isobel was dead. There was a trial, and he was found guilty, but since she was only a slave and he was a judge, his sentence was not hanging. No, he had to live the rest of his life with a rope tied around his neck, just like Black Isobel. He finds a very expensive silk rope and wears it like a necktie, but the ghost of Black Isobel doesn't let him sleep, and one night he can stand it no longer. He rides back to the Falls—our falls here at Smyrna—and, still wearing the noose around his neck, jumps and is killed. The body is washed away and never found, but during full moons his ghost still walks along the creek and around the Gnomes' House at Smyrna."

"What a dreadful story," Ziza said, "dragging that woman to her death—it must have given the younger children terrible dreams."

"No," said Naomi, "if it had been about a little boy being killed or an animal, a dog maybe, it would have given them nightmares. But she was only a black woman. It was the ghost of the judge that made them wet their beds."

"As local color this is all very charming," said Melody Horn, giving Naomi her warmest smile, "and I suspect Sherman Benedikt may be able to work up something about the judge and Isobel—I suggest that we drop the black slave aspect—but I think we're getting far afield from poor Llewelyn."

"He told 'Black Isobel and the Evil Judge,' " said Charley, "and we all sang the parting hymn—"

" 'Now the day is over,' " Frank half sang, half spoke, " 'Night is drawing nigh, / Shadows of the evening, / Steal across the sky.' "

"The fire had become terribly smoky—"

"Not all the brash was as dry as it had seemed."

"So after the counselors led the campers back to their bunks, Frank and I stayed behind to help Llewelyn rake down the fire."

"But he said no."

"But he said no, he'd let it burn down some more, he said, and then come back to the camp later."

"He sent us on our way. And we never saw him again."

"Never."

Mrs. Van Schoonhoven had seen to it that the wineglasses had been kept full, but no food had appeared, and Mr. Van Schoonhoven still had not arrived. Naomi noticed that there were pencils and small yellow pads next to the places of Melody, Mills and Benedikt. They all seemed to have been making notes. It was, she assumed, her turn.

"He never came back," she said and almost reached for the untouched wineglass in front of her.

"And?" asked Melody Horn.

"He never came back. He never slept in his bed. The next morning he was gone. That's all."

They all waited, as though they did not, in fact, believe that was all.

Ziza waited, hoping that the old silence trick might stir something up. It didn't, so she finally said, "I'm curious about the Van Schoonhovens. Harry *was* the camp director, at least in name. Was he there that night? Were you, Gwen?"

"Oh, no," said Mrs. Van Schoonhoven, "we didn't attend evening events. The camp was really Llewelyn's show. We usually ate dinner with the boys in the mess hall, but that was our only contact. As a rule. We were newlyweds, you know, just like Llewelyn and Naomi. The last thing in the world *we* wanted to do was to spend our time with dozens of little boys." The inference, clearly, was that Llewelyn and Naomi were not so discerning.

"But you were there at the birthday bonfire," said Charley.

"The smoke," said Frank.

"You complained about the smoke," said Charley, "that no matter what side of the fire you stood on, you still got smoke in your eyes."

"Someone always says that at a campfire," Mrs. Van Schoonhoven said. "You are confusing me with someone else."

"I remember as though it were yesterday," said Charley.

"Wrong," said Mrs. Van Schoonhoven.

" 'We remember,' " Frank sang. " 'We remember.' " It was another old camp song. " 'We remember thee, Zi-on. . . .' "

"Perhaps Naomi remembers," Ziza said.

"No, she doesn't," said Naomi.

"I think we should begin without Mr. Van Schoonhoven," said Mrs. Van Schoonhoven. Without any obvious signal the waiter appeared, pushing a cart, and began passing out bowls of what smelled like hot corn soup.

"Perhaps our mistake," said Melody Horn, taking her first sip of the soup, "—my, isn't this delicious, an old community recipe I'm sure—our mistake, perhaps, is that we are focusing in on the last moment. Perhaps, perhaps, we should try to recall the last whole day."

"At seven-thirty, the bugler played reveille," said Charley. "I remember as though it were yesterday."

There was an audible groan, but everyone was intent on the soup. ("Imagine how even better it must be with *fresh* corn.")

"No, no, Charley, you're forgetting first call, five minutes before reveille," said Frank.

"By God, I lied," said Charley. "I forgot first call. However could I?"

"Charley always slept through first call," Frank said to Ziza, since no one else seemed to be paying any attention.

"Why would you have a bugle call before the wake-up call?" she asked, more out of politeness than curiosity.

"Why? For the skinny-dippers. We allowed skinny-dipping in the stream from seven-thirty to seven thirty-five. But no one ever went. Young Father Quick had once said there was no better way to greet the day. So it was, you might say, a traditional option."

The waiter had come back to pick up the empty bowls, when a lurid red light cut across the ceiling of the Dining Room. It swung past and was followed by a white light, then another red. By the time Nick Story came through the door everyone was expecting the police or an ambulance driver. Mrs. Van Schoonhoven stood first. The others followed.

"I'm sorry to interrupt," Nick Story said, "but Mrs. Van Schoonhoven, would you mind coming with me? There's been an accident. . . ."

"Where?"

"Over at the old boys' camp. You better come, too, Naomi."

By the time they got to the front door and into the waiting cars, everyone had decided to go except for the Butler brothers, who stood on the front steps and watched the others drive off. They turned toward each other, stood silently for a moment, and then Frank said, "It must be time for the main course. It shouldn't go begging, whatever it is."

"Indeed not," said Charley.

Naomi and Ziza rode with Nick Story and Mrs. Van Schoonhoven in his car. The others squeezed into Mills's pickup and followed along behind. Story did not try to make small talk. Mrs. Van Schoonhoven did not ask any questions. When they pulled up to the Gnomes' House, an ambulance was waiting, its wide back door open, an attendant sitting inside, his legs dangling over the edge. He was having a cigarette. Two other police cars stood nearby, empty, their radios squawking.

"This way," Nick Story said. "We have to go down into the cellar." The screen door was wedged open. "That's how they found him," Story said. "One of the workmen saw the door and became suspicious. The house was supposedly all locked up." They walked into the kitchen—living room that took up the entire first floor. Upstairs was the dormitory where the youngest campers used to sleep. Except for dust, the place had not changed since Naomi had last seen it. There was a wide stone fireplace that still smelled of ashes although it hadn't been used in years. Over it hung a flintlock rifle that she remembered. They used to tell the campers it had belonged to Daniel Boone.

"I'll lead the way downstairs," Story said. "The steps aren't the best."

They headed down, Story first. Ziza paused at the top—she did not want to go down there—then reached out to help Mrs. Van Schoonhoven. As they came down the badly leaning stairs, they moved into blinding light. The police had rigged up a portable unit that made the place as bright and shadowless as a television studio.

What struck Naomi was that never, in all the times she had visited that cellar, had she realized how beautifully fitted together the stonework was. What struck Ziza was the number of policemen who fit into the small space and how quiet they all were. What struck Mrs. Van Schoonhoven was the long white sheet stretched over a mound in the corner.

"It may well have been a natural death," Story said, "probably was. Heart attack, more than likely. But we would like you to take a look."

"We expected him for dinner," Mrs. Van Schoonhoven said. "A place had been set."

Story nodded to one of the men, who pulled back the sheet. It was Mr. Van Schoonhoven, doubled over as though he had a pain in his stomach. His eyes were open. He did not look terrified, only mildly surprised.

"Of course it's him," Mrs. Van Schoonhoven said. There was some scuffling on the stairs as Melody Horn pushed past Mills and Benedikt. They could hear her footsteps run across the floor above them. A door slammed. The policeman replaced the sheet.

"Did he have a heart condition?"

"Not a serious one. Or so he said."

"Why would he have been down here? Any idea?"

"We expected him for dinner."

"I think we should go," Naomi said. Story nodded. Naomi and Ziza led Mrs. Van Schoonhoven toward the stairs, but she pulled away from her comforters and walked quickly up the steps alone.

"Sir," said the policeman who had pulled back the sheet, "while you were gone we did some looking around and found this on the shelf over there, just above the body." He held up a rusted coffee can half filled with bone fragments so shiny they looked as though they had been licked clean by a hungry dog.

9

❧

Naomi sat at the old camp table in the mess-hall kitchen and thought about making coffee—thought about rinsing the kettle, filling it, throwing out the old grounds in the Melitta filter, throwing out the filter, rinsing the pot and filter holder, attaching the filter, dumping in the new coffee, French blend (grinding it first, though, in the old Dutch hand grinder mounted on the wall), waiting for the water to boil. And while waiting she would just start thinking about the things coffee making was busywork done to forget. Or was it just to avoid? Waiting for the boiled water to drip through the filter, smelling the coffee, thinking of the old days. Think On Death, said the gravestones, the petulant angels.

"We remember, we remember, we remember thee, Zi-on," sung as a round, three parts, Lew leading one group, she leading one and Frank Butler the third. First group begins: "By-y-y the wa-a-aters of Bab-y-lon, we lay down and wept and wept for thee, Zi-on" (second group begins at the beginning; the first keeps singing) "we remember, we remember, we remember thee, Zi-on" (third group comes in; the others keep going). Sing it through three times. Sometimes they repeated it more than that. One night the round went so well they went through it ten times, the boys' voices echoing off the cliff, drowning out the waterfall and the roaring bonfire. The heavy smoke, blacker than usual. It was the last night. Lew had seemed so happy. Everyone could feel it. Round and round the song went, everyone intent on not losing his place but also listening to the others, to the wonderfully harmonic chaos.

Gwen Van Schoonhoven had indeed been there that night. Naomi could see her still, her white T-shirt and shorts shining in the firelight, her legs brown after a long summer, her eyes intent on Lew. Gwen was in Lew's group, and Naomi remembered watching her while waiting for the moment when her own section would join in the singing. Harry Van Schoonhoven was there, too, but not near his wife. He stood in the back of Naomi's campers. She remembered being surprised at seeing him. He never turned up for evening activities, and she remembered noticing him because he wasn't singing. He was staring, maybe at Gwen, maybe at Lew, maybe at her, but he stood just within the circle of light, and he waited.

Naomi decided she would make coffee after all. It was late, but she had a feeling it would be a sleepless night anyway. It's not every evening that a new corpse turns up. And more of those damn bones. Think On Death. Now she would have to think about Harry Van Schoonhoven curled up like a baby taking a nap on the hard dirt floor under the Gnomes' House. It was a silly place to die. It had all the elements of a new camp ghost story. The Body in the Cellar. "We expected him for dinner," Gwen had said, cool, controlled. Surprised? Maybe. "A place had been set."

Footsteps moved across the floor of the mess hall above the kitchen. A steady tread, not ambling, a man, a man who knew where he was going but saw no need to rush. She got out another heavy china cup. The last steps she had heard running across a floor above her had been Melody Horn's at the Gnomes' House, steps full of panic or fear, the sound of someone escaping.

These new steps came down the stairs, and the kitchen door opened. It was Nick Story, of course.

"I heard the sound of someone grinding coffee beans," he said.

"Coffee will be ready in a minute, but I'm out of milk."

"It's the right time of night for black," he said.

If it had not been for that faint sound of New York in his speech, Nick Story could have passed as a local, Naomi thought. The straight Will Rogers hair, the collar a size too large, the trousers so short that when he sat down you could see his white, hairy legs above the tops of his plain black socks. His hands were too large for his arms, and the backs of them were knotted with veins. He looked like a farmer. Without his shirt, Naomi imagined, his body would be as fish-belly white as that sliver of exposed leg, with deeply tanned hands and neck—a farmer's coloration, or a soldier's.

"Rough night," he said.

"I've been thinking about Gwen Van Schoonhoven. She must be in shock."

"There are two widows now," he said. "I think we've been taking the first widow for granted."

"A widow is not how I think of myself. My marriage— sometimes it's more like looking back on the senior prom. Who was my date? Was the prom at the gym or the Holiday Inn ballroom? Whose car did we go in? Was anyone old enough to drive?"

"And the theme? Proms, as I remember them, always had a theme. April in Paris, Nights in Hawaii, Mardi Gras. What was yours?"

"Brave New World? Great Expectations? Peter Pan and Wendy?"

"I think it was more than that. After all, you came back to Smyrna."

"After all. Yes."

"Why?"

"I was invited," she said, saying it before she thought about it.

"Oh?"

"Smyrna's home. The only one I ever had, really, after my parents'."

"You were invited?" His voice had become alert, on duty.

"There had been some newspaper story about plans to rejuvenate Smyrna, and I began to think about the old place. Then there was Aunt Nan's obituary."

"Which you took as an invitation?"

"So I hopped in the car and headed north."

"With a loose bottle of whisky in the trunk."

"Whatever works, right?"

"Been back to any more meetings?" He was now in his old-buddy mode again.

"In Catskill? No. I will. I need a meeting. I can feel it. You can only drink so much coffee alone."

"If you don't want to go alone you could try the Butler boys. I don't think I'm breaking their anonymity. The Butlers are regulars, and they like company."

"And there's you." He did not react. "You're there most meetings."

"Don't count on it." There was a long pause. "So you came north in your car to Home Sweet Smyrna and found more than you expected."

"Oh, yes," she said, more confused than ever about what Nick Story was really up to. "Bones." She said it with a bitterness that surprised her.

"It can't have been easy."

"First that skeleton in the sleeping bag, which I never actually saw. Then those horrible table decorations at breakfast, then that damn coffee can tonight. It's sick, disgusting." She was out of breath, gripping her coffee cup with both hands. "And Harry Van Schoonhoven," she said, as though reaching for a straw, anything to change the subject. "Was it a heart attack?"

"Too soon to know. Would a heart attack surprise you?"

"Well, he had the look of someone with a heart condition,

that soft, sweaty look. He always seemed to be panting, having trouble catching his breath. But that was true even thirty years ago. No, I suppose it wouldn't surprise me. But in the cellar of the Gnomes' House? At night? That does surprise me. Why there? Why was *he* there?"

"Perhaps he had an invitation."

Nick Story wasn't giving up.

"And why are *you* here tonight?" she asked.

"Maybe I get tired of drinking coffee alone."

"Tried the Butler boys? I hear they're always looking for company, good souls that they are."

"Maybe I sensed that there was something you were ready to tell me."

"Maybe you sensed a lonely widow when you saw her kitchen light on at one o'clock in the morning."

"Maybe I thought I had an invitation."

He reached across the table and took her hand. It was cooler than she had expected—and she had expected it—as though it had been holding cold metal.

"Are you getting ready to ask me if I killed my husband?"

"Not yet."

"Do you want to ask where I hid his body?"

"Not now."

"Do you want to know how I got that sleeping bag into Aunt Nan's room?"

"Maybe later."

He smiled at her, a simple, rather silly smile, the hired man smiling at the farmer's wife, knowing the farmer has gone to town and won't be home for hours.

"Let's go upstairs," he said.

He left his coffee cup on the table. She took it and rinsed it with her own and left them in the sink. She led the way and he followed, turning the lights out as they went. On the stairs going up to the mess hall he asked about the scaffolding on the back of the building.

"The phantom housepainter," she said. "They seem to be

fixing this place up, but I've seen no one out there since I arrived."

The mess hall itself was dark, and they walked toward the light coming through the open door that led into the original farmhouse. Nick Story closed the door and slid the bolt shut.

"We never lock that," said Naomi. "There Are No Locked Doors at Smyrna. Saith Young Father Quick. It's in the book."

He unlocked it.

She led the way down the hall to the stairs and stopped at the front door, where she extended her hand. "It's bad luck to leave by a different door than you entered. . . ."

"Saith Young Father Quick?"

"No, my Grandmother Dunn." She kept her hand out to be shaken.

"There's another flight of stairs," he said.

"Oh, really?"

"Right behind you."

"And there is a door right behind *you*."

"I suppose there's a bedroom up there, too."

"You are shameless, Nick Story. Now, shake hands and leave."

"Without hearing about your invitation? I think you're flirting with me, Naomi Quick."

"Good night, Mr. Story."

"I heard that it said something on the order of 'Llewelyn returns on the weekend of the twentieth.' "

"Returns home."

"Home?"

"Returns home on the weekend of the twentieth. Did Ziza Todd tell you that?"

"As a matter of fact, no. It was Sherman Benedikt. She seems to have told him."

"We are surrounded by gossips, Mr. Story. I'm shocked."

"Yes," he said, shaking her hand. "We should all be on our best behavior."

He made a gesture as though he were tipping a nonexistent hat, opened the screen door and headed across the porch. She turned on the outside light so he would not trip on the uneven stones on the walk. There were still a few police cars parked next to the Gnomes' House, although they had turned off their revolving lights. Naomi was indeed shocked, just a little. She had thought Ziza Todd would keep the secret. Or maybe she would tell Nick Story after a lot of cross-examination. She even expected that. But Sherman Benedikt? A public-relations man? A common flack? That was shocking.

10

ð

It rained during the night, a hard, pounding rain that began soon after Nick Story walked down Naomi's front steps and continued until just before sunup. High in the mountains, upstream from Smyrna, rivulets still muddy from the melting of winter snows flooded again and ran down to the Kaaterskill Creek, which carried along leafy mountain loam as it rushed, gathering force, downhill toward the Hudson, spilling—as the old camp cheer went—over the rocks and cliffs at Kaaterskill Falls, Bastion, Fawn's Leap, Bridge Falls, Dog's Hole, Niobe, Fern Wood, Little Falls, High Falls, until it made one final giant leap at Smyrna before broadening and beginning its slow, meandering way across gently sloping farmland toward the great river.

The rain was over by dawn, but the still-damp air at Smyrna was rich with the smell of the mud carried along by the stream, a thick brown stew of rotted plants and bark and the decayed remains of hundreds of small animals that perished during the past winter or winters before that. The stony banks of the creek, before it turned and cascaded over Smyrna Falls, were littered with a new supply of driftwood, entire trees skinned clean by the miles of rocks they were dragged across, broken limbs, small polished slabs of old beams and fence posts. There was also a fresh supply of empty Clorox bottles and aluminum cans and one untouched six-pack of Genesee lager, still in its transparent plastic carrier, washed away and lost last fall at some upstream beer party.

The sun rose in a fresh, cloudless sky, warming the rock cliffs above the stream before it touched the buildings at Smyrna. It was the day when spring, no matter what the calendar said, really began, the day when the budding trees that yesterday had been only smudged with green produced fresh full-grown leaves unmarked by blisters or mold or acid rain.

Well after dawn a black station wagon pulled around the Heart and stopped in front of Mansion House. Two men in dark suits and black ties got out and walked up the front steps. One of them carried a black attaché case. Mrs. Van Schoonhoven was waiting for them. As they went inside, a police car pulled up. The driver was in uniform. The man sitting next to him was not. They parked behind the station wagon and turned off the ignition. Neither man got out. The man behind the wheel rolled down his window and lit a cigarette. The other closed his eyes. It had been a long night.

"I've requested a Full Unknown," Nick Story said.

"Oh, Christ," said the driver. "They're going to love you at the lab. Those things can take six months, doing all those tests to find every conceivable cause of death."

"No, I have a pretty short list of drugs I want them to look for first."

"You think you're on to something? It looked like a run-of-the-mill DOA heart attack to me."

"Just wait," Nick Story said. "Just wait."

All of Smyrna seemed to be waiting. In his office—his real office and not the table in the library—Sherman Benedikt sat in front of a manual typewriter, a blank sheet of paper in place, preparing to write a press release announcing Mr. Van Schoonhoven's untimely death. He had written the first sentence in his head (Harry Van Schoonhoven, sixty-eight, newly appointed chairman of the board of Olde Smyrna Community, Inc., died yesterday of a sudden heart attack at his upstate home in . . .) but was having trouble actually typing it out. He stared at the keys. He stared at his fingertips. He leaned back in his chair and studied a crack in the plaster ceiling, a line that ran straight across the room and then divided like twigs at the end of a dead branch.

Melody Horn was not in her own office. She was in Mr. Van Schoonhoven's, at his desk, slowly reading through the entries in his Rolodex. She had brought 3 × 5 cards to make notes. So far she had copied down only one number. It had been written in his own hand, not typed, like most of the others, by a secretary. No name, just initials—GB & H— and a number. She had read it over several times. Area code 212, Manhattan. She read it again.

The Butler boys were in their room, in their beds, both awake, each knowing the other was awake, both silent. The beds were the size of camp cots, narrower than standard single beds but with real mattresses and springs. They were arranged end to end along a wainscoted wall in a room just down the hall from Aunt Nan's in Mansion House. They slept feet to feet with only a small rustic end table between them. On the table was an owl Aunt Nan had made years ago out of birch-bark and pieces of driftwood. The two of them lay in bed and listened to the distant rumbling of the freshly swollen stream. If either sat up, the first thing he would see would be his brother.

Naomi, too, was still in her room at the old mess hall, still in bed, listening. She had been awakened by what she thought was an animal gnawing on something. It seemed to be on the second floor, as she was, but on the other side of the house, slowly, steadily chewing away, probably on the house itself. Then she heard footsteps and the rattle of loose boards on metal pipes, and she realized that someone was on the scaf-folding on the back of the building. The phantom house-painter was finally making his appearance, and from the sound of things he was scraping away old paint. She lay back and watched the bright morning sun move across the familiar wallpaper, fantasy flowers now bubbled and water-stained with age. No, they had always been bubbled and water-stained, and they were not fantasy flowers but mums, chrysanthemums and ivy. She listened to the scraping and the gnawing and wondered when Nick Story would be back with his next round of questions.

Mrs. Van Schoonhoven sat on a Morris chair in the parlor of Mansion House, slowly turning the pages of an expensively bound leather album. She was not really looking at the color photographs. The two men in black sat on a couch facing her. They did not lean forward, and they believed their silence was both respectful and comforting. When she had greeted them at the door she had said she wanted them to do just what they had done with Aunt Nan, and they had said they understood her wishes perfectly but wondered whether Mr. Van Schoonhoven, who was indeed a community leader and an important figure in the world of business, required a different honoring. While Mrs. Van Schoonhoven thought about the word "honoring" they handed her the album and suggested she browse through it at her leisure. They would not want to rush her but suggested she might be interested in looking at the Executive Suite on page three.

The Executive Suite turned out to be a large silver-gray metal coffin with mahogany trim and exclusive, one-of-a-kind engraved decorative panels. She slowly turned the pages and thought about the police car that she had seen follow the undertakers' station wagon around the Heart. As long as she was with these men, the others would wait outside. She framed her question carefully. Just what, she asked the men in black, would be engraved on the one-of-a-kind decorative panels? And how many panels could there be?

Out in what was called the Children's House Hagadorn Mills was also looking at pictures. Melody Horn had inspired him. Several days before, just after her breakfast announcement, he had pushed together long mess-hall tables and carefully arranged on them more than a hundred photographs and prints selected from the archives. They were going to be a key part of his presentation. Naomi Quick was coming by this morning, and Melody was scheduled for that afternoon, although Mr. Van Schoonhoven's death might call for a change of plans. He had begun to see that he had more options than he had ever imagined. Once more, and it would not be the last time, he studied each picture.

They were vaguely in chronological order, pictures of the earliest days of Smyrna, of Old and Young Father Quick, of workers in the box factory, of the mill when it was new, of a schoolroom full of community children (taken at the very spot where Hagadorn Mills was standing). There was a special section for pictures of visitors to Smyrna (Mills was especially proud of this; it would make the tourists feel part of a great tradition): city people at the weekly Smyrna open houses, eating lunch in the Dining Room, watching a community chorus in concert (young editions of Frank and Charley at either end of the third row), gawking at another group of Smyrna children, all suspiciously well dressed. And there were some old camp photographs he especially wanted Naomi to see. One showed a younger, thinner, but not particularly prettier Naomi surrounded by a group of very small campers in Smyrna T-shirts. A young man was with her (Llewelyn surely; his shirt had STAFF printed beneath a golden crown). His arm around her waist was protective (or was it proprietary?), but otherwise he seemed to be utterly ignoring her, staring off at something outside the photograph. Naomi was wearing a skirt that even then must have been unfashionable. Perhaps it was supposed to make her look more mature.

Mills carefully straightened the last photograph, although it was already perfectly aligned. Captions would come later. And with his text, which was all but finished, it would come together as just the sort of book Melody Horn wanted. He looked again at the young Naomi. Last night's meeting had been something of a botch-up, but she had said she would come by and see him. Perhaps on his own turf things would go better. She had, after all, if he remembered correctly, taken his suggestion and called him Andy.

Ziza Todd woke up when the rain stopped, and she could not get back to sleep. Some things that had happened yesterday needed to be sorted out. Others were best forgotten. The tiny room she had been given on the third floor of Mansion House, overlooking the Heart, seemed to catch sounds and magnify them. When she realized that she was not going to get back to sleep, she got up to put down on paper the lists she was making in her head. Under the heading "Them Bones Gonna Rise Again" she cataloged all the people who could have put the sleeping bag in Aunt Nan's suite: Aunt Nan herself (unlikely—she was too frail at the end), Mr. Van Schoonhoven (no—he was too frightened by the jawbone Ziza had dropped on his desk), Mrs. Van S. (but why?), the Butler boys (ditto), Melody Horn (too physically bizarre for her—if she were up to something she would not bother messing around with Halloween decorations to get it done), Naomi Quick (why *is* she here, how real was that note, how strong is her claim on any Smyrna stock?), Sherman Benedikt (a hired gun at best; if he did it, he did it for someone else). Ditto for Hagadorn Mills. But what did Benedikt mean when he hinted that Mills knew something about that outfit called Great Bear and something?

The next list was titled "Heart Breaker." If Mr. Van Schoonhoven had not died of a heart attack, who prospered? Mrs. Van S.? Melody? Naomi? The Butlers? The Smyrna stockholders? Herself? It was an index without page numbers, a useless column of names. She simply hadn't the information, at least not yet. Another list: "Why Am I Still Here?" Followed by "Reasons to Leave." Both were still blank when she heard the two cars pull out front. There were footsteps on the stone steps, then the now-familiar muffled squawk of the police radio.

She looked back at the list of names and, without thinking

much about it, circled her own. Todd, Ziza. Herself. Like it or not, she had to think about yesterday afternoon. She had to think about her visit to the Gnomes' House.

She had wandered over to the camp to see Naomi about nothing much in particular. Research could be the excuse if she had to come up with one. In fact, she was simply bored and looking for someone to talk with.

As Ziza came around the side of the old mess hall on her way to the kitchen door (for this kind of visit, she thought, the kitchen door was the one you used), she had noticed that the front door of the Gnomes' House was standing open, just ever so slightly, but open. The dark stone cottage was a building she had been curious about, and the one other time she had tried to get in, it had been locked up tight. So she went over, pushed the door open the rest of the way and called out what she hoped sounded like a friendly hello. When there was no answer, she went in for a quick look around.

It had been dark and damp-smelling, not rotten or even moldy, but a chilly, green smell she vaguely associated with pet turtles. The first floor was all one room, and as in most seventeenth-century Hudson Valley houses (a crude 1689 had been carved into the keystone over the fireplace), the ceiling was low and heavily beamed. One entire wall was taken up with a fireplace big enough to walk into, if she ducked down a bit. Over it hung a flintlock musket. The small, dusty windows were cut deep into the three-foot-thick walls. In one corner a steep open stairway went straight up, without pausing for a landing, to the second floor. In another corner was a simple kitchen that looked as though it dated from the early 1950s. There was a small sink with a dripping faucet, a gas stove with enough curves and chrome to rival a postwar Mercury convertible and an oversized refrigerator with a cooling cylinder on top. The refrigerator—its original owners probably called it an icebox, the way Ziza's parents always did—was unplugged, and its door was propped open for ventilation. Ziza looked inside and decided mice had had the run of the place for years. Next to the sink was a door that led down to the cellar. It, too, was open, and Ziza looked in. At the bottom of the slanting stairs a very dim light was shining.

Not a sound could be heard. Instead, there was the exaggerated silence of someone holding his breath. Her breath? Ziza suddenly felt her heart beating. She held her own breath and was flooded with a sense of unreasonable terror. Someone was down there. She could not have sworn it to Nick Story or in court. But someone was there, standing out of sight at the bottom of the stairs, trying as hard as possible not to breathe, somehow absorbing all the random noises in the shadowy room—the dripping faucet, the wind in the ivy, the creak of the wide floorboards. Ziza was about to call out again and try another jolly-sounding hello, but stopped. Saying anything would just warn whoever was down there that she knew he was there.

She backed away from the top of the stairs and slowly crossed the room to the front door. What had she seen in the dim light at the bottom of those stairs? Was there a shadow? Had there been movement? Had she seen any signs of a body? The outline of a shape, maybe? The mound of a back? No, she had thought, there was probably nothing to see. Probably there was no one there at all. Just herself, frozen in place like a deer caught in the glare of headlights, holding her breath. But she did not really believe that, not now. Someone was there.

I have seen nothing at all, she told herself as she went outside and tried to leave the door exactly as she had found it. There was no one there, she told herself as she decided against going to visit Naomi and headed back toward Mansion House. There was nothing there but mice, she told herself.

And last night when she and the others went down those stairs she told herself that, no, she could not have heard anything. She had looked at the policemen watching them as their eyes adjusted to the bright work lights, at the curled-up body that lay at their feet, and thought, no, she could not have seen anything. Whatever caused the death must have happened after her visit. Mr. Van Schoonhoven's hair was still wet with sweat.

So she said nothing to Nick Story or anyone else. But what, she thought now, what if the silence she felt as she stood at the top of those stairs was the silence that follows a gasp? What if the person she sensed down there was simply Mr. Van Schoonhoven? Alone. What if he were lying there passed out, with a heart attack, clutching his stomach, on the brink of death but still alive, still somehow savable if the person who sensed he was there would only run down the stairs to help? Had she, who over the years, from Girl Scouts on, had sat through God knows how many classes in first aid and CPR, passed up her chance to save a life?

Could she have made a difference?

When in doubt, she told herself, go for a run.

She put aside her file cards with all their blank spaces, splashed water on her face from the sink in the corner (the toilet and shower were down the hall), brushed her teeth and then put on her sweats and New Balance running shoes and went downstairs.

She hit the cobblestone hallway running. Out the open front door she went and then clockwise around the Heart. The first time she passed the police car, Nick Story simply stared at her. The second time, she waved. The third time, he waved back. The air smelled muddy, the way she imagined a small town outside New Orleans might smell with the Mississippi lapping away at the levee. Her warm-up over (she knew she should do stretching exercises but never did), she headed for the open road. Her daily route covered about five miles: three times around the Heart, down the hill and through the woods to the old summer camp, back up the hill (a killer), along the community drive to the Olde Smyrna Road, past the church to where the road meets the main highway and then back to Mansion House. On the way back she usually stopped at the church to wander around the old graveyard. To look at the stones, she told herself, although she knew better. She was not knocking back those five miles as easily as she used to.

The roadway this morning was full of puddles, and although one of the running guides she had read said serious runners did not avoid them, she did, trying not to break stride. Old songs set the rhythm: at first it was "The grand old Duke of York, he had ten thousand men, he marched them up the hill and he marched them down again," and then she sped up to "The kids in Bristol are hot as a pistol when they do the Bristol stomp. It's really sumpin', the joint is jumpin' when they do the Bristol stomp."

Bristol, England, or Bristol, Pennsylvania? The same question passed through her mind at just about the same spot every morning (halfway down the hill leading to the old box factory parking lot), and she always gave herself the same answer: "Hot as a pistol" is an Americanism; it must be Pennsylvania. Or maybe Bristol, Connecticut. Running is a ritual. The same thoughts at the same rhythm until there is no thought at all, no notice of the puddles or the frogs brought out by the fresh rain, and then time evaporates and all memory is washed away.

And that was why she did not see him until she ran into him. She hit him head-on and would have fallen over if they had not caught each other. Her first impression, before she could see his face, the impression on impact, was of youth and strength, of someone her age or even younger, solid, healthy, a warm body as though fresh from bed, a smell of sweat, two kinds—new, fresh sweat and the vague hint of old, sour-smelling clothes.

"Sweat," he said, maybe reading her mind but making her suspect what she could smell was herself and not him. "The long-distance runner."

She apologized. She was sorry. She had not been looking

where she was going. Her thoughts were a million miles away. In fact, she was astonished to see that she was in front of the Gnomes' House; she had lost track of where she was.

She could see him now. He was young, younger by at least a few years than she was, in his very early twenties. He was not tall, and he had long blond hair tied up by a rubber band into a ponytail. There was something wrong with his eyes. They were not crossed, but they didn't seem to quite focus on the same spot. When he looked at her she sensed that he was also looking at someone behind her. He wore a crisp, new Camp Smyrna Staff T-shirt, so new she could see the crease marks where it had been folded.

"I like redheads," he said, and he smiled. He had a small gap between his front teeth. She began to suspect their meeting was not an accident.

"It's more like strawberry blond," she said.

"You come by here every morning," he said.

"You're *here* every morning?"

"I'm the housepainter, and that's my baby," he said, pointing at the mess hall. "They've given me a place to stay and an allowance, and by the end of the summer that mother is supposed to be scraped and painted. Tim Jacobsen." He extended his hand.

"Tim Jacobson," she said, shaking hands. "Ziza Todd."

"It's *sen*, not *son*," he said. "Jacobsen. Norwegian. Squarehead. Hardworking but dumb. That's why I took on that piece of shit. Didn't know any better."

"I'll bet," she said. There was a long pause, and she could not be sure if he was watching her. To make conversation: "Where did you get that shirt?"

"Found it. Found a whole box of them," he said. "You'd be surprised what you can find around here." Which seemed to remind him of what he really wanted to ask: "What was going on here last night? Do you know?"

"Mr. Van Schoonhoven," she said, "had a heart attack and died."

"The Schooner?" He seemed genuinely surprised. "In there?" he said, pointing at the Gnomes' House. "He was my boss," as though that made death in the Gnomes' House impossible. "I saw the lights down here and thought the cops had found some sort of drug stash, so I stayed away. The ambulance, though, didn't make any sense if it was drugs."

"I suppose not."

"People are jumpy about drugs around here. The stuff keeps turning up in funny places. Couple of months ago a house on Olde Smyrna Road caught fire, and when the volunteer fire department got inside it was full of plastic bags of pot, big plastic bags, the kind with little yellow handles for leaves that you rake up from your lawn. Dozens of them. Roomfuls of them, and the place was supposedly empty. No one knew nothing."

"Of course."

"Of course, of course. I used to be a volunteer fireman, but I quit. All you did was turn up every Saturday, drink beer and polish the fire engine. Actually the old guys would sit around watching the young guys polish the fire engine and talk about famous barn fires where they had to shoot all the horses. You even had to buy your own beer. It's hard to figure the old Schooner dead, although he never did look too healthy."

"You're from around here, then?"

"You got it. You're looking at an authentic local, Catskill High, class of 'eighty-seven. Or should have been. My mom had a trailer that she called a mobile home down the other side of the Dutch Reformed Church, and that's where I used to live. Now I'm here." He gestured off toward the woods. "Want to see it? It's too wet to work until the sun dries things out, anyway. It's a place of my own."

What the hell, Ziza thought. "Sure," she said.

Tim Jacobsen led the way, talking as he went, about his mom's trailer (he always called her Mom and never mentioned his father), about an older brother in the Air Force and how hard it was to get a job around here anymore, about kids in his high-school class who had gone to Alaska to get rich, about lucking into this job at Smyrna. "I was at the Pizza Inn one night back in February, playing the machines and drinking beer, and the old Schooner asked me if I wanted a job in the spring. Outside work at the camp. Lots of guys there, but he asked me. Go figure, right?"

"Mr. Van Schoonhoven would hang out at the Pizza Inn?"

"Hang out? No, but he would turn up a lot, usually after stopping off at a couple of other places, if you know what I mean. He'd come in late for a beer and a couple of slices. A couple of beers."

"A regular guy?"

"Trying to be. Never played any of the machines, but he could talk a good game. I thought the job offer might be just talk and beer, but I called him up about it, and he said, sure, he remembered my name, Dottie Jacobsen's kid, and that I should come by the old place to set things up. And here I am. And here's my place."

They had walked uphill, past the mess hall (Was that Naomi watching from behind a curtain in an upstairs window? Ziza thought so) and through a grove of hemlocks, the ground slippery with rain on the fallen brown needles, to a small open field gradually being made smaller with the inroads of young quaking aspens and birch trees crowding around its edges. Set back into the maple woods beyond the field were cabins, maybe a dozen or so old camp bunkhouses. Many of them had been fixed up and vaguely winterized. Some had been repainted in combinations of primary colors Young Father Quick would surely not have approved of. Plastic sheeting had been stapled over the windows, although most of the doors hung open in the breeze. Stovepipes were jury-rigged through rough-cut openings. A refuse pit of bottles and tin cans was alongside one of the buildings. In front of another were sheets of rusted metal that might have been junk or sculpture. It all looked hastily abandoned, as though the residents had fled in panic.

"How many people live here?" she asked, amazed at this combination of rural Appalachia and 1960s bohemianism.

"None, now, just me. But when it gets warmer, people will start to turn up. Since the pipes are aboveground there's no water in the winter. But now that we've had the last thaw, there's all the comforts. And more room than my mom's trailer."

"And the Smyrna people don't mind?"

"Shit, we *are* Smyrna people. Employees, mostly. Some crashers, maybe, but they say the old Schooner didn't seem to mind, and he was the only honcho who gets involved over here, him and sometimes the Butler boys."

"Involved?"

"You might say he's the mayor of this little village. Was."

Tim ushered her into his cabin with the pride of a man who has bought his first house. "Mind the step," he said. It was the smallest of the bunkhouses, farthest back into the woods, and seemed to have been the least remodeled. Inside, it was clean, amazingly clean, Ziza thought, the floor even looked scrubbed. The furniture consisted of one old camp cot, a ragged star quilt, a rustic bentwood couch with a number of missing twigs, six solid rustic chairs, a small four-burner yellow enamel-and-chrome wood stove dragged in from somewhere and polished up and what Ziza recognized as one of Aunt Nan's collages, a mountaintop profile.

"Haul all this down to New York City and you could make a fortune," Ziza said.

"It's just stuff I found." There were also a tape deck, a portable radio, a hot plate (where Ziza suspected the cooking was actually done) and an electronic keyboard. "Mostly. Like a drink of something? We can have a housewarming. You're my first guest. My first outsider."

"Your mother hasn't seen this?"

"She's not around these days. It's sort of a case of My Mom the Junkie. She's a pill popper, can talk any doctor she's ever seen into writing any kind of prescription she's ever heard of. And now she's down to the state hospital for the cure. But I expect she'll come back. She always has before. Now, for a drink."

"Coffee sounds great."

"I have beer."

"At ten o'clock in the morning?"

"It's not refrigerated."

What the hell, Ziza thought. "Sure," she said.

11

It's amazing, Ziza thought, what a couple of warm beers can do for a damp morning. Tim was an attentive host. He didn't offer drinking glasses, but he did have napkins (THIS BUD'S FOR YOU, they said) and half a bag of Fritos that he had wrapped tightly with a rubber band to keep fresh. He had her sit on the fragile-looking couch, and he took the nearest chair, picking at the bark on its armrest as he talked. He talked with the eagerness of someone who spent more time thinking about talking than actually doing it.

He interrupted himself from time to time to say that he couldn't believe the old Schooner was dead or to check if Ziza needed another beer. He tried to remember the last time he saw his boss (only a day ago, maybe; he had come by to see if Tim needed anything, he had said, but actually, Tim knew, to see if painting had begun yet). He talked about building the scaffolding on the back of the mess hall (a mother of a job for one man, especially with the old Schooner coming by all the time to see if work had begun—begun!—yet).

Words just tumbled out of him. Ziza listened and tried to keep track of where the conversation was headed.

"Do you think I still have this job?" he suddenly asked her. "I mean, with the death and all, do you think I'm out of here?"

"You have an agreement, right? They'll stick to it, I'm sure. They're a pretty decent bunch. Anyway, the mess hall really does need painting. . . ."

"The mess is a mess," Tim said, which struck Ziza as very funny. Beer on an empty stomach, she thought.

". . . and you've already started," she said. "It's easier for them to stick with you than find someone else."

"The Schooner, though, paid me in cash taken out of his own wallet. Off the books."

"I'm sure you'll get it. Remind Melody Horn. No, let it rest, but if you don't get paid next week, remind *Mrs.* Van Schoonhoven. I've a feeling she's going to be the one to deal with."

Tim thought about that for a moment. "There are lots of stories about this place, you know. In the old days. No marriage. Everyone screws everyone, with the Quicks first in line. No rules apply. The old-timers around here can tell all kinds of things."

Ziza wondered if this was an attempt to turn the conversation toward sex, flirtation Tim-style. "No," she said, "there was marriage, and from what I've learned about Smyrna, there was nothing but rules."

"Sure there were. For who?"

"Rules is rules," said Ziza, draining her second beer.

"There's one more," he said, crushing his beer can with one hand the way they do on television commercials. "Want to share it?"

"Maybe we should both get to work."

"Yeah, maybe."

"Show 'em they have a busy housepainter on their hands."

"You mean, one that doesn't fall off his scaffold after downing a hearty breakfast." He pitched the can, a clean foul shot into an old wooden peach basket.

As they reached the door, Ziza, sensing that her visit had indeed been a major social event, said all the things a polite guest says, and Tim replied with all the hearty good grace of a genial host. She must come back again. Soon. Now that she knew where he lived.

The sun by now had baked the dampness out of the air and was warming the ground. But the tall grass in the open field was still wet, and it soaked through Ziza's running shoes as they crossed it. Going down the hill through the stand of hemlocks, Ziza slipped, and Tim caught her and steadied her. They both laughed. "I knew I shouldn't have taken that second helping of breakfast," she said. Instead of letting go when she regained her balance, Tim took her hand.

Do people still hold hands? she wondered. It was a warm hand, large and solid but softer than she would have expected, more the hand of a high-school boy than a housepainter. When was the last time Ziza had walked along holding anyone's hand? After a prom. Whoever she was with was wearing a tux. He had taken off his jacket, and she was wearing it to keep warm. His suspenders had been bright red, only not the classy kind that hooked onto buttons but the pinch-on kind, and with his jacket off she could see that one of them in the back had come loose. She remembered that but could not remember his name. Holding hands, though, and walking was something she associated with her father, long Sunday walks when she was very small, off through the park to the zoo, endless walks that usually ended with her tired and crying and—finally—happy and riding on her father's shoulders back toward home.

Perhaps sensing that holding hands with this strange woman was, well, strange, Tim began to swing their arms back and forth in an almost musical-comedy parody of young lovers walking hand in hand through the woods.

"There are things *I* could tell you about this place, too," he said, hopping back to the safety of what they were talking about before. "It's not just the old-timers. I've been around long enough to have seen some sights."

Ziza was suddenly aware that she and Tim, themselves,

were becoming one of the sights. A Smyrna pickup was in front of the mess hall, and next to it, watching Ziza and Tim walk down from the woods, were Naomi Quick and Melody Horn.

"Morning, ladies," she said, letting go of Tim's hand, but he still held on. "Do you know Mr. Jacobsen? Mr. Van Schoonhoven hired him to restore the exterior of the mess hall."

"The Phantom," said Naomi. "We finally meet." She almost said something about the Camp Smyrna Staff T-shirt but thought better of it.

"Tim," said Tim, dropping Ziza's hand and shaking hers.

Melody Horn ignored him but turned her warmest smile on Ziza. "I just came by to give Naomi a ride to Mansion House. There have been some, shall we say, developments. Want a lift over? Although perhaps you don't want to interrupt your morning run."

"No, I would appreciate that. No more running today. Tim, here, waylaid me and fed me breakfast, and I can only run on an empty stomach." Naomi and Melody Horn, weighing what that might mean, turned to look at Tim, who was backing slowly toward the mess hall. He waved. Ziza waved back. "Later," she said to him.

"You bet," he shouted to her and ran around the corner of the building. Before the women got into the truck, they could hear the metallic rattle of the pipe scaffolding as Tim raced to the top. Ziza pictured a monkey on monkey bars or children scampering around a jungle gym. Naomi, for the first time, began to wonder what someone could see from that scaffold.

The three women fit snugly into the truck. Melody drove; Ziza sat next to the window, which she opened, thinking the breeze would blow away any smell of beer on her breath. She exhaled through her nose, mouth tightly shut, hoping that, too, might help.

But she couldn't outfox Naomi, who knew beer when she

smelled it. Naomi was surprised, but she refused to make a judgment. That's what she told herself: I refuse to make a judgment. But she filed away the fact that Ziza Todd, the Reverend Ziza Todd, was someone not above having a wake-up beer. With the Phantom, no less, a Phantom in a curiously new-looking staff T-shirt.

"What *are* the new developments?" Ziza asked, speaking out the window into the wind.

"Oh," said Melody Horn, "it was just that Nick Story was around this morning doing his farmer-in-the-dell act, pulling his forelock and asking about when we all saw Mr. Van Schoonhoven last. 'Do you know why he would choose that time to visit the Gnomes' House?' And so forth. Lots of hints that it may not have been a heart attack. And lots of statements that it was 'too early to be certain' about this and 'awaiting the lab reports' on that. But he clearly believes the dear man met with foul play. He doesn't have to spell it out."

"Could anyone add anything?"

"Hardly. I think we all know—knew—that Mr. Van Schoonhoven liked to buzz over to the camp at odd moments, when he had a free half hour or so. He never seemed to have gotten over being camp director. . . ."

Naomi made a snorting sound. "When he *was* director he certainly never acted like one."

"As men get older you never know what things in their past suddenly become more important," said Melody Horn with the gravity of someone who subscribes to *Psychology Today*. They had pulled up in front of Mansion House. "Mrs. Van Schoonhoven has asked to see Naomi," she said, speaking across Naomi to Ziza. "But perhaps after you freshen up you might like to drop by the Parlor to say hello. She is taking all this remarkably well."

There was probably a rebuff tucked into that statement, Ziza thought as she walked up the stairs toward her room. Maybe two. "Freshen up" certainly had connotations. The

comment about Mrs. Van S.'s doing 'remarkably' well was a
nice reminder that she had never asked how the widow was
holding up. The politesse of mourning. That's one of the first
things you're supposed to learn: worry about the survivors,
not the victims. Emotional triage. But for some reason Ziza
found it very hard to worry about Mrs. Van S.

The main staircase ended on the second floor. To get to
her room on the third, Ziza had to walk down a long hallway,
past Aunt Nan's door—still marked by a plastic Day-Glo pink
crime-scene police tape—to the narrow back stairs. The door
to the Butlers' room was ajar. They could not—could they?—
have been waiting for her, and she was certainly walking as
quietly as possible, but she was barely past before Frank
popped out and called her name.

She waved, said hello and kept walking. A shower was
definitely her first priority.

"Oh, Ziza." Frank again. She stopped. "Do you think we
could have a word—"

"A *brief* word," added Charley, unseen, from somewhere
behind Frank in the bedroom.

"I was just going up to change," she said, motioning toward
the stairs.

"A *very* brief word," said Frank.

"Oh, sure," she said and headed slowly back toward him.

Charley was immediately out the door, which he closed
behind him. The brothers were wearing their usual dark business suits and vests, but they had left their jackets in their
room, and they were going tieless. "We will be more comfortable talking down here," Charley said, leading the way
back along the hall, beyond the main staircase toward the
open balcony of the Meeting Room. Frank made elaborate
ushering motions to show that Ziza should follow.

Behind the back row of pews on the balcony were group-
ings of overstuffed chairs that did not look as though they
had been used—or dusted—in years. On the back of each

was placed a yellowing lace antimacassar. "These chairs used to be popular with the older folks during meetings," Frank said. "They have a lovely view of the podium but are a good deal easier on the bottom—if you will pardon the expression—than the pews."

"But only with special permission," said Charley.

"Only senior citizens, as we would now say, with special permission from Young Father Quick could use them."

The three sat down amid a gently rising cloud of dust and the groaning of aged springs. If, Ziza thought, the chairs had once, indeed, been easy on the pardon-the-expression bottom, those days were long past. The brothers exchanged glances. Each nodded to the other, and Frank began.

"Do you love Smyrna?"

"Love it?" she asked.

"We think you do," said Charley. "We've been watching."

"Watching, yes," said Frank. "Keeping our eyes open. We see you. We see the professor—"

"Professor Hagadorn Mills," said Charley.

"And we can tell who loves this place and who has something altogether else in mind."

"And you are the lover," said Charley.

"Love is a pretty strong word," Ziza said. "Fascination says it better."

"No, no," said Charley, "the word is 'love.' "

"We are becoming concerned by the turn of events," said Frank.

"The shocking death," Charley interrupted, "of Mr. Van Schoon . . ."

"All the talk of change . . ."

"The terrible business with the bones . . ."

"Poor Llewelyn . . ."

"And Naomi, too."

"Yes," said Frank. "None of us has thought enough about Naomi, but we are getting concerned with the impression that observers such as yourself and even Professor Mills must be getting of Smyrna."

"Death," said Charley, "is not what Smyrna is all about. We never thought about death, and that's all you hear about these days."

"Death and money."

"Well, we often did concern ourselves with money. . . ."

" 'But thou art rich.' "

"Indeed, we 'art.' All the stockholders, and there aren't all that many. Smyrna is a very successful business, and don't forget it. But we aren't kooks and crazy people."

"I've heard the talk about free love," Ziza said.

"There you are. It's nonsense," said Frank. "Stuff and nonsense. Neighbors got that started. Smyrna was—is—a very moral place, but Old Father Quick and then Young Father Quick believed in the importance of genetics. Detailed records were kept on how smart people were, on their physical condition, on skills, and the community tried to make matches that were to the glory of God and that would produce offspring that would be to the glory of the community. All very scientific."

"But the stories?" Ziza asked.

"Stories are stories," said Frank.

"The refuge of the small-minded," said Charley.

"In one press account," Frank said, "an outsider wrote that there were no priests or pastors in our faith—which is true—because Young Father Quick said that, based on Christ and his disciples, who had begun life as Jews, only converted Jews—male Jews—could be ministers, and no one at Smyrna qualified."

"Which he did say," said Charley. "Young Father did say that. Once."

"As a joke," said Frank. "It may have been the only joke the old fellow ever made, but some reporter was there to write it down deadpan. People were all too ready to believe it was another of our silly notions. The very idea that we have no ministers because we never converted a single Jew . . ."

"The same way they keep repeating the story about Aunt Nan having her doll taken away . . ."

"And about free love," Ziza added.

"We weren't Baptist or Methodist or Dutch Reformed. We stuck to ourselves, worked together, had our own school, and we lived well. So people thought there was something funny about the whole setup. Yet they would pay good money to come out here, eat our food and gawk at us. Rich people—freethinking rich people—would send us their sons for the summer camp because the air here was healthy and our program was challenging. Half the high-school seniors east of the Rockies still wear our rings. But we came close to being Greene County's only freak show and zoo." Charley seemed about to lose his temper.

"This is what you wanted to talk to me about?" Ziza asked. "You're afraid that's going to happen again?"

"Well, yes . . ."

". . . and no."

"It's about Mr. Van Schoonhoven," said Frank. "We hear they're talking murder, and we think maybe he got involved with the wrong crowd."

"A bad element."

"He does seem to have been a regular at the local bars," Ziza said.

"Not a local bad element," said Charley, "although there is some truth to that."

"No," said Frank. "It's the outsiders we're thinking about. City people. Funny deals of some kind. Something was up. More than just Melody Horn's *wonderful* plans."

"We think whatever happened was outsiders' work, and as someone who is around and asking questions . . ."

"And as someone who we believe loves Smyrna . . ."

"We think you should be keeping your eyes open in that direction."

"What direction?" asked Ziza.

"A jaundiced eye," said Charley, "that's what you will be watching out for. Be alert. Not everyone, we suspect, is what they seem."

"Catch our drift?" asked Frank.

"Not entirely," said Ziza.

"You will," said Charley.

With that, the two brothers rose and bade her a very formal farewell, with handshakes and wishes for a good day. She remained seated and watched the bright band of sunlight slowly moving across the trompe l'oeil marbling on the wall of the Meeting Room below her. She could see that the room was in far more shabby condition than it seemed in shadows. The paint was actually cracked and crumbling and would soon be in even worse shape unless something was done to preserve it.

She heard the double doors open below her and the sound of someone entering—more than one person, probably. The door was closed slowly and pulled tight. Footsteps moved across the floor, and a pew creaked as they sat in the shadowy side of the hall, out of sight from Ziza.

"We will keep this brief," said a woman's voice. Mrs. Van Schoonhoven's.

"We always have." It was Naomi.

"I want you to know that I appreciate your condolences. I don't believe I ever formally expressed to you Harry's and my profound sadness about the discovery of poor Llewelyn's remains. Consider it done."

"I'll make a note of it."

"Don't be snide. This is a difficult time for us all. My point, and the reason why I wanted to talk to you away from the others, is that that detective friend of yours tells me it is possible that death from natural causes may be ruled out."

"What can be ruled in?"

"Let me finish. It may have been a heart attack, but it may have been induced somehow. Had Harry come over to see you? That's what I want to know."

"I was with you, if you remember, having a gracious fireside dinner at Mansion House."

"I'm talking about that afternoon."

"No."

"Any afternoon? I know Harry spent more time than he admitted nosing around that old place. Were you on his regular rounds?"

"Never."

"Never?"

"You expect me to now say, 'Well, hardly ever'? This isn't Gilbert and Sullivan. Never. Period."

"You were never fond of Harry. Of us."

"Is that a question?"

"No."

"Good."

Neither woman spoke. Ziza sat very still, afraid that the ancient springs in her chair might begin to sigh. The dazzling band of sunlight had moved to the center of the platform and was now illuminating the shining Smyrna crown. *Did* she love Smyrna? Hardly. Did she want to solve its mysteries? Of course. Did she want help? Maybe Sherman Benedikt was not the answer, but if the Butlers were right, whom could she trust as a partner?

"I should be getting back," said Gwen Van Schoonhoven.

"A widow has responsibilities," said Naomi.

"Yes."

"I *am* sorry. About Harry."

"Indeed?"

"Indeed. Death is something you have to share."

12

Naomi noticed that she seemed to be following a pattern. The day after Llewelyn's bones were discovered, she had gone into Catskill for a meeting. Now, the day after Harry Van Schoonhoven died, she wanted to go back. Needed to go back, was more like it. She gave the Butler boys a call to see if they wanted to go with her.

Confusion followed. Frank answered, but instead of replying to Naomi's invitation, he passed the phone to Charley, who did not seem to know what Naomi was talking about. He handed the phone back to Frank, who, when asked again if he wanted a ride into town for a meeting, claimed that Naomi was mixing them up with someone else. Naomi decided to play her ace. "Nick Story," she said. "He told me you like to attend the evening meetings at the church and that you might appreciate a ride." The phone was now muffled, and the brothers talked with each other until Charley got on the line to say that Frank thought it against the code for Story to have told her without their permission. Then Frank got on to say that Charley said they would greatly appreciate a ride, provided that she was going herself. In the background she could hear Charley saying that they'd better leave right away or they would be late. She agreed. In fact, she was calling them from the front hall of Mansion House and they would leave as soon as the boys came down. There was some sputtering about suitable notice, but within five minutes they were coming down the stairs, coats and vests on, Smyrna ties neatly knotted.

The rain had started again, but now it was soft and misty, the way spring drizzle is supposed to be. Frank climbed into the front seat next to Naomi after first opening the back door for Charley. He did not hold the door, however, and Charley closed it himself. A nice bit of protocol, Naomi thought. They were all silent until she made the sharp turn from the entrance drive onto Olde Smyrna Road. A long, rolling rumble came from the trunk.

"That sounded like a bottle," Frank said.

"It was," Naomi said.

"Oh," Charley said.

"For luck," Naomi said, and that seemed to break the ice. Charley laughed first, and then Frank joined in. "For good luck," he added, and she started laughing, too—meaningless, relieved laughter, the kind heard at wakes or outside the church after a funeral. It had been too long, they all agreed, since they had been together, just themselves, and had a good talk about the old days—no one said "good old days"—and what they had been up to since then.

Driving east on a narrow blacktop country road, alone in her car with two old men she had known best—which was really not very well at all—back when they were prematurely middle-aged bachelors and she was a bride, Naomi felt more at home, more at ease than she had at any time since returning to Smyrna. That morning she had kept her "penciled in" appointment with Hagadorn Mills in the old Children's House, and that experience may have been why she had called the Butlers.

Oddly enough, Ziza Todd had been there, too. Andy—Mills insisted that Naomi call him that—seemed a bit flustered about having both women there at the same time. The Reverend Todd had just dropped in, he said. Rather unexpectedly, he said, and Ziza said something about having had an open invitation. Andy quickly agreed that she certainly had one and was very welcome to stay. And stay Ziza did, although Naomi thought Andy made it perfectly clear that he would have been happier if she hadn't. Unfortunately, he said, he had only two teacups, but Ziza said that was quite all right. She was trying to cut down on her caffeine intake.

He guided Naomi around the carefully arranged displays on the green mess-hall tables. The material about Old Father Quick coming west from New England to establish the community and the early days of evangelism and the founding of the box factory was skimmed over, but when they came to the newer camp pictures, Andy wanted details. Did she recognize this person? that camper? what year did she think this was? This fellow in the back row was clearly Llewelyn, and this girl, the short, pretty one with all that dark hair, was obviously her. But who was that? A young Gwen Quick Van Schoonhoven, Naomi said. She was in a lot of the pictures, Andy noticed. Naomi agreed that she was. Often rather well dressed for a summer camp, he noticed. Naomi did not reply to that. The only pictures Mills said he found of Mr. Van Schoonhoven were in the annual group shots of all the campers and staff. Naomi said that didn't surprise her. Ziza stood behind them, looking over their shoulders.

There were some boxes of photographs he wanted Naomi to look through in case there was anything of interest he had missed. Naomi poked through one, Ziza another, and it was Ziza who came up with the prize, a blotchy and curled series of pictures of a young man scaling a cliff—the cliff above the waterfalls, by the look of it. The photographer had probably been a camper, and the prints had obviously been made in the camp darkroom by a beginner, but there was Llewelyn doing what he did best, climbing a rock face.

Ziza spread them out on an empty table and then rearranged them so that they were in order, a young man in shorts and heavy boots starting at the bottom of a sheer wall of rock and making his way diagonally upward until, twelve

8½ × 11's later, he was at the top. Waving. And smiling broadly enough to register on the stained and foggy print.

"Oh, my God, he's blindfolded," Ziza said. "He must have been a mountain goat."

Naomi dug through the box until she found another curled sheet of photographic paper and laid it down at the beginning of the series. It showed her tying a bandanna around Lew's eyes. "It was his favorite stunt," she said. "He called it the Blind Man, and he would do it a couple of times a summer. To pass his climbing course, the boys would have to go up a much smaller cliff blindfolded, one farther downstream. Lew said you really didn't have to see to climb. It was all a matter of touch, he claimed, and doing it blindfolded just improved the kids' feeling of self-confidence. He was proud of the fact that no one who ever tried it fell. But, then, I think he was pretty careful about who he let try it."

She remembered the day those pictures were taken. It was toward the end of the last summer. Water in the stream was so low it had not even shown up in the photographs. It was a windy day, and she was very nervous. Remember, he had said, no one ever falls doing the Blind Man. But on his knee he bore a jagged silken scar from a fall years before (the result of a stupid mistake, he told her), proof that he did not always make it to the top. The boy taking the pictures was especially inept, and he kept yelling up at Lew, asking him not to move for a minute so he could get a better shot. And Lew would hold on, not so much a mountain goat, as Ziza said, as a spider. His smile when he got to the top was broader than usual, the wave a little wilder. It made her suspect that he, too, had become frightened.

"Unfortunate that the film quality is so bad," Hagadorn Mills said. "Definitely not reproducible, but look at some of the things over here, Naomi. There are some more people I would like you to identify."

It all went on for longer than she could stand, faces she could recognize with names she could not remember. No rush, Andy said more than once, if you wait a minute or two it may all come back to you. It did not. At least what she wanted did not. She was vaguely aware of Ziza Todd—and she was even more aware of Mills's being aware of her—poking into this box and that, going through items Mills had obviously discarded, and every now and then looking at a photograph for an especially long time. Every time Ziza did that, Naomi could sense Mills wanting to rush over and see what she had. Instead he would grit his teeth, smile and call Naomi's attention to another photograph, a boy standing on the gunwales of a canoe, say, and holding a long pole with a boxing glove fitted over one end. What do you suppose this is all about? he would ask. Visitors' Day Water Carnival, she would say, and they would be off on more trivia: what year, do you suppose?

"I have a question," Ziza interrupted at one point while Naomi was trying to dredge up the name of a particularly officious water-sports director. She was holding a battered maroon book, *The Social, Mercantile and Ecclesiastical History of the Smyrna Community of Greene County, New York.*

"Idris Quick's history," Mills said. "Mrs. Van Schoonhoven's father."

"Yes," Ziza said, "but there are pages missing."

"Pages 303 to 306 in a chapter called 'Well On With The Work.' Right?"

"Right."

"They're all that way," he said.

"Yes," Ziza said, "but what do you suppose is being hidden?"

"It is a mystery," Andy said, "unless Naomi can clear it up. Whatever it was got Idris dropped as official historian. Rumor is that lots of papers, family papers, were also destroyed."

They both turned to look at Naomi, hoping for a comment.

"Scandal," she said.

"Yes?" they said.

"Or at least what passes for scandal around here."

"Yes?" they said, waiting for more.

But Naomi—perversely—said no more, and when she told the Butlers about it as they drove toward Catskill that night, they thought it was a great joke.

"Only at Smyrna," Naomi said, "would the news that Young Father Quick was the natural son of Old Father Quick be considered a scandal."

"But it was one of Old Father's theocratic rules," Charley began.

"Rule Number Five," Frank said.

Charley continued, "Set forth that leadership could not be inherited. It was a gift from God, and the child destined for leadership must be sought after and found."

"Old Father simply found the new leader sleeping in a crib in his own bedroom," Frank said. "Probably saved a lot of time."

"Not a joking matter," Charley said. "He ought not to have done it."

"But who could have led better than Young Father?"

"But still he should have admitted it and found Scripture to explain it."

"Or maybe Idris, who had been passed over and maybe had his nose out of joint, should just have kept quiet about the whole thing in his official history, pages 303 to 306."

"But it ruined his life. Or ended it. No sooner did that book come out than old Idris died."

It was an old argument, a familiar, comfortable, comforting argument that contained no surprises and no questions, a family secret that was no secret to anyone in the family. It was the sort of thing Naomi needed to hear after a morning with Andy Mills's prying questions and his boxes of dusty photographs. The conversation in the car drifted on to other subjects: how the Butlers had often thought about her over the years, how they wished they all had kept in touch. And what was she doing these days? Still working on a newspaper?

"Copyediting, freelance," she said, "working at home. No

more city rooms and drinks after work to prove I was just one of the boys." It was an attempt to allude to the purpose of their trip to Catskill, but the brothers refused to pick up on it, so she went into her usual rap about what a copy editor did, masking the long hours and the endless detail by saying it was mostly a matter of being able to tell the difference between *farther* and *further, eager* and *anxious,* and knowing where the comma goes after a quotation.

"As for spelling," she said, "you have to know three things: that *cemetery* has an *er* not an *ar,* that *McDonald's* begins with *Mc,* not *Mac,* and that the only *e*'s in *Edgar Allan Poe* are at the beginning and the end. Those are three things few writers seem to know."

They rode in silence as the windshield wipers squeaked across shiny glass constantly being repeppered with new rain, and they thought about spelling.

"How about *judgment?*" said Frank. "I always have to think twice about that one."

"Luckily it's a word you don't use often," Charley said. "But do you know that the letter *a* doesn't appear in any number word until you reach *thousand?*"

"He used to win money on that one," Frank said.

"A great barroom bet. You say you can talk for five minutes without repeating yourself and never use a word with an *a* in it. Take the bets and then start counting slowly."

"Very slowly. One. Two. Three. Four. Five. Bored the daylights out of everyone he tried it on."

"And you couldn't have a drink for five minutes."

"A terrible way to make a living," Frank said.

"It's a terrible thing to say," Naomi said, "but I'd forgotten how much I missed you."

"Well, we've never forgotten you," Charley said.

"We've been the Guardians all these years," Frank said, "and we knew a time would come when things would have to be put right."

"We just waited . . ."

"Bided our time . . ."

"And now it looks as though the time has come."

She was probably driving faster than she should have, but they had been off to a late start and she was trying to make up for lost time. She never liked it when people came in late for meetings, bumping into chairs, apologizing louder than they should. It always seemed to show a lack of seriousness, a lack of respect for the poor soul up there spilling his guts. Or her guts. But now as they were going down a steep hill that led to the overpass that crossed the Thruway, she looked up into the rearview mirror, astonished at what Charley was saying, puzzled over his meaning, as though if she could catch a glimpse of him it would all make a great deal more sense.

She could see him only as a shadow. Behind Charley the lights of another car, going even faster than she was, gained on her through the rain. The lights moved out into the empty oncoming lane as though to pass and then pulled back behind her again, following closer than she liked.

"You probably wondered what it was all about when you got that strange letter," Charley was saying.

"Did Ziza Todd tell you about that, too?" she asked. The lights pulled into the other lane again. It looked more like a pickup truck than a car. She slowed down. She could hear Frank, next to her, stamping on the floor as though he, too, were putting on the brakes.

"Ziza Todd? Why, no . . ."

The pickup was alongside and then just enough in front to splash up a sheet of water from the road that overwhelmed the windshield wipers. She slowed down again. The car seemed to slide sideways. The only thing she could see was gray water, but somehow she sensed the truck was pulling back into her lane too soon. Frank was stepping on the brakes again and clutching the dashboard.

There was a crash that felt as though she had driven into the incoming tide. A wave—or was it the back of the pickup truck?—caught the front edge of the car. For some reason she said, "I hope everyone remembered to buckle up," and then they began to roll, ever so gently, ever so slowly, down the side of an embankment.

Some things remained perfectly clear. She remembered the sound of Frank pounding on the floor with his foot, the sound of Charley inhaling a great gulp of air as though he were about to submerge. She remembered the brake lights of the pickup going on, then off, and the truck speeding away. She remembered the Butlers saying they were her Guardians, and she remembered the rich smoky smell of scotch. Her last thought before passing out was that she had broken another damn bottle.

13

❧

"That does it," Melody Horn said, slamming down the telephone. She was in her office, behind the highly polished four-inch-thick slab of white oak she used as a desk. Sherman Benedikt sat in an armless side chair, not one of the two leather club chairs in front of the desk. He held a pad and a felt-tipped pen and looked for all the world like an old-fashioned stenographer. But he was not taking notes.

"Shall I list, shall I just list all that I have to deal with at the moment?" she asked, not speaking directly to Benedikt, who was not one of the people at Smyrna she had to charm. "I think I shall.

"Number one: a dead Mr. Harry Van Schoonhoven, who the yokel Keystone Kop wants to believe was done in by foul play."

"A drug unknown to science?"

"Wouldn't that be lovely? But you are interrupting my catalog of woe.

"Number two: a company that should be just on the brink of becoming a multimillion-dollar baby.

"Number three: another outfit . . ."

"Great Bear and Highfield, Limited . . ."

"Thank you, Sherman, but I'm well aware of the name. Great Bear and Highfield Not-All-That-Limited, which seems to think it was invited by the late, dear Mr. Van

Schoonhoven to buy out this place lock, stock and barrel.

"Number four: a bag of bones . . ."

"Poor Llewelyn . . ."

"Was that his first name, Poor?"

"So it would seem."

"Poor Llewelyn, whose considerable stock in this place, now that a body has turned up to prove that he is really dead, seems to be owned by his poor widow. Who also conveniently turns up just at the right moment to claim it."

"She hasn't claimed it yet."

"Just a matter of time. The lawyers say there's a written agreement—'instrument,' if you will—with Van Schoonhoven saying that he would control the stock, in trust for the community, as long as there was any doubt about the boy's fate. When doubt is settled, and it certainly seems to be settled, the Widow Naomi inherits."

"Speaking of whom, number . . . what are we up to, Sherman?"

"Five."

"Number five: That was the Widow Van Schoonhoven on the phone. Naomi, it seems, got into some sort of god-awful automobile accident last night."

"Fatal?"

"Not."

"It could have certainly tidied things up if it were."

"But it was not. She has a bloody nose and some sprains or something, and her insides are shaken up. The Butlers, of all people, were with her. I can never remember which one of them is which, but whoever was sitting in the back seat just received bruises. The one in the front . . ."

"In the death seat."

". . . has broken bones. A leg, maybe two, and I think an arm. Anyway, Mrs. Van Schoonhoven's message was that we are going to be playing *General Hospital*. The Butlers will be convalescing in their own room, of course, but Naomi is being graciously offered Aunt Nan's old suite until she is on her feet again. That way, Mrs. Van S. says, the nurse she has hired will be able to handle all three."

"Handy," Benedikt said.

"Isn't it?"

"Now, what do we do about Great Bear and Highfield?"

 ❧   ❧   ❧

The door to Mr. Van Schoonhoven's office was ajar, and Ziza Todd peeked in because there was no good reason not to. Mrs. Van Schoonhoven was at the desk. The direct morning sunlight had not yet reached the windows, but no lights had been turned on. She sat in the oversized desk chair and held the telephone to her ear, not speaking to anyone. At first Ziza thought she was eavesdropping on someone, but no, she was simply leaning on the phone, using it as an improbable headrest. The desk in front of her was empty except for the antique wooden box Mr. Van Schoonhoven had used to hold papers and a half-filled bottle of vodka. She had a glass in her other hand.

Ziza was about to duck back out the door when she realized Mrs. Van Schoonhoven was looking directly at her. "Have a seat," she said. "Pick a comfortable one."

"I don't want to interrupt," Ziza said.

"Interrupt what? More telephone calls? Sit."

Ziza sat.

"If you want a glass there are some over in that cabinet. Baccarat, I think. Something fancy and expensive. And if you want anything to put in the glass there's vodka, cheap and handy."

Ziza just shook her head. Beer before breakfast yesterday was bad enough. "I am so sorry about Mr. Van Schoonhoven . . ."

"Do you think widows mourn? Is that what they teach you at your seminary, that widows mourn? They don't. We don't. Widows talk on the telephone." She put the receiver back on the cradle, very carefully, as though she might have been eavesdropping after all. "We make arrangements. We hear about arrangements that have been made for us (just to simplify things, they say), which then we have to change with another telephone call. In the old days people used to bring casseroles and leave them in the kitchen. You could judge how popular someone was by how many casseroles were lined up on the sideboard. Nowadays, they call up the widow and ask if there is anything they can do. The answer is yes, they can get off the telephone. So I appreciate your stopping by."

Ziza could not very well say it was unintentional. "I never really got to know Mr. Van Schoonhoven."

"My first reaction is to say, 'Just as well you didn't.' Isn't that terrible? People never much liked Harry. He got the job done around here, but when people called him the Old Schooner I don't think it was done with much affection, if you know what I mean. He was a foundling, you know. In the days before birth control and easy abortions a lot of foundlings ended up at Smyrna. And he never left. He was a teenager when Llewelyn was named heir. He never quite got over that. He was older. He was clearly the one to run things, but when Young Father Quick—and I mean a very, very old Young Father Quick—had to name an heir he picked a little kid, lovely little Llewelyn. He was just a couple of years younger than me, Llewelyn was, and, oh, I once had such a terrible crush on him. That's what we called them then, crushes, and they were thought to be very innocent. They weren't, of course.

"So while Llewelyn got older and took up things like that jazz band—they were truly terrible, but everyone was so enchanted with Llewelyn no one would admit it—and rock climbing and spending every summer being the wet-dream hero of a bunch of adolescents at the camp, Harry took charge of things and made them work. He didn't marry the boss's daughter. There wasn't one. But there was a handy niece, and I was it. Together, we made this place work, although lately he'd begun to get ideas about changing things. Or maybe I should say he picked up a lot of ideas about changing things."

She took a sip from her glass, a slow, dainty sip as though she were nursing a drink until closing time.

"Harry, you know, was someone who thought he was born to be a star. He acted in outrageous ways just like stars do. In bars or restaurants people always knew he was there. Waitresses took special care of him. He had a way of being given treats such as personally heated bread or free after-dinner drinks. When the bills came, there was a routine he would go through that would be embarrassing if someone else did it. He would go through every item. 'Now, did she *get* the Lasagne Lago Como?' he would ask, with just the slightest hint that perhaps something inferior might have been substituted instead. 'And there were four martinis and three Manhattans and *two* carafes of house wine?' The waitress would defend the fact that there were indeed two carafes, although you could tell that she'd begun to doubt it herself, and by the time he was checking to see that the right percentage had been taken out for taxes you could tell that they knew he was someone not to offend. That's when the after-dinner drink would arrive. On the house. That wouldn't be a bad epitaph for Harry Van Schoonhoven: On The House."

"Have you been able to get much sleep?" Ziza asked, thinking maybe she should find a way to get Mrs. Van S. away from the bottle.

"You don't get much sleep when there are phone calls to answer. And make. That silly Naomi goes out on the town with the Butler boys and drives off the road, and now I have a second floor of invalids to deal with. I had to call a half-dozen practical nurses before I could find one to come out here. They kept saying no. I kept wanting to say, 'Well, send an impractical one, then.' But I suppose that's a joke those people have heard more than once too often."

It was the first Ziza had heard of Naomi's accident, and

she had questions to ask. But there was no stopping Mrs. Van Schoonhoven.

"And then there's Nick Story. One minute he's here, the next he's on the phone, and always there are questions. Did Harry have a heart condition? A mild one, yes. Was he taking medication for it? No. Did he have a special diet. Yes and no, but he didn't follow it, anyway. Did he exercise? Are you kidding? And oddest of all—and this is the one he keeps harping on—Was Harry under any sort of treatment for alcoholism? Harry? He can drink everyone under the table and never be the worse for it, never show it to speak of. I've never known a better drinker. Never even a hangover that needed a cure. But Story wants to know if it could have been something Harry was doing secretly, without telling me about it. Had I noticed if he had stopped drinking for extended periods? Harry, I asked, a secret abstainer? Never. And then he started hinting about this and that. Nothing definite. Just one little hint after another, a lot of it about drinks. Drinking. Maybe that it was not just a simple heart attack."

"Not suicide?" Ziza said.

"Oh, he asked about that, too, but right out front. No hints. Did I think Harry was suicidal? Did he resent being kicked upstairs in the company? Surely not, I said. The move was his idea. He spends all his time now—" She caught herself. "He spent all his time on the phone making some sort of special deal that he couldn't have made before. Hush-hush. Big man's big secret. Not the sort of thing to trust with the little woman. No, murder is what Nick Story has in mind, and he claims his lab people are going to prove it."

"But not yet?"

Gwen Van Schoonhoven sat there in the morning shadows, glass in one hand, back straight, dwarfed by the high-backed leather chair she sat in, the woman, Ziza remembered, whose reaction to seeing her husband's dead body was to say, "We expected him for dinner."

"It must be someone here," Ziza said. "The murderer. If it was murder."

"So it would seem."

"Someone we know."

"Yes."

The door to the hallway, which had not been pulled shut, opened. Light cut across the floor and splashed against the far wall. It was as astonishing as a shout, and both women jumped. A thin shadowy figure stood in the center of the light. He held something in his arms, a tumbling bouquet of flowers.

"Mrs. Van Schoonhoven," he said, following the path of light toward the desk.

"Timmy," she said, putting her glass down and coming forward to meet him.

"I'm very sorry for your troubles," Tim Jacobsen said as though it were a sentence in a foreign language he had memorized.

"Timmy," she said, throwing her arms around him. He passed the bouquet to Ziza, whom he was clearly surprised to see, and put his arms around Mrs. Van Schoonhoven, slowly patting her back as though he were calming a nervous animal. "Flowers," she said, "you brought flowers." Her tears began before the sobs. "He was very kind to you."

"I guess."

"This would have pleased him, Timmy. Bringing flowers would have made him very happy."

In the dim light, Ziza could not tell if one person was crying, or two.

14

&

Tim Jacobsen went upstairs with Ziza to see the invalids. She had tried to slip out of the office, thinking that Tim and Mrs. Van Schoonhoven might want to be alone. But he would have none of that. Where was she going? he wanted to know. To give herself a destination, Ziza said that she was going to look in on Naomi. And the Butlers, too? he asked. Of course, she said, although that had not been her intention at all. Tim said he would come along.

She handed the flowers over to Mrs. Van Schoonhoven and, without thinking much about it, placed a quick kiss on her damp cheek. She could feel the older woman stiffen on contact. Nothing was said. Mrs. Van S. only nodded, but Ziza knew she had made a terrible mistake: not the kiss itself but simply being there.

"You never know what you're getting into when you walk through a door," Tim said as they climbed the stairs. "I was thinking, you know, how you're always supposed to send flowers to dead people, which seems a waste. So why not take them to a living one instead. They at least know what's happening. Instead I open a can of worms."

Looking sideways at his face, Ziza could not be sure he had not been crying down there in the dark. "It was a very nice gesture," she said.

"Gesture? That was no gesture. I did it."

The plastic crime-scene tape had been taken away, and Aunt Nan's door stood open. Ziza looked in. Naomi was lying in bed reading what looked like a magazine. Before Ziza could step inside, Tim pulled her arm. "I thought we were looking for the Butlers," he said. "Next," Ziza said. "Since we're here we might as well say hello."

Hearing the whispers at her doorway, Naomi looked up. "Come on in," she said. "I'm not the ghost of Aunt Nan, if that's the problem."

"What happened?" Ziza asked, remembering too late that she should have begun by saying how well Naomi looked.

"It was a terrible night, last night," Naomi began, sounding as though it were not for the first time. "The weather was simply awful, and we were late. I suppose I was just careless."

"I'll be down the hall," Tim said to Ziza. "Nice seeing you again," to Naomi. "You'll be up and around in no time."

"That's what I've been saying. Thanks."

"You know Tim, of course," Ziza said to Naomi, but he was already out of the room.

"Of course. Yesterday morning, with you. The Phantom. I think it makes him uneasy being in the same room with a woman in bed."

"Think so? Now, tell me details. What happened?"

"Take a chair." This time, Ziza got the details, at least most of them. She heard about the truck, especially about the truck coming to a stop and then speeding away. ("That sounds funny to me," she said.) She did not hear about where they were heading or what the Butler boys had been saying just before the crash.

"So I escape with a bumped head, a sore nose and some bruised ribs. The patient will survive, but I think I should tell you that I'm cross with you," Naomi said. "You told that Sherman Benedikt about my mysterious letter. And maybe you told more. Gossip. Loose lips sink ships, and I don't like it one bit."

"Gossip?" Ziza was shocked. "Good Lord, no. We were

exchanging clues, trying to come up with some answers to what's been happening around here."

"You think of all of this as some sort of murder mystery, something that can be tidied up in two hundred or so pages?"

"Well, there is a mystery, and now there has been a murder."

"Harry?"

"Nick Story's been asking Mrs. Van Schoonhoven all kinds of vague questions . . ."

"Harry Van Schoonhoven was not colorful enough to kill. You know the type. When you read their obituaries it's always a surprise because you thought they'd died years ago."

"Nick Story says—"

"Nick Story, Nick Story." She shooed his name away with her hands as though it were a fly. To change the subject, she showed Ziza what she had been reading. It was not an old magazine but a Camp Smyrna catalog for the year 1937. On the cover happy boys waved from a swimming raft. "This room is where you and Hagadorn—pardon me, Andy Mills— should be doing your research. Aunt Nan had more material about Smyrna squirreled away than you'll find in the library or Andy's cardboard boxes." A mischievous look crossed her face. "That even looks like the maroon spine of Idris Quick's history over there on the bookshelf. Maybe Aunt Nan had an uncut copy."

Ziza pulled it out and turned to the chapter called "Well On With The Work." There were no missing pages. She began reading right where she was standing.

"Take it with you, and maybe you'll find one of your beloved clues. Just try not to share it with the first good-looking man you run into."

That sounded as though it was a hint to leave, so Ziza did not sit down again. She would have liked to have another look at the little room where she had found Llewelyn's skeleton, but that could wait for another day. In spite of her good spirits Naomi seemed pale and tired. She wore the look she would have as a very old woman. Ziza did something she had never done before at Smyrna: she asked if Naomi would like her to say a prayer before she left. Naomi looked startled. Then she smiled and held out her hand.

"Only if it's a silent one," Naomi said.

"You've made a deal," Ziza said and took her hand. If they had listened in their silence they could have heard the distant stream—still swollen by the night rains—and the laughter of Tim and the Butlers spilling down the hall. They could have heard the household sounds of a far-off vacuum cleaner and footsteps on the creaking stairs. But they were not listening.

"If Gwen Van Schoonhoven asks you to take part in Harry's service, please accept."

"I don't expect—"

"Please accept."

She gave Naomi's hand a squeeze. "I'll see you tomorrow."

By the time Ziza got to the Butlers' room the laughter had stopped, and the three of them looked at her as though she had caught them at something they would rather not talk about. Tim was sitting on the floor, his back against the wall, his legs stretched out straight in front of him. Charley lay on his carefully made bed, but he was fully dressed. He was even wearing his shoes and a vest, although the vest was unbuttoned. Frank was much more the worse for wear, and when he saw Ziza coming through the open door (without knocking, he would mention later), he tried to rearrange the blanket into a more modest drape. One arm was in a cast, and by the look of it, one leg as well.

"Oh, poor Frank," said Ziza. "What's the tally?"

"One each," Frank said. "One arm, one leg, one left, one right."

"His crippling is balanced, but asymmetrical," Charley said.

"And he," Frank said, "has had a serious shaking up."

"My ribs are taped," Charley said. "The back seat is not without its dangers."

"The less said about women drivers the better," Frank said.

"But it was a terrible night," Ziza said, "and there was that crazy truck."

"There was a crazy truck?" asked Tim.

"It missed my notice," Charley said.

"It was a time of considerable confusion," said Frank.

"And the less said about driving skills . . ." Charley began.

"What's that?" Frank asked, pointing at Ziza's book. "It looks like Idris Quick."

"It is Idris Quick," Charley said.

"On loan," Ziza said. "Naomi said it would be all right if I borrowed it."

"I don't know that it's Naomi's to loan out, assuming it's from Aunt Nan's collection," Charley said.

"It is."

"Mind if I have a look?" asked Charley.

"They're all the same," Ziza said.

"But are they?" asked Frank.

"Of course they are," Ziza said and started for the door. "I'll be dropping by again. Take care."

Tim sprang up, and before Ziza was out of the room he plucked the book out of her hand. Ziza could not believe he could move so quickly or that he would move so fast against her. They stood facing each other, and Tim slowly raised the book an arm's length over her head, a confident center keeping the basketball away from a pesky forward. She refused to jump for it.

"Hand it over."

"Make me." He said it with a smile and a taunt, bigger brother to smaller sister.

"Sure," she said and kneed him in the groin. Not a hard knee, not the sort of thing that would knock him to the floor, but a well-aimed knee, a surgically precise strike, as they used to say about bombing raids, and Tim doubled over just long enough for Ziza to snatch the book from him.

She ran out the door and down the hall, passing Naomi's door, which was now closed tightly. He was right behind her,

and she suspected he could speed up and grab her anytime
he wanted. She cut back through a side hall that she knew
would come around and meet the back stairs. The old house
seemed to be vibrating to the rhythm of their running, and
it was not until she reached the stairs to the third floor that
she realized they were both laughing. This is absurd, she
thought. She was acting as though she were a silly teenager,
a way she could not remember actually acting when she really
was a silly teenager. Tim seemed to turn her into someone
on a television sitcom. But what the hell, she thought, just
this once, in for a penny . . . She raced up the stairs toward
her room, and he followed.

The Butlers, stretched out on their beds, heard Ziza's door
slam, but they could not tell whether it slammed with Tim
inside her room or out. Try as they might, they could hear
no other sounds. No more laughing or running; no one banging on a door.

"Children," Charley said. "They are nothing but children."

Naomi, too, was listening, but she was no longer in Aunt
Nan's old bed. She listened to the laughter and the running
as she lay on the narrow cot in the small side room where
Ziza had found Lew. She had come in to see the pictures
they had told her were on the walls—the Llewelyn shrine,
someone called it. But after only a minute or so she felt so
tired she had to lie down. Her ribs, held tight by heavy taping,
ached when she breathed deeply, and her nose—which the
doctor insisted was not broken—felt as though it were spread
across her face. She was afraid to touch it, afraid the bleeding
would start again. She lay on the rough cotton mattress cover.
The sleeping bag, of course, was gone, hauled off with everything else by Nick Story.

How long had Lew, what was left of Lew, rested on this
bed? Not long, according to Story's men, days, a couple of
weeks at the most. Long enough for her to receive a letter
and come north to Smyrna, long enough for the Guardians
to finish their work.

She lay there surrounded by pictures she could not bring herself to look at and forced herself to think of that last night and the memories she was now sure of but which she had for so long refused to allow herself to remember. Lew had been in their bedroom in the old mess hall when she got back. That was a surprise. She thought he had stayed behind after everyone else left the birthday bonfire—everyone, of course, but Gwen. It was the end of the season, one of those last nights before the boys went home when kids who had stayed out of trouble all summer began to slip. It was the time each year when discipline crumbled, when limits—now that threats of punishment could only be empty—were tested, when everyone tried to see just how much he could get away with. It was a time when no one even pretended to be asleep after lights out.

She had run into Harry Van Schoonhoven that night. That, too, was a surprise. He had indeed been at the bonfire, staying in the shadows at the back. He had been there, she assumed, to keep an eye on Gwen, who had become more and more outrageous in her flirting with Lew. They met on the path through the tall lilac bushes near the Gnomes' House. It occurred to her that he might have been following his wife. She said nothing about that. She and Harry did not mention Gwen or Lew. It was not the sort of thing you spoke about: What's my husband doing with your wife? My wife, your husband. Had they spoken at all? There were distant shouts and war cries as the boys from Tuscarora raided the Seneca cabin. A counselor was halfheartedly blowing a whistle for order. She walked down to the stream with Harry, then along the narrow path that led to the bottom of the Falls and on to the swimming pavilion. Neither of them spoke. The war cries were farther away now, but there were more of them. Inspired by the Tuscarora, other raiding parties moved through the camp. Harry's hand had been on her shoulder, she remembered that, but had it been she who led the way? She suspected it had. What they did was not something either of them much cared about. It was something to get away with, a moment of private revenge, a silent raid with no resistance and no booty worth boasting of later. As she remembered it now, her mind was not on Harry (although Harry was far more seductive than she would have suspected; he really had not been bad-looking at that age) but on them. Gwen and Lew. Where were they? Where did they go?

And when she got back to the room, there was Lew, stretched out on the bed, one reading light on, his arms crossed on his chest, waiting. Not reading, not pacing, not messing around with the climbing equipment that lay piled in the closet and always seemed to need some sort of special attention.

"Get lost?" he asked.

Had she and Harry had something to drink? A pocket flask would have been in character. "Did you and Gwen?" A challenge.

"Gwen?" A dismissal.

She had decided to become frank. There had been talk about him and Gwen, she said, enough of it even to get back to her. (They must have had drinks at the swimming pavilion, warm, too sweet, and some of it had spilled, she remembered now, across her throat and down between her breasts.) To all her charges, his reply was the same: "Gwen?" in disbelief. And then, to shock him into a different reply, she mentioned Harry, threw Harry at him, she and Harry down at the swimming pavilion, a gauntlet across the bed, never raising her voice, never shouting, no tears, just a flat statement.

His reaction was to freeze. He made no answer. He did not move. There was utter silence, and then he sprang up, stood facing her. One last, disbelieving look before he turned to the shadows of the corner, and with one hand pressing each wall, Samson bringing down the temple, he said, "No. No. No. No. No," a cry without tears. With the torn William Morris chrysanthemums on the dark-green wallpaper heaped around his bowed head, he kept pressing against the walls, a climber seeking a grip.

She had not gone to him. She stood stock-still on the other side of the bed, shocked by what she had caused to happen, frozen just as he had been, and when she was able to move, he was gone.

She lay now on the cot in the little room off Aunt Nan's bedroom. Splayed out on the wall above her were dozens of photographs of Lew, but all she could see was his face that last night, the face of the betrayed as disbelief turned to utterly unacceptable belief, his last, stunned look at her.

15

᳕

Nick Story had been playing it by ear. As a detective with the state police he rarely encountered killings in which mystery played any part whatever. Some drunk in a highway bar pulls a gun on another drunk, usually over something as important as who paid for the last round, and shoots a bystander. A husband, out of work, the unemployment payments run out, hits his wife once too often. A hunter mistakes his oldest son for a deer. He had never been involved in a case in which the killer was a woman.

He read somewhere that a former Pinkerton detective—this was back in the 1940s—said that in his experience city killings were over money, country killings over sex. That sounded clever, and Story had dealt with his share of jealous husbands, more than his share of hotheaded teenage boyfriends, but had the people they killed—or tried to kill—really come to grief because of sex? Usually it was just a silly mistake. Everything would have been different, say, if the killer had caught the red light at the intersection of routes 23A and 32 and arrived home three minutes later. Nothing was ever planned. There was no deception. No one ever had an alibi. The wrong guy happened to turn up at the wrong time. And when Story and his men would drive out to arrest the killer ("murderer" was too grand a term), the guy usually was waiting to be picked up, sitting on the front porch with what was left of a six-pack beside him.

Now that drugs were moving into Greene County he suspected the kinds and styles of local crime would change. But so far no one had killed anyone, other than hopped-up kids smashing their cars into one another. No "kingpins," as the papers and the politicians liked to call them, had flexed any muscle in Nick Story's territory. That day, no doubt, would come, but now he had to deal with whatever was going on at Smyrna.

How many murders were there? One? Two? None? How many murderers?

Exhibit one: a fairly new mummy sleeping bag stuffed with some fairly old bones. Other bones from the same corpse turn up (just about all of them now accounted for), and the skeleton turns out to be—to no one's particular surprise— the long-lost son and heir. And what does that prove? How did he die? A number of the bones were broken. He could have been beaten to death. He could have fallen. Jumped? Pushed? People seemed more curious about how the sleeping bag got into the old lady's bedroom than about how he died.

A tidy solution would have been that the old lady killed him (or simply found him dead years ago) and kept the body as some kind of relic. Horror-movie stuff. Maybe sleeping with him on the cot. Fashionably kinky stuff. But the facts and the lab reports would not support that. Then, who had the body, the bones, all those years? How did that person get them? Was he the murderer? (Was there a murder?) Did the person who had them stuff them in the sleeping bag and put them on the cot? Or did someone recently stumble across them and stash them hurriedly in the bag—leaving some of the pieces behind in the panicky rush—and dump them on the cot to be found, sticking that god-awful mask over the skull? And why the mask? Halloween humor? A hint of the occult?

Exhibit two: Harry Van Schoonhoven curled up on the dirt

cellar floor of the Gnomes' House. Dead. A coffee can of Llewelyn's bones nearby. A place set for dinner back home. Heart attack? That would solve everything. He had a heart condition, a mild one, so they said. But Nick Story had his doubts. He called for the medical office to pull a Full Unknown, a series of tests that would not end until every possible cause of death had been explored. Medical examiners claim to hate Full Unknowns. Back when he was a rookie cop in Brooklyn, no one below a deputy inspector could request one. But this was not Brooklyn. Up here, with a tediously steady supply of mangled highway fatalities, they might even rise to the challenge. A change of pace. Anyway, he had some specific drugs he wanted searched for, anything that, mixed in the stomach with alcohol, might trigger a heart attack in someone leaning in that direction. It was only a whim, and he always distrusted whims, but he especially wanted them to look for traces of disulfiram, Antabuse.

Story himself had once messed around with Antabuse, years ago back in Brooklyn. "Back in Brooklyn," to Story, was almost code for "back in the bottle." Those were his drinking days. He had not been born in Park Slope, but he grew up there (Berkeley Place, below Seventh Avenue, way below, where it had never been fashionable), grew up long before the neighborhood had been discovered by the lawyers and publishing people and Wall Street types who spent fortunes "restoring" the place to a Victorian quaintness even the oldest old-timers could not remember. He had become a cop at a time when city boys became cops in groups of twos or threes, he and Mike Concannon from down the block.

Years later Mike had been the one who had given him the Antabuse. Concannon had been spotted as a potential problem and was sent to a series of special departmental alcohol-counseling sessions. Story had once been sent to one, too, but a lower-level affair, not something for serious cases like Mike's. In Story's group they were given a lecture on alcoholism's danger signals, and then a chaplain and a doctor (at least someone dressed as though he were a doctor) told them what sympathetic help was available—at no cost and strictly confidential—within the department. And no more was said. In Mike Concannon's group, they had to show up twice a week for therapy ("sitting around in a circle and bitching," Mike had said) and were eventually given a supply of Antabuse. Half a tablet every morning. The stuff would not stop you from drinking, they said, but if you did drink after taking it, it would make you very sick.

Fuck that, Concannon had said. He parked the tablets in his locker, kept on drinking and at the semiweekly circle jerks bitched like the best of them. He might have fooled a couple of people, but not many. The last time Story saw Mike, when he had gone to the 87th Precinct on Flatbush Avenue to sign his separation papers, Concannon was working as a temp duty clerk/typist, still in uniform but without a gun, hunched over a typewriter stuffed with a wad of papers and carbons, carefully and slowly trying to peck his way through some sort of departmental paperwork. Next to the typewriter was a pile of forms half a foot high. Sweat was running down Concannon's puffy face, and the bulky uniform made working at a typewriter difficult. He formed each letter he typed with his lips, and he was out of breath, panting slowly as though he had run half a block too far. Story was sorry to have seen him, but it was an image he liked to remember.

He had borrowed the Antabuse from Concannon one hung-over morning when, in a moment of crystal clarity, he knew he had to stop drinking before he really got into trouble. Borrowed, hell, he just grabbed an envelope of them from the pile when Concannon left his locker door open. He did not drink that night and the next morning took a tablet, a whole one. For two more nights he skipped the booze and took a pill every morning, and he was feeling as clean as hell. Then came Friday night, an off-duty Friday night and an empty Saturday ahead, so he dropped into Harkin's at the corner of Berkeley and Seventh Avenue (as a good Brooklyn boy he was still living in his parents' house: you don't move out until you have a bride). It was just to say hello. Just because you gave up drinking did not mean you had to give up your friends.

In the old days—the weekend before—he could start at Harkin's and drink his way south along Seventh, hitting the bars on every corner, and the few mid-block ones as well, down the west side until he hit Third Street and then back the east side (for some reason, perhaps zoning had something to do with it, there were more than twice as many bars on the west side of the avenue as on the east), getting back to Harkin's, an east-side place, for closing.

None of that tonight, he had told himself. His first order of a Coke ("No ice, Tom") caused all the drama he had hoped for, but by his third the joke was over, he was getting restless, the game on TV was boring and it was not much past 10:30. So he tried a scotch and soda. Nothing much happened, if anything it made the drink better, with one drink feeling more like two or three. He felt a bit warm, as though a bank of heat were building up, but that was about all. He had a second, and then it hit him. He was having a heart attack, he was sure of it. His chest was pounding so hard he could not believe the others couldn't hear it. He was burning up. His heart was going crazy. The stomach cramps began, and he stumbled toward one of the booths in the back (no one in Harkin's ever sat in a booth) while Tom dialed 911 for an EMS ambulance.

He never tried Antabuse again, even several years later when he did stop drinking for good. That came when he left Brooklyn and his parents' house, still without a bride. He had discovered upstate New York and effected—although it was not easy—a transfer to the state police. He had made his "discovery" through the PBA, the Patrolmen's Benevolent Association. They ran a summer camp for cops and their families near Tannersville in the northern Catskills. He went up for a cheap vacation (East Durham, a town of Irish bars,

Seventh Avenue without the dog shit, was only about a half
hour away) and found that he loved those scruffy little mountains with their improbable waterfalls and their trashy towns
full of pizza parlors and real-estate agents. He found that he
felt totally at home in a local diner named Warm's, where
the old coots met every morning over good coffee and leaden
doughnuts to discuss sports scores and the previous evening's
traffic accidents. He felt that this might be his way out, his
way to avoid ending up as a burned-out typewriter puncher
like Mike Concannon. Anyway, buying land around there
might even be a smart economic move.

After the state police agreed to accept him (his superiors
on the NYPD wrote suspiciously praiseful recommenda-
tions), he picked up the mortgage on a tiny farmhouse in an
apple orchard in East Jewett. It was on a dead-end road that
went to a lake, a short drive from Warm's and a longer one
down the mountain to the police barracks in Leeds. And now,
fifteen years later and still without a bride, he had advanced
to the point where he didn't wear a uniform and had enough
clout to get away with spending more time than he could
honestly justify trying to figure out what was going on at
Smyrna.

And he was winging it. Every day he spent a little time at
Smyrna, hanging around, asking questions, listening to the
answers. Over the years Story had learned that the answers
people give rarely have all that much to do with the questions
asked. The questioner should not count on hearing what he
expects to hear, and he should never expect to hear what he
hopes to hear. Usually, he found, if he was really paying
attention, the answers were more provocative than the
questions.

As yet, he had no proof that Harry Van Schoonhoven's
death was not natural. The lab tests were still going on. But
no need to tell anyone that. No need, in fact, not to suggest
that he did have damaging proof of some kind. He had also
come to suspect that the person he was looking for was a

woman, and even though he had never encountered a female killer, he felt, just felt, deep down that this was woman's work if he ever saw it. No need to let on to that, either.

He tracked down Ziza Todd at the old mess hall. She was high up on the scaffolding with Tim Jacobsen, both of them scraping away at the weathered clapboards and causing a flurry of yellow paint chips to drift down and be scattered by the wind. After thinking the better of it, he swung onto the ladder and made his way toward the top. The two of them stopped working and watched him climb but did not say a word until he reached them.

"Welcome aboard," Tim said. "I have an extra scraper, if you want to use it. There's no work to it, the paint's so old. Touch it and it falls off."

"Tim's perfecting his Tom Sawyer fence-painting act," Ziza said. "And don't believe him. This is hard work. My arms are going to be killing me tomorrow."

"The scaffolding was the hard part," Tim said. "But she's a pretty fair helper."

"And my pay's right," Ziza said.

"Can't complain about that," Tim said.

They both waited for Nick Story to say something. He must have had a reason for being there. But he just stood and admired the scenery.

"Hope you aren't bothered by heights," Tim said.

"I'm fine," Story said. "You have a good view of the Gnomes' House from up here. No one could come or go without your seeing him."

"Or her," Tim said.

"Of course," Story said.

"Assuming I was here. And watching," Tim said.

"Were you?"

"When?"

"The afternoon Mr. Van Schoonhoven died."

"Don't think so. If I was, I didn't notice. The Schooner

was around all the time. Seeing him isn't the sort of thing that would stick in your mind. Not like seeing someone trotting around in her little red sweat suit."

"I thought you told me Mr. Van Schoonhoven had been around bugging you about getting started on the mess hall," Ziza said, perhaps to change the subject from red sweat suits.

"That was up at my place, not here."

"That afternoon, the afternoon he died?" Story asked.

"I think."

"Up at your place, what time?"

"Late afternoon. Four. Four-thirty. That's about the time he usually came around. He'd bring a six-pack with him and we would talk about chores he wanted done. It was all stuff in the future that didn't need much discussion. What kind of paint he wanted used. Primer. Doing the wood trim on the Gnomes' House after I finished the mess hall. I think he just wanted someone to talk to. And he liked to do a lot of hinting around about how big changes were coming to Smyrna and how there was a future for an industrious young man like me. He always said 'industrious.' Not 'smart.'"

"You think it really was murder," Ziza said.

"Where did you hear that?" Story asked.

"Mrs. Van S."

"Really? People seem to tell you a lot."

"No. I ask questions, is all."

"And you get answers?"

"Of course. People are dying to talk about themselves."

"Dying?" Nick Story asked. "Tell me about it."

"Naomi has a story to tell," Ziza said, "and I suspect she's just about ready to tell it. So do the Butler boys. What do you think the three of them were up to the night of the accident? If it was an accident."

"You have doubts about that?"

"There was this truck, or so Naomi says . . ."

"Frank and Charley didn't see one," Tim said.

"Frank and Charley," Ziza said. "It's always Frank *and* Charley. I'd sometime like to hear what Frank said without Charley, or Charley without Frank."

"I don't think they work that way," Tim said. "Which reminds me: Tim has to get back to work, and so does his helper."

"I think," Ziza said, stretching out her scraping arm and turning it slowly, "his helper is pulling up lame. She's going back home to soak in a hot shower."

Tim and Nick Story both seemed to consider that a minute, and then Tim began scraping away at the house again. He worked quickly, and dried paint spun off his putty knife like sparks from a grinding wheel. "I'll be here when you've recovered," he said but did not look up.

"Want a lift back?" Nick Story asked.

"Sure."

The unmarked police car was parked behind a towering lilac bush on the other side of the Gnomes' House. "I've been poking around this place," he said as they walked through the tall grass, "looking through windows, opening doors with broken locks."

"All with a proper search warrant, I suppose." Beware of policemen making small talk, she thought.

He laughed. "You bet. There's a shed up there full of broken green mess-hall chairs, dozens of them, maybe hundreds, just scattered around the floor, piled on top of one another. There's another shed, it must have been the old craft house, that has roll after roll of boondoggle, you know those plastic strips kids at camp make lanyards out of. Red, yellow, blue—you name the color—all cracked and brittle with age. Bend it, it shatters. People have been living up there in the old cabins, what they used to call hippies, by the look of things."

"Any sign of drug use?" she asked.

"Who knows. I'm not trained like a K-9 to sniff it out, but I would guess, sure, why not? You've got to believe your eyes."

"One thing I've been taught is that you can't always believe your eyes. It is not always as simple as that."

"That was in divinity school, right? You know what a career as a policeman has taught me?" They were at the car, and he opened her door for her, reaching out as though to protect her head as she ducked inside. When he slid into his seat, he continued, "It's taught me that it *is* as simple as that. Things are just about always what they seem to be. People who look like druggies are druggies. People who dress queer are queer. Mobsters look like mobsters. Politicians who are too good to be true, are. Too good to be true. That kindly old priest who loves the homeless kids, does."

"Does what?"

"Love them. What I'm saying is not that there's always some dirty little secret. It's just that there is a good deal less mystery in this world than we would like to believe."

"I can't accept that."

"You're young and—"

"What?"

"Inexperienced."

"You were going to say, 'a woman.' "

"Well, maybe." They were pulling around the corner of the Heart. "I'm going to be dropping in on Naomi. Why don't you come along?"

"For moral support?"

"No, but I suspect you could be useful. Humor me."

Humor? It was not a word Ziza associated with Nick Story. "I was going to take a shower."

"Not really," he said. "You just wanted to get off that scaffold. That, and you wanted to show me you didn't have to hang around with the Jacobsen kid if you didn't want to. I turn up. You get a little embarrassed playing handy helper to some dropout kid who still keeps a tube of Clearasil next to his bed."

"What?"

"I saw it there when I was looking around this morning."

"You planning on booking him for acne?" she said.

"It's a beginning. Are you coming or not?"

"OK, but I'm only humoring you."

"That, and you want to be in on it."

"On what?"

"Whatever happens."

Naomi's room was empty when they got there. The bed had not been made properly, but the blanket had been pulled up to the pillow and smoothed down. A number of books—old ones—had been taken out of the bookcase and were arranged in piles on the floor. All of Aunt Nan's collages had been removed. Ziza looked into the little side room, the Llewelyn shrine. The bed in there was disturbed, too, but all the old photographs were still on the wall.

"Let's try the Butlers," Story said.

The three of them were waiting, Frank, Charley and Naomi. No one was speaking, and by the look of it no one had spoken for quite a while. Naomi and Charley sat in matching wooden chairs from an old dining-room set. Frank was stretched out on his bed. Ziza, at first, thought he was asleep. But his eyes were open, and he was staring furiously at a crack in the ceiling.

"Good morning, Naomi, boys," Story said. "Ziza and I were just passing, so we thought . . ."

"We were expecting you," Naomi said. "Have a seat." She motioned to two other chairs from the same set. "Ziza, you sit next to me."

"The Mills fellow and that pansy Benedikt were up here first thing this morning," Charley said, "and they warned us that you were around."

"You need warnings about things like that?" Story asked.

"Mills was going through Aunt Nan's books and papers," Naomi said. "Maybe Ziza told him there were some goodies there."

"No, I . . ."

"He's certainly welcome to them," Naomi said. "Mr. Benedikt was collecting all of Aunt Nan's art for some exhibit he's organizing."

"Melody Horn's organizing," Charley corrected. "He even took our owl," he said, pointing to the empty night table between the two beds.

"Borrowed," Frank said, not taking his eyes off the ceiling. "Made him sign for it."

"Made him sign for it, although he didn't want to. Claimed it was property of the community. But finally he wrote out"— Charley took a piece of paper from his inside jacket pocket, carefully unfolded it and read—" 'Anna May Quick untitled owl sculpture, wood and bark, condition: fair to good, loose bark, on loan from Frank and Charles Butler to the Olde Smyrna Community.' "

"And dated it," Frank said. "Today."

"He said you were nosing around over to the camp and that we would be wise to expect you," Charley said.

"But we had already made our decision by then," Naomi said. "Charley, Frank, you have something to tell Mr. Story."

"Our confession," Charley said.

"Someone should take notes," Frank said. "Ziza?"

"Just tell me now, and we can worry about writing it up later," Nick Story said.

"We did it," Charley said. "Frank and I." He said it, and he sighed a sigh of relief. The confession had been made.

"We did it together," said Frank. "And we don't regret it. Not one bit, except maybe for leaving Naomi out."

Nick Story said nothing. Naomi waited. Ziza became impatient. "What did you do?" she asked.

"Poor Llewelyn," Charley said. "We've been his Guardians."

"Charley found the body," Frank said. "We're talking about the morning after the birthday bonfire."

"I had gone down for the morning dip. Between first call and reveille, from seven-thirty to seven-thirty-five, the kids were allowed to go skinny-dipping. I always supervised that, but no one ever showed up. The stream is too cold that early in the morning for anything but a hangover cure. And that morning seemed the same as always. I was bundled up in a sweater and long pants—after the first week in August, mornings get chilly in this valley—and waited on the swimming dock just in case."

"But it wasn't the same as usual," Frank said.

"No, there was a body washed up on the bank next to the canoe racks. I knew who it was right away . . ."

"Llewelyn," Frank said.

". . . but I ran over pretending I didn't. Even rehearsing in my mind the surprise I'd feel, the shock, the horror, when I turned the body over and saw who it was."

"But it was even worse than he expected."

"He was wearing just his climbing shorts and those heavy boots of his. He was white and blue, a horrible, unnatural white, and his lips and fingers were blue and all the cuts— no blood—where he had crashed against the rocks when he went over the Falls, blue gashes everywhere. His eyes were open, but he was looking far beyond me. I couldn't believe he had done it, not Llewelyn."

"Done what?" Ziza asked.

"Why, killed himself, of course," Frank said.

"No," Ziza said, "maybe he fell."

"Llewelyn couldn't fall," Charley said. It was an unshakable statement of belief. "He would go up that cliff blindfolded. He couldn't fall unless he wanted to."

"So we had to do something," Frank said. "The heir to Smyrna's leadership couldn't be a suicide."

"We hid him," Charley said.

Nick Story made a motion to Ziza to keep quiet, but she ignored it. "But why kill himself?" she asked.

"It's hard to understand Smyrna's sense of scandal. You've seen Idris Quick's book, so maybe you do. Our neighbors always distrusted us. We always had to be above reproach.

It was a scandal that Old Father Quick chose his own son to be his heir, something to hush up and keep hidden. Something to tear out of a history book. So imagine what news of a suicide would mean."

"We had to hide him," Frank said.

"But suicide was the first thing you thought when you saw that body?"

"Yes," Charley said. "He couldn't fall." Naomi seemed about to say something.

"Naomi?" Ziza said.

She just shook her head and then said, "No boy had ever been loved more than he was."

"But now he was reaching the age when he actually would have to do something," Ziza said, working out her own reasons.

"We had to hide him," Frank said.

"It was still before reveille. I wrapped him up in an old piece of canvas and hid him away in a shed behind the boat house."

"That night we did him up properly. Cleaned him up, said some holy words. Then we sewed him into some clean canvas the way they do sailors who die at sea and hid him away in the root cellar of the Gnomes' House. He stayed there for almost twenty-five years."

"Who else knew?"

"No one," said Frank.

"No one at all," said Charley. "We became the Guardians. Keeping watch."

"You sent the letter to Naomi?" Nick Story asked.

"Yes," Charley said. "We found an old stash of notepaper and a typewriter in the attic of the mess hall. The time had come for Llewelyn to return."

"Dollars and cents," Frank said.

"Something funny was going on with the company," Charley said.

"Still is. It seemed time to get that stock away from Harry Van Schoonhoven and put it back where it belonged. Back in Llewelyn's hands. In Naomi's hands."

"You put him in Aunt Nan's room?"

"We had some help," Frank said.

"Some inexpert help," Charley said.

"Who?" asked Ziza, afraid that she knew full well who.

"Timmy Jacobsen, a helpful boy," Frank said.

"But not a careful one," Charley said. "He lost a lot of the bones and then thought it would be funny to leave them around at that breakfast of Melody Horn's. That was not our idea."

"Indeed not. He heard from us about that."

"We may be guilty of many things. You have heard our confession. But we are not guilty of bad taste of that ilk."

"Naomi," Nick Story asked, "what is your role in this?"

"I finally came to my senses and figured it out. Then I had a talk with the boys."

"And Llewelyn, what do you think happened to him that night?"

"I think he went climbing and he fell."

"Fell?"

"Fell."

"Climbing at night? Alone?"

"He fell," she said firmly, putting an end to it.

"We're ready," Charley said. "Frank and I are ready for our punishment."

16

Cars gleaming with professional wax and polish jobs were once again parked around the Heart at Smyrna. They had come for another memorial service. At least their passengers had come dressed for another memorial service, but their thoughts were on other things. There was a conspicuously aloof delegation from Great Bear and Highfield, Ltd. More of the community stockholders than one might have expected so soon after the annual meeting were clustered in a group that admitted no outsiders. By actual count, the largest percentage of the crowd was made up of community employees, men and women from the ring factory and the printing plant. They, too, stuck together, and their cars, not nearly so well polished, were parked out of sight at the side of Mansion House.

There were also officials from Catskill and the county, politicians duty bound to miss no such gatherings as this, and even some neighbors from along Olde Smyrna Road. They, too, tended to band together and keep track of who had not turned up. Sherman Benedikt, on the job, greeted everyone he thought was a journalist, but he was especially attentive to a small group that was dressed just a bit more stylishly—and more obviously expensively—than the rest. The art crowd, Melody Horn called them, and she had invited them. They were there to see the special exhibition afterward. As the different constituencies made their way along the cobblestone hallway to the Meeting Room, Nick Story loitered at the wide front doorway, planning on being the last one in.

Benedikt had tracked down a student string quartet at the State University in New Paltz, and they played something properly somber, slow movements from several different early Beethoven quartets, as the crowd settled down. The group's only other public appearances had been in the great hall of Grand Central Terminal in New York, where they occasionally appeared at noontime and the evening rush hours on Fridays, usually picking up enough change from passersby to pay for a weekend in the city. This was the first time anyone had actually sat down to listen to them (not counting the homeless in Grand Central who were sitting on the floor), and they appreciated it. They had never played better.

Nick Story, though, was not the last one seated. After everyone was in place, a single file made its way down the center aisle to the front row. Mrs. Van Schoonhoven, unassisted and striding with more dispatch than the people behind her had expected, led the way. Then came those who would be speaking at the service: Melody Horn, a representative from the factory, the minister of the Dutch Reformed Church outside the gates, Hagadorn Mills, Ziza Todd (who had indeed been asked to take part but was told to read nothing biblical—that was the preacher's territory—or historical—that was Mills's), and at the end, although they would not be speaking, came Frank Butler in a wheelchair pushed by his brother. Both wore downcast expressions suitable for men who had confessed.

Ziza did not pay any particular attention to the speakers. Their voices rumbled on, words such as "leadership," "duty," "upright man," "stewardship," "tradition," and "community," "community, "community" drifted past. She was thinking about what she had chosen to read. It was likely, she thought, that everyone else would pay as much attention to her as she was paying to the others. But she was going to be provocative, and with luck the right person would notice. She read "A Poison Tree," which, when it came her turn, she chose not to announce. She simply said, "A poem from *Songs of Experience,* by William Blake," and began:

> I was angry with my friend:
> I told my wrath, my wrath did end.
> I was angry with my foe:
> I told it not, my wrath did grow.
>
> And I water'd it in fears,
> Night & morning with my tears;
> And I sunned it with smiles,
> And with soft deceitful wiles.
>
> And it grew both day and night,
> Till it bore an apple bright;
> And my foe beheld it shine,
> And he knew that it was mine,
>
> And into my garden stole
> When the night had veil'd the pole:
> In the morning glad I see
> My foe outstretch'd beneath the tree.

She glanced up from the lectern and saw a wall of blank faces. Mrs. Van Schoonhoven seemed puzzled. Melody Horn looked as though she suspected Ziza might have made a serious faux pas but was not quite sure why. The Butler boys studied the floor in front of them. She could not find Naomi in the crowd. The others in the room simply shifted about and waited for the next speaker, who, if they counted correctly, was probably the last. As she turned to leave the platform she saw a shadow standing against the light at the rear of the empty balcony. She could not see the face, but she recognized the slim outline. He must have seen her looking at him, because Tim raised his arms and clasped his hands together like a boxer hearing the referee's winning announcement.

The last speaker was Mrs. Van Schoonhoven, who said nothing at all about her husband. She was being the perfect hostess, thanking the guests for coming and hoping they would drop by the Parlor for coffee and cake. The students began sawing away again on their instruments—this time, brisker movements from early Beethoven quartets—and the crowd shuffled toward the door.

Ziza felt a sudden weight on her shoulder, a hand pressing down. The words "You will come quietly" sprang to mind, but when she turned she was looking into the sunny, smiling face of Melody Horn.

"Beautiful, simply beautiful," Melody said. "Just the right touch of class. You made it all come together." Melody gave her a quick kiss on the cheek. "But," she added, lowering her voice so only Ziza would hear, "I didn't quite get what it was all about." The dazzling smile froze. "Just what are you up to, dear?"

"You know Blake," Ziza said.

"I don't know that I do. Not in this context."

"All that mysticism."

"That didn't seem so mystical to me," she said, forgetting to whisper.

"Apples are always mystical," Ziza said, moving away as quickly as possible. "Adam, Eve, the Garden, Snow White . . ."

Melody turned to tell the Dutch Reformed minister that his remarks pulled the entire service together. Naomi stepped up and she, too, gave Ziza a quick kiss. "Just what *are* you up to, dear?"

"Fishing, I suppose. Fishing for a murderer."

"Don't we have people like Nick Story for that?"

Ziza chose not to answer. Instead, she said, "You and I

haven't really talked since the other morning with the Butler brothers. It must be a relief to you, having all that settled once and for all."

" 'Once and for all' has a nice storybook quality to it. I'm not so sure it's a phrase that applies much to Smyrna. We tend never to hear the end of anything."

Nick Story slipped in behind them in the line that inched toward the Parlor, where Mrs. Van Schoonhoven stood at the door. Ziza had never seen her looking better. She was smiling. She was chatting. In fact, she was spending far more time with each person in line than protocol demanded. She was even acting as though she were actually glad to see everyone.

As they waited, Nick first nodded to Naomi in a way that made Ziza think they had been talking earlier, and then shook Ziza's hand with a formality she found hard to take seriously.

"Why did you come to pick that poem?" he asked.

"She was fishing," Naomi answered.

"It was some choice," he said. "You're lucky people stop listening to poetry after the first rhyme."

"Don't be so sure of that," Ziza said.

As if to prove Story's point, a woman with an expensive but out-of-date fur piece—a tangle of fox snouts and paws—stopped to shake Ziza's hand. "A lovely poem," she said, "lovely. A touch of verse does so much for an occasion such as this. What better buttress than the poet's?" She left without waiting for Ziza's answer, and as a local dignitary—president of the Friends of the Library, perhaps—she obviously saw no need to introduce herself.

"Expecting some reactions, then?" Story asked.

"Maybe a few nibbles," Ziza said.

They had reached Mrs. Van Schoonhoven, who gave Naomi a big kiss and then squeezed her hand with both of hers. "Thank you for coming. It means so much to me." Naomi did not speak, but she put her arms around Gwen and gave her a kiss of her own.

"Mr. Story, I hope this is not official."

"I'm here as a neighbor," he said.

Her handshake with Ziza was coolly proper. "Thank you for reading," she said, "but I think you are a troublemaker."

"I'm sorry."

"Don't be," she said as she turned to the next person. "Not yet."

The Parlor was so crowded Ziza suspected some people had gone directly there and skipped the memorial service. There were tables with coffee, tea and sherry. (Ziza took the sherry. Well earned, she thought.) And high-school girls hired from town passed what looked to Ziza like tiny hot cross buns.

The entire west end of the room had been turned into an art gallery of Aunt Nan's sculptures and collages, which gave people something to do after they had said the usual things about Mr. Van Schoonhoven and the service. The second biggest attraction seemed to be Frank Butler's arm and leg casts. Perhaps because he and Charley had established themselves next to the table with the guest book, people had begun stopping at the wheelchair to sign messages of good cheer on the fresh and gleaming plaster of Paris. "Do the book first and then Frank," Charley said. And once the cast was signed, most stayed long enough to hear ever more dramatic versions of the accident as well as mysteriously vague hints about their confession. From time to time the word "Guardian" could be heard over the low rumble of conversation.

"What will happen to the Butlers?" Ziza asked Nick Story, Naomi having gone off with some people who were showing her a pocket-size album of snapshots.

"On what matter?"

"The Llewelyn business, of course. Is there anything else?"

"No, and probably nothing much will happen. We can pull them in for mishandling a corpse and unauthorized placement of remains. And we could have got them, I suppose, on interfering with a police investigation. Not reporting a death and so on. But statutes of limitations have run out on all of that, and look at them. Why bother? It's yesterday's newspapers. No jury is going to find them guilty of anything."

"And the money, the stock?"

"Who did it profit? Not them. If Mr. Van Schoonhoven were still around and we had been able to prove he knew about the whole story, we could have nailed *him* for something. I'm sure the IRS could find something for the Feds to use. But these old gents?"

"What if Naomi knew?"

"What if she did?"

"Wouldn't that make a difference?"

"Perhaps. And if you'll excuse me, I'm going to circulate."

"Remember, you told Mrs. Van Schoonhoven you were not here on official business."

"No, I didn't. I told her I was here as a neighbor."

"A nosy neighbor?"

"You got it."

Naomi had been shown photographs of "lost" Mayan ruins that were reached by taking a hazardous mule train from Tikal, of an anthropological *QE2* cruise to the Falklands, McMurdo Sound and Tierra del Fuego, and of a maharaja's private parlor car that could be booked only on very special tours of India. This was, she sensed, the way community stockholders communicated with one another (something one of those *QE2* anthropologists might have been able to explain) and was sorry she had no photographs of her own to show. Of what, though? A weekend in Atlantic City? A very special rowboat that could be booked only on very special tours of Central Park?

But once this almost stately show-and-tell was over, talk turned to business. What was happening with the community stock? What information, they wanted to know, did Naomi have on Great Bear and Highfield? As they spoke they all turned and looked toward the corner where the Great Bear and Highfield people were chatting—and looking at snapshots—with another circle of community stockholders.

Naomi said she was afraid she knew nothing about them beyond their name. And when, they wondered, trying to sound offhand, was Naomi actually taking possession of poor Llewelyn's old shares? Just how many were there? On that last question they began to sound a bit desperate. But Naomi only smiled and shook her head and said she thought she had better get a lawyer. Three of the men suggested good Manhattan lawyers in solid old firms she might want to look up.

As they talked they kept their eyes on the Great Bear and Highfield corner. Hagadorn Mills had spoken briefly, very briefly, with one of the men on an outer ring of the circle, and now Gwen Van Schoonhoven was approaching it. The Great Bear men in their expensive suits handed the photographs they were looking at back to their owners, smiled warmly in appreciation for having had a chance to look at them and stepped forward to welcome Mrs. Van Schoonhoven.

Did it look, the people with Naomi wondered, as though they were meeting her for the first time? Naomi thought it did. The handshakes seemed a bit stiff, Gwen's smile a bit guarded. But that might simply be a product of the occasion, the man with the Mayan ruin photographs said. But, look, said the man who had booked the maharaja's parlor car, look how one of the Great Bear people has put his hand on her shoulder. Comforting, said Naomi. All too familiar, said the wife of the man with the parlor car. Not a first meeting at all, she said. The wife of the man with the *QE2* pictures agreed. Naomi had her doubts. She tried to read the body language. The Great Bear people were leaning toward Gwen and smiling. She was leaning away. But smiling, too. No longer a stiff smile, Naomi said. The wife of the man with the parlor car pictures agreed.

Gwen Van Schoonhoven made a sudden gesture toward

the door. Was she throwing them out? No. The Great Bear people were actually bowing, just the slightest bit, and then they followed her out of the room. The man with the *QE2* pictures gasped.

"Doesn't mean a thing," Melody Horn said. They all jumped in surprise. Their interest in the Great Bear corner was so intense they had not seen her join them. "With Naomi here becoming a member of our community stockholder family"—she smiled with a warmth that would have melted a terrorist—"poor Gwen hasn't the goods to pull anything off alone. Now, let me see your pictures. It's been ages."

Ziza had wandered over to the art exhibit. Most of the local people were there, trying to guess the locations of the different collages. Some were obvious: the old Catskill Mountain House with its tall columns, perched for years as a ruin on the edge of the cliff up near North Lake; the double cascade of Kaaterskill Falls; the distinctive overstuffed-chair shape of Hunter Mountain (before the ski lifts were installed).

The second major topic of conversation (no one was mentioning the Van Schoonhovens) was how clever Aunt Nan Quick had been, how with just bits of wood and twine and a few swatches of cloth she could make up a picture of something you could recognize. There were a few attempts to identify the different textures of bark—a smooth beech, a pebbly black birch, heavy sheets of red oak—but spotting the different kinds of cloth was more popular. This white splash was obviously from an old dress shirt, that blue cloud a patch from someone's jeans. Here was something that looked like a piece of flowered upholstery; here was mattress ticking, there bits of weathered canvas . . .

Ziza spotted the sunset landscape that had been hanging in Tim Jacobsen's cabin. (Sherman Benedikt was very thorough in his roundup, she thought.) Someone behind her identified it as the narrow entrance to Stony Clove, and no one disagreed with him. The same voice said, "Everything is really in remarkably good condition, don't you think, Ziza? Especially when you consider that no one has taken care of this stuff in years." She turned. It was Hagadorn Mills.

To say something, she congratulated him on his remarks at the service, though she honestly could not recall a word he'd said.

"I want to talk to you about that," he said. "Come." He took her arm, a stern high-school principal escorting a rowdy pupil to detention hall, and headed away from the art show. Although she could have resisted, Ziza allowed herself to be dragged along. The route was not a direct one. They headed for the far side of the room and ducked behind Naomi's group and then around the Butlers and their circle, which now included Nick Story. People were still signing the cast, Ziza noticed, and the unsuccessfully stifled laughter suggested that the written comments had become comic, perhaps even a bit ribald. Then they headed for the corner where the Great Bear people had been, but at the last minute ducked out the doorway into the hall. Tim Jacobsen was waiting there, but Mills did not seem to notice him.

"What we need is a breath of fresh air," he said, and before Ziza could do more than say Tim's name, Mills had her out the wide front doors. "You simply must excuse me," he said, a bit out of breath, "but we have just effected an escape. From Benedikt and that jumped-up art crowd." He stretched his neck to see if, perhaps, they had been followed, but only Tim was back in the hallway, and he seemed to remain invisible to Mills.

"Benedikt—which, of course, means Melody Horn—wants me to give that woman's so-called art my imprimatur. They were closing in on me when you arrived. Can't you just hear his line? 'And here is our prize-winning historian. Why don't you tell our friends from New York all about Aunt Nan's artistic genius, Andy?' I've done a lot for this company, but I'm not giving my blessing to those rags and twigs. Most of it, if my guess is right, was rigged up or, shall we say, soi-disant 'restored' by Mr. Van Schoonhoven and his man-of-all-work. What's his name, the pimply housepainter sulking back there in the hall?"

"You don't mean Tim Jacobsen?"

"Of course I do. The ever-so-handy handyman. And now that we indeed have fresh air, I can talk to you about what you brought up inside. You complimented my memorial remarks. For which I indeed thank you. They were actually— except for that first bit about Mr. Van Schoonhoven himself— excerpts from the Olde Smyrna guide I've been working on. And good taste now requires me to say something about your contribution. I confess that my reaction is the same as it has been to everything else you have done around here. And that is a question: What does she know?"

"Not as much as you, clearly."

"I have my doubts about that, my dear. But I would be careful if I were you. Using Blake was cute. But I don't believe it was prudent. Yes, indeed, I suggest that you remain a good deal more careful than you've been."

He shook her hand and brushed his anachronistically boyish forelock back into place—it was a gesture she had seen on dozens of *Masterpiece Theatre* television shows set in Oxford—and to her surprise gave her a quick kiss on the cheek. "Even foxes have their holes," he said with a wink, "and I'm off to find mine before Benedikt and the chic art world join us in the fresh country air." He went down the front steps and off around the side of Mansion House, heading, she suspected, for his office in the old Children's House.

"Prize-winning kisses," said Tim, who had come out onto the porch. "What next?"

"You've been eavesdropping. I want to talk to you," she said.

"No, you don't. You want to ask me a lot of questions," he said.

"Yes, and then I want to talk to you."

"Let's walk first. I'll show you something you haven't seen before. It's only a short hike."

"I'm not dressed for a hike."

"Then change. You want to hang around here and be kissed by more people like Andy Mills? I'll wait for you where the road enters the pine plantation. Don't wear silly shoes."

"I don't own silly shoes."

"Then you're the only one who doesn't."

"One what?"

"Girl." He said it in a way that was oddly dismissive, Ziza thought. "I'll wait for five minutes, and then I'm gone. I don't want Nick Story and his boys pulling me in for lurking in a suspicious manner."

"Then just lurk in your usual unsuspicious manner. I'll be there as soon as I can."

Hiking through the pine trees was the last thing Ziza wanted to do, but she had not seen Tim since the Butler boys confessed. There was a lot to talk about, even without getting into Mills's hints that Tim had a hand in Aunt Nan's folk art. And at least she would not have to listen to more vague warnings of one kind or another.

She got to her room without running into any of the crowd from the memorial service and was half undressed before she noticed the mess on her desk. The 3 × 5 cards with her numbered research notes were spread across the desktop as though someone had fanned them out like playing cards. Books were also out of place. Noyes's *History of American Socialisms,* Bestor's *Backwoods Utopias,* Holloway's *Heavens on Earth* and a few others dealing with nineteenth-century utopian communities had been pulled out, riffled through and left where they had been dropped. (The Graham Greene, Anne Tyler and Angela Carter paperbacks were ignored.) Her pocket-size spiral notebooks were lying as though someone had shaken them out looking for loose pages and then discarded them. On her bed lay Aunt Nan's copy of Idris Quick's history of Smyrna. She turned to the "Well On With The Work" chapter. Pages had been torn out. Now it was just like all the other copies stored away in the library.

Ziza decided to play it cool. She would leave everything exactly where it was. She took one deep breath and then another, hung her dress in the tiny doorless closet, pulled on a Colgate-Rochester sweatshirt and stepped into an old pair of jeans. She was crawling under the bed, looking for her running shoes, when she noticed the wastebasket. There were printed pages in it. Printed pages torn in half and discarded. Without looking—although she did look—she knew they were ripped from Quick's history. She checked the page numbers. All of them were there. It didn't make sense.

"Sure it does," said Tim a few minutes later when she told him about it. They were walking toward the creek between two of the hundreds of perfectly straight lines of pine trees in the plantation. The trees were so close together Ziza could not see the sky, but the lower branches had been cut to a uniform height of six feet. Everywhere she looked everything was uniform, straight and changeless as in a military cemetery. For a forest it was organized to look as man-made as possible. But whoever planned it could not control springtime. As they walked Ziza and Tim stirred the deep bed of pine needles, now heated by the spring days, and the air became pungent with the warm smell of pine and the promise of summer.

"It doesn't make sense to me," Ziza said.

"Sure it does," said Tim. "Why search a bunch of books you got out of the community library? Why go through boring notes that were mostly just a bunch of page numbers? Why rip out a bunch of pages and then leave them behind?"

"I'd read them already, anyway."

"Why make a mess and leave it for you to find?"

"To scare me?"

"Clear as a bell."

"Someone thinks I know something."

"No shit. You've certainly tried hard enough to give them that impression."

When they got to the stream Tim went first and told Ziza to follow him and step on the same rocks he did. The way across seemed simple enough, but one rock that stood steady enough for Tim wobbled when Ziza stepped on it, and she slipped sideways. Tim reached out and grabbed her hand before she went into the water. She squealed, and they laughed and went slower. For the rest of the way across, she held on to his hand. On the other side they scrambled up the dirt bank and were again in a pine grove, this one natural and utterly random. The trees were far apart and small birches and maples, still leafless, were springing up among the pines. The ground was littered with pine needles and dried leaves from last fall. A clearly marked trail ran uphill. Tim more or less followed it, although at times it meandered one way, and he kept moving steadily upward until the trail rejoined them.

"How did you know the notes were mostly page numbers?" she asked, following along behind and keeping up with his pace like a good scout.

"I saw them when we were up in your room a couple of days ago, them and the books."

She could not see his face. He did not turn to her when he talked. "I wasn't aware that you were looking at books," she said.

"I keep my eyes open," he said.

They were off the trail again, and Tim was ducking under some low pine boughs. Ziza had let him get farther ahead, so she would be out of reach of the branches that snapped back in his wake. When the first one hit her she called out for him to be more careful, and Tim said—in a way that made her think he was quoting someone else—that in hiking it was the responsibility of the follower to stay far enough back to avoid being hit. He seemed to be making a philosophical point—or maybe a test—out of whether or not she ran into a rebounding branch.

His movements, she thought as she crouched down to follow, were still those of a teenager, a teenage athlete's— direct, unfussy, thoughtlessly graceful. But his voice, when she heard his voice without seeing him speak, seemed to belong to someone older and more guarded. It was flat, almost monotone, a voice careful not to give too much away.

"We're there," he said as the steep incline leveled off. He pulled aside the low branches of a mountain laurel as though he were opening a garden gate. "You first," he said, and then, as an afterthought, "Watch your step."

She stepped out onto a wide rock ledge smooth as a sidewalk, and she gasped. Six feet in front of her the world fell away into dazzling nothingness, and although she was in no real danger of going over the edge, she stooped down and put her hands on the sun-warmed rock for support.

Tim laughed. "Gets you right in the gut, doesn't it? Never fails." He walked over to the edge, showing off, getting closer than Ziza thought safe. She crawled along behind.

Far below them was the soundless stream, beyond that all of Smyrna, the red-brick Mansion House, the Heart still lined with expensive cars, their chrome glittering in the bright sunlight. She could see the camp mess hall and the roof of the Gnomes' House, although the cabins where Tim lived were hidden by the trees. Farther off was the stone tower of the Dutch Reformed Church and on the horizon the smudged sprawl of Catskill and the dusty smoke of its cement factories. The river was over there, too, just out of sight, but every now and then, there was a flash of light reflecting off the water, a gaudier version of the glistening limousines at Smyrna.

"If you stand up, you'll see more," Tim said. Ziza stayed where she was. "There's my mom's trailer, just beyond the church. I don't think you can see it from down there."

"I can see it fine," she said, although she could not.

"Want one of these?" He sat down with his legs dangling over the edge and offered her a homemade cigarette.

"I don't smoke."

" 'I don't smoke.' " He mimicked her voice. "You don't smoke these to smoke."

"This is a stupid place to do that."

"No, it's the best. My favorite." He lit up and inhaled and lay back flat on the stone.

"What if you decide you're going to fly or something?"

"Grow up. You watch too much TV."

"I know what that stuff can do."

"What did you do, take some high-priced college course and now you know?"

"I'm not a prude. I'm not inexperienced."

"Prude?" Tim laughed. "You sound like the Butler boys. What's a prude to you?"

She almost answered but thought better of it and stretched out on the sun-drenched rock next to Tim. It was like lying in warm bathwater. She cupped her hands behind her head and watched the cotton-ball clouds scatter across the robin's-egg-blue sky.

"Shoot," he said.

"What?"

"You have a list of questions, right? So let's begin with number one and then move along."

"Number one? Resurrectionism."

"Oh, for Christ's sake . . ."

"Digging up dead bodies. Resurrectionism."

"There was no digging up of anything. The bones were bundled up in canvas. I just had to unroll the thing and dump what I found in that sleeping bag. It smelled like old socks."

"The Butlers didn't seem to think you did a very good job."

"A lot of help they were. They weren't even around. For them it was just a matter of handing me the sleeping bag and a key to the Gnomes' House and wishing me Godspeed. No shit, that's what they said, 'Godspeed,' as though it were some kind of new designer drug or something. Putting the mask over the skull was my idea."

"Nice touch," she said dryly.

"Think so?"

Ziza sat up. The heat was making her sleepy. "Of course

I don't think so. The damn thing nearly scared me to death. This is serious business, Tim. A young man died. Lord knows how. The police were never notified. He was never given a proper burial, his widow never knew what happened to him and twenty-five years later two old coots egg on some kid with a lousy sense of humor to play Halloween games with what's left of him."

Tim sat up and dragged heavily on his cigarette, letting the healing smoke move at its own speed through his lungs and out his nose. His eyes were closed. "What do you mean by 'egged on'?"

She reached over, pulled the cigarette out of his mouth and threw it over the cliff.

He spun around, every nerve tense, his eyes clear and full of rage. He grabbed her arms and pushed her down. "Get off my case, lady." He almost said "bitch." She could hear the unsaid word. He held on to her and began to rock slowly. "It wouldn't take much," he said, almost whispered—she could feel his breath in the words, smell the smoke—"not much at all to roll us both right off this cliff. We could follow the route of poor Llewelyn right to the bottom." He rolled slowly sideways so that she was briefly on top, and then she was held down again by the weight of his body. She could feel the heat of the smooth rock beneath her, the warm weight of Tim above her. "This must be pretty close to the spot where he went down." His lips were so close to her eyes that their tiny cracks looked like dry canyons in a desert. She thought of those children's books illustrated with impossibly magnified photographs. The most beautiful pictures always turned out to be of revolting things such as hairs from a fly's leg or slime from a swamp. The ugliest things were never bomb craters but close-ups of human skin.

His lips moved slowly, mouthing the word once in silence before he said it aloud: "Splash."

And he burst out laughing. "Splash, splunk." He rolled again, this time away from Ziza. "I'm splash. You're splunk.

Last ones into the pool." He squinted at her through the bright sunlight, shading his eyes with his hand. "Not funny?"

"No," she said. There was nothing to fear now. She would never show him that she had been afraid. "Why did you agree to help them?"

"I haven't gotten you off this subject?"

"No."

He reached out across the rock and took her hand. "No?"

"No."

"I'm just someone who likes to help out."

"Simple as that?"

"Look, I'm just a neighbor kid, what's-her-name's son from the trailer. There's not a hell of a lot to do in a trailer, and there are no kids around here to speak of. To get to school in Catskill you get on the yellow bomb every morning and ride for half an hour. Same thing at night unless you can hitch a ride from someone. So as a kid I started exploring pretty early. First the crazy cemetery next to the church. Half the gravestones aren't even in English, Dutch I guess, but you can figure it out. 'Here lies . . .' 'Here in his grave is . . .' And most of them have carvings of these really obnoxious angels. They all look as though they have pokers rammed up their asses.

"It didn't take long for graves to be as boring as anything back in the trailer, so I made my way through the pine trees and found this crazy world back here. All kinds of buildings. No one much around. The stream to swim in. Rocks to climb on. The waterfall. There are even ruins down at the bottom of the Falls. Foundations. Frank and Charley said it was some sort of con game that went on before the Quicks arrived and built Smyrna. Some guy had turned up, sunk the foundations, said he was building a flour mill and sold shares to all the dumbhead locals. Then, when he had all the money he could bilk out of them, he skipped out. That's how the original Father Quick got his hands on the place. The dumbhead locals were looking for a way to get their money back, and this crazy preacher said he would buy out the land around the Falls."

"You learned all this from Frank and Charley?"

"Sure. I'm not totally dumb, you know. Anyway, I guess I hadn't been as invisible as I thought. The Butler boys noticed me poking around, and we all got to know each other. They did a lot of talking, and I listened. I was available for odd jobs. They even gave me presents. Living in a trailer with a mom who's often kind of confused—hell, most of the time she was completely spaced out—I didn't get many presents. They were nice to me here. They introduced me to Mr. Van Schoonhoven, and as Smyrna started coming back to life he had all kinds of things that needed doing. Like I told you before, he even gave me the cabin."

"So the bones were just another odd job?"

"Odd, sure, but Frank and Charley said it would be a way of saving Smyrna. They talked a lot about stock and shit like that, but I didn't pay all that much attention. Moving the bones would be a way of helping to keep the place for ourselves. That's what Frank and Charley said."

"What about forging the art?"

"What art?"

"Aunt Nan's pictures."

"That's not art. I was just helping out."

"Frank and Charley? Mr. Van Schoonhoven? Melody Horn?"

"Mr. Benedikt. He said he had some old pictures and shit that were in pretty bad condition and wondered if I'd help out."

"And you said, 'Sure, why not?' Always ready to help, that's our Tim."

"No, he mentioned money first, and then I said, 'Sure, why not?' Pay the money, take your choice. These new people around here have real cash to spend. I even put little bits of the canvas that was wrapped around the bones in some of the pictures."

"Another little joke?"

"I guess so. Sure, why not?"

Ziza realized that Tim was still holding on to her hand. She sat up again. "Most of the limos have left," she said. Nothing had been said about Harry Van Schoonhoven's death. "You told Mrs. Van Schoonhoven that her husband had been good to you."

"Once."

"Once as in 'one time' or once as in 'once upon a time?'"

"Are you into word games or what?" Impatience was back in his voice again. "Let it go, okay?"

They were both looking out over the valley again. Ziza slid closer to the edge and looked over, straight down onto the creek. Because of the angle she could not see the Falls, but she could see the water roiling around in the box factory pool. Beyond that was the old swimming area, the Frog Pond, where Charley Butler had found Llewelyn's body washed up next to the canoe rack.

"This was all under water once, back in the dinosaur days," Tim said. "All this, all the way over to the Berkshires in Massachusetts. The shore on this side was up above us in the mountains, the cliffs up there. Down here was the bottom of the lake. Look at this." He pulled away some of the loose stones at the edge of the cliff. "Look."

The rock seemed amazingly fragile, and Tim pulled it apart with ease, layer after layer. "Fossils," he said. The rocks were solid with them, and the more Ziza's eyes got used to looking at them, the more she saw. Small shells and long wormlike shapes, little fans, tiny snails. "They were all alive once, right here, all crawling around over each other, and then whammo they're rocks." He pulled more rocks apart looking for better samples.

"The best grade I ever got in science was because of these things. I'd seen some people in the cemetery doing gravestone rubbings of those asshole angels. They taped thin paper to the stones and then rubbed them with plumber's chalk, and the pictures and the inscriptions came right through. So I did that with a lot of these fossils—there's one huge beauty of a shell down near the top of the Falls, but you can only find it when the light is just right—and then I looked up to find their real Latin names and labeled everything. I got an *A* out of it. Rescued me from failing the course."

He started throwing the scraps of rock out over the cliff and watched them arc down toward the creek below. "They're all dead bodies, you know. That's what fossils are. One dead body after another." He was standing now, throwing the fossil rocks out as far as he could, and Ziza watched him, thinking of all those little Smyrna boys of the past who were led to the creek and watched to see whether they would throw stones or float twigs. Tim would have passed the test.

17

Naomi did not knock on the door. She simply threw it open and walked into Harry Van Schoonhoven's old office, as big as life. Although she still felt stiff from the bruises of the accident—every move of every muscle sent a twinge through her body—she pushed the door so hard the brass knob banged onto the wall, chipping off a patch of trompe l'oeil wainscoting. The men from Great Bear and Highfield who were drawing their chairs up around Gwen Van Schoonhoven jumped to their feet, more out of surprise than deference.

Naomi was tired of all this sweetness and light, bored stiff with everyone's questions about poor Llewelyn, as they insisted on calling him. She was sick of Nick Story's sly innuendos, sick of the Butler boys' knowing looks, sick of Ziza Todd's sorority-girl-with-a-conscience perkiness, sick of having to kiss—one more time—Gwen Van Schoonhoven's dusty, wrinkled cheek.

She was sick to death of having to sympathize with Gwen. The Widow Van Schoonhoven. The grieving Widow Van Schoonhoven. The grieving Widow Van Schoonhoven with a firm handshake and a ready smile for those tall bastards from the city—every one of them was tall, and she was sick of that, too—with their expensive suits, courtly manners and a brace of company lawyers who waited out in the limos with the chauffeurs just in case something needed to be signed.

Most of all she was sick of herself, the Naomi who played along and put up with all of this. She was sick of being the patsy, the Naomi who came when she was called. She had been cooperative for far too long, ever since that confused day so long ago when she was deep in her own grief and Harry Van Schoonhoven talked her into deferring her claim on Lew's stock. Perhaps it began even before that, on the night she went to the swimming pavilion with Harry. Who knows?

Well, there would be no more of that, she thought. Seeing the tall suits from Manhattan bowing ever so slightly to Gwen and following her out the Parlor after the memorial service had been the last straw. Gwen Van Schoonhoven was not the Queen of England, but just a middle-aged lady with something to sell. The suits, Naomi decided, could damn well start bowing to her instead. So she followed them out of the Parlor, down the hall, and even the closed door of Harry's office did not slow her down.

The men from Great Bear and Highfield did not remain surprised for long. There were introductions. ("Mrs. Quick, we had so hoped to meet you, an honor." A hint of a bow.) Naomi felt her anger dissipating into curiosity. Chairs were rearranged. A space was found for Naomi, far from Gwen. Coffee cups were being handed around, and Gwen devoted all her attention to instructing the high-school waitress on just how much cream to pour into her coffee.

When she decided to notice Naomi, her tone was suspiciously gracious: "Your timing is perfect, dear. We were about to begin a discussion of Harry's affairs."

"Fine," Naomi said, "just fine," which was not at all the tone she wanted to establish.

"Harry, it seems, had an agreement with these gentlemen."

"Not so much an agreement as an initialed letter of intent to sell," said one of the men.

"Initialed?" Naomi asked.

"Not signed," said a second.

"But dated," said a third.

"Dated?" said Naomi.

"Yes." In unison. Tenor, baritone and bass. It sounded like the Harvard glee club.

"A month ago," said the lead tenor. "The fifteenth, a Friday." There were six of them in all, Naomi counted, not as young as they seemed at first glance, late forties maybe, and they kept their long legs tucked away as neatly as storks.

According to what she could learn from Andy Mills, Naomi knew that Great Bear and Highfield began as a Pennsylvania soft-coal company, with a half dozen or so mines scattered southwest of Pittsburgh and on across the West Virginia border. Except for a strip mine just outside Wheeling, that operation had been out of business for years, but the name remained as a parent company for a conglomerate of radio stations, motel chains, fried-chicken franchises, Caribbean commuter airlines, soft-drink bottlers and—most successful of all—sports equipment manufacturers. From the very beginning—back in the Depression, when a handful of near-bankrupt small-town mines were bought up by a Dartmouth dropout with a terrible stutter—the company's top management had closely reflected their leader. Over the years, the bright young men near the top at GB & H ranged from stuttering Dartmouth graduates, to nearsighted Princetonians, to acned, balding Columbians, to spectacularly short Yalies (a particularly dicey period), to the current batch of gracefully aging giants from Penn (all of whom were especially loyal to the firm's successfully overpriced line of running shoes).

"I don't think Mr. Van Schoonhoven's initials—even if they are dated—are worth much these days," Naomi said.

"But the sense that He Would Have Wanted It This Way must indeed have some bearing," said the tenor, clearly the senior man, not that much younger than Naomi.

"Not with me," she said.

"But surely with Mrs. Van Schoonhoven?" The six leaned forward like sprinters awaiting the starting gun.

"I'm not sure . . ." Gwen Van Schoonhoven began.

"I'm not sure Mrs. Van Schoonhoven's views are worth that much more than her late husband's," Naomi said.

"*I'm* not sure," Gwen Van Schoonhoven continued, "just what my husband's wishes actually were. You have a piece of paper that says he promises to deliver the majority block of Olde Smyrna stock."

"Something he couldn't do then and certainly can't do now," Naomi said.

"Something," Gwen continued, "I must say, I think he had no right to offer. He wasn't even, you know, a Quick. I am the Quick in our family." The six slumped back in their chairs.

"There you are," Naomi said.

"But," Gwen continued. They sat forward again. "But there is also the matter of all those plans he was making for Smyrna, he and that Melody Horn."

The very name sent the six into uncontrollable laughter. It was not a matter of guffaws building to knowing chuckles and then exploding into belly laughs. They were roaring immediately, laughing so hard they had to put their half-finished coffee cups on the floor to keep from spilling them.

For the first time since Naomi entered the room, she and Gwen Van Schoonhoven exchanged glances, puzzled glances.

"Surely you know," said the tenor, "Harry's little joke? No? I can't believe this. He fooled you, too."

"I trust you are not suggesting," Gwen began, but rather than finishing her sentence she stood and looked toward the door as though she were about to leave. The six leaped up (Naomi stayed where she was) and made enough soothing comments for her to sit down again.

"He fooled us, as well," said the tenor. "Well, not fooled exactly, but Melody Horn's purpose was to catch someone's attention, and she caught ours."

"Solid old company with more capital than it knows what to do with," said one of the others, "suddenly shows signs of coming to life."

"Revitalized."

"New blood."

"Diversification."

"Rumors were going round the Street," the tenor said, "that Smyrna—whoever had heard of Smyrna?—was alive and kicking with a bright young heir apparent—or should I say heiress?—who was being given all the space she needed to get things done. Or should I say all the rope she needed?"

That got the other five laughing again, but this time in a more subdued, boardroom sort of way.

"Melody was the bait, then?" Naomi said. "Harry never planned to put her plans into operation?"

"I suppose he would have proceeded in a suitably cautious manner until someone bit," the tenor said. "We just happened to bite right away."

"And we were smart to do so," said one of the others.

"Damn tootin'."

"He didn't trick you?" asked Gwen Van Schoonhoven.

"Indeed not," said the tenor. "It was all marketing, inspired marketing. We were smart to move in and get an agreement before anyone else."

"And what about Melody Horn?" asked Naomi.

"She has a wonderful future within the Great Bear and Highfield family."

"Did she know she was bait? Did she know it was only inspired marketing?"

"I think it is safe to assume she believed she was taking command of Smyrna," said the tenor.

The boardroom chuckles began again.

"But of course she won," Naomi said.

"What do you mean by 'of course'?" asked the tenor.

"She won. She *is* running Smyrna. Your agreement is worthless. It couldn't be more simple than that."

"We have an initialed letter of intent."

"Dated, I know," Naomi said. "From a dead man. For a good deal more stock than he actually controlled. I'm afraid you have been bluffing long enough. And Lord only knows what grief you are putting poor Mrs. Van Schoonhoven through." She looked over at Gwen with a show of concern she hoped did not seem too outrageously false. "Gentlemen," she said, "I'm the person you have to deal with now. Most of the stock Harry Van Schoonhoven offered you is mine, you know, and I suggest you make an appointment to see me at my earliest convenience." With that she walked toward the door, feeling better than she had at any time since her return to Smyrna.

She felt sick of nothing at all, and indeed her exit would have been most impressive if Nick Story had not entered the room when she was halfway to the door. He had not knocked, or at least he had not until he had the door open and was well inside. Then he reached back and rapped twice. Seven pairs of eyes swiveled from Naomi to him.

"Sorry to interrupt," he said far too gleefully for anyone to believe. "But I've had some news. I suppose it won't be a big surprise to everyone, but it seems as though Mr. Van Schoonhoven's death was not a natural one, not by a long shot. It's official now, lab reports and everything, so I think I should get to work on it right away. Mrs. Van Schoonhoven, why don't you excuse yourself from these fine gentlemen so we can have a talk."

18

Ziza was at her desk. Her note cards were back in order. The books were back on the shelves. She had even taped together the torn pages of Idris Quick's history and tucked them inside the old book.

She was thinking of Harry Van Schoonhoven's body as he lay doubled up on the hard dirt floor of the Gnomes' House cellar, the harsh glare of the needlessly bright work lights, the knot of uniformed men crowded into the far corner watching the wine-flushed newcomers from Mansion House as they saw the body for the first time. She saw Nick Story watching Mrs. Van Schoonhoven's reaction, Naomi's, her own, watching Melody Horn rush up the stairs. It was theater: You know I'm watching you; I know you know I'm watching; you know I know you know. And none of it meant a thing to Harry Van Schoonhoven, his hair still soaked with sweat, clutching his stomach, a final look of surprise—but not horror—frozen on his face. It was the look not of a man facing eternity but of someone about to complain about something as trivial and as upsetting as a very bad stomachache.

Ziza was looking at the notes she'd begun, and instantly discarded, the morning after Mr. Van Schoonhoven died, the morning she met Tim for the first time. Now that his death was officially murder—it did not take long for news of Nick Story's announcement to get around—she'd pulled them out again. Under "Heart Breaker" she made a new list of the people who would prosper by Mr. Van Schoonhoven's heart attack, just a list of names on a 3 × 5 note card. This time each suspect—the word took her back for a minute, but, yes, that is what they were, suspects—had a card of his or her own, and under each name she listed what that suspect stood to gain or lose from Harry's death.

GWEN VAN SCHOONHOVEN: Rumor had it that she was the first person Story questioned once he announced he was looking for a murderer. Had she known that her husband made a deal to sell the community? As someone who prided herself on being the last of the "real" Quicks, she may well have wanted to keep outsiders outside. She herself was a major stockholder. The only stock Harry "owned" was, in fact, Llewelyn's old shares. Did Gwen know that Naomi could claim them? Could she have thought that by doing away with Harry she would have a block of shares that could have put a stop to any sale? Would she be heartbroken to learn she had killed for no purpose whatever? Would she simply be happy to be rid of a husband who had worn out his welcome?

NAOMI QUICK: If she had wanted to put the kibosh on Harry Van Schoonhoven's deal with Great Bear and High-field, why bother killing the old boy? She had enough stock, once she claimed it, to create a pretty effective roadblock. Did she even know about the deal? Could Naomi have had a reason for wanting to get rid of Harry that had nothing to do with money or stock or Wall Street lawyers? It did not take much of a detective to see that there was no love lost between Naomi and Gwen. Did the real motive behind the murder date back to the old days of Camp Smyrna? Was Naomi as harmless as she tried to seem?

MELODY HORN: She had the world by the tail, or so it seemed. Harry, surely, was in the palm of her hand. Smyrna was hers to do with what she wanted. And the plans she had would have spelled success for both herself and the company. Then, kapowee! Had she found out the truth about what

Harry was up to? Was that reason enough for her to kill him? Not really. Not logically. Melody could easily have wheeled and dealed her way around him to keep control of Smyrna. But was Melody always logical? And when was murder logical? Could Harry have been killed simply out of malice? Could Melody have done it out of rage for having been played with?

And then came the men. Who could take any of them seriously? Sherman Benedikt? Andy Mills? The Butlers? Even Tim? They didn't even seem to require separate 3 × 5 cards, so she put them all on one, leaving a bit of space after each name (the Butlers were, of course, one entry) in case something came up.

And what about herself? If Nick Story ever bothered with 3 × 5 cards he certainly would have had one for her. She wrote ZIZA TODD on a fresh card. After all, she had been at the Gnomes' House the afternoon Mr. Van Schoonhoven died, although no one, not even Nick Story, seemed to have noticed. With the thought of those shadowy stairs and the memory of that unnatural silence broken only by a dripping water faucet, a familiar sense of dread returned.

Could she have made a difference?

What if there had been no murderer at the bottom of those stairs, what if Mr. Van Schoonhoven had been alone and still alert, awake, on his feet, waiting for someone else to come down the steps, someone with an appointment, a date? What if he were standing there in the shadows, waiting, knowing by the fact that she had stopped at the top of the stairs that she was not the person he was meeting, perhaps even recognizing that her footsteps were not the ones he was listening for? If she had walked down those stairs could she have prevented a murder? Or would she have walked into a double murder?

Ziza put her own card at the bottom of the pile on her bed and drew another one from the pack. Now she would begin a list of people, suspects, who had the opportunity to meet Mr. Van Schoonhoven that afternoon. Naomi Quick? Yes. Melody Horn, Sherman Benedikt, Tim, the Butlers, Hagadorn Mills, even Gwen Van Schoonhoven? Yes, yes, yes, yes, yes, yes. Yes to everyone, although meeting Gwen in a cellar made no sense. Was there something down there she had missed, something to show someone, something besides that can of bones? She was getting nowhere asking herself the same old questions. It was time to get back to minding other people's business. She would make another list of . . .

"Door's open," Melody Horn said, breezing into the narrow room and sitting down in the only chair, "so we won't insult you by knocking." In fact, Ziza thought, the door had not been open, and she would not have been insulted in the least. She looked into the gloom of the hallway to see who "we" was. Sherman Benedikt was out there, dawdling, as though to say this visit was not his idea. He was carrying his metal clipboard. Perhaps he, too, had been making lists.

"Sit," Ziza said, tucking the 3 × 5 cards under her pillow. "Please."

Choosing between sharing the bed with Ziza and sitting on the floor, he opted for the floor. Ziza thought she noticed a pause, as though he were considering dusting it off first or sitting on the clipboard, but good manners won out and he simply sat. His knees made a popping sound.

"Don't you think Sherman was a silly name to pick for a southern boy?" Melody said, smiling broadly. If he had been closer to the desk chair Melody would have reached out and rumpled his hair, Ziza thought, as though he were a friendly dog who had followed her home.

"My parents were immigrants," Benedikt said without much enthusiasm. Clearly, they had been through this number before. It was a curious conversational gambit for someone who called herself Melody Horn. "They wanted an American name. At least they didn't come up with Lincoln."

"Or Arnold," Ziza said.

Silence.

"Arnold comma Benedikt," Ziza said.

More silence.

A voice out in the hallway said, "Knock. Knock." Ziza's visitors seemed as surprised as she was.

"Who's there?" she said.

"Andy."

"Andy who?"

"You want me to say 'And deliver us from evil,' as though this is some silly knock-knock joke? It's Andy Mills, of course." He sounded annoyed.

"Come on in," Ziza said, "join the party. I hope you brought lunch."

Hagadorn Mills looked behind him before he came in and then carefully closed the door and made sure the latch had caught.

"Lunch? Of course not. This was strictly spur-of-the-moment. I just happened by. Hadn't expected a crowd." He sat on the far end of the bed and looked around with the deliberation of someone expecting to be quizzed on what he had observed. "A very cozy room. Wonderful view of the Heart and the stream."

Silence.

"You can even hear it up here," Mills said, "the stream." He seemed to be waiting to be told something.

Silence.

"OK, all right, no," he continued, "I'm not surprised. I'll admit it. I followed you guys, saw you going up the steps to the top floor and said to myself, 'Who's up there but Ziza?' and came along. Frankly I smelled council of war." He paused, waiting for a reaction. "I wanted to be in at the kill."

A smile spread across Melody Horn's face. With a flick of her head, her champagne-colored hair fell into place, and then, after individual eye contact all around, she said, "I'm so glad we are *all* here because we are the ones who can save this place. We're the ones with our heads screwed on right."

Hagadorn Mills sighed. Sherman Benedikt seemed to be making a correction to something on his clipboard. Ziza waited for the other shoe to drop.

"We came up here to talk with Ziza about Smyrna's future. The widows, Naomi and Gwen, are just that—widows. They have too many memories to worry about, and they are prone to confusion. We have to see that they are not misled by the wrong people. Naomi is the key, and she seems, Ziza, to be partial to you. She would put a lot of trust in what you say."

"And you want me to tell her to stay clear of the Great Bear people?"

"Frankly, yes. The future of the company, at least for now, lies in its independence. We have plans. . . ."

"How much did Mr. Van Schoonhoven tell you about what he was up to?" Ziza asked.

"Mr. Van Schoonhoven was not, it turns out, a very honorable man."

"When did you learn that most of Mr. Van Schoonhoven's so-called stock was really owned by Naomi?"

"Right after you discovered those stupid bones. Until then, poor Llewelyn was just part of the local mythology, a particularly boring part. They say 'poor Llewelyn' and their eyes mist over, the whole pack of them. I had never thought of him as a ghost stockholder. And then, right on schedule to walk into a wad of money, Naomi turns up."

"And Great Bear and Highfield, when did you learn about them?"

"After Mr. Van Schoonhoven died."

"Was murdered."

"Well, yes."

"Only then?"

"Yes."

"Sherman," Ziza said, "don't you remember tipping me off about GB&H up in the library the day we talked about being a detective team, Mr. Inside and Ms. Outside?"

"I wouldn't call it a team, and I wouldn't call it 'tipping off,'" Sherman said.

"What's this all about?" Melody asked.

"You never told Melody?" Mock surprise.

"There was nothing to tell."

"You knew about Great Bear?" Melody asked. "Even before he died?"

"What I knew—overheard—was a name, some initials," Sherman said. "I noticed Mr. Van Schoonhoven jumped when calls came in from them, but I didn't suspect it was very important. Even Andy seemed to know about them."

"Not really," Mills said.

"You didn't tell me," said Melody. It was not a question.

"How could anyone *not* have heard of Great Bear?" Andy said. "They're always in the newspapers buying someone out. Friendly this. Unfriendly that."

"Not my line," said Sherman.

"Really?" Ziza asked.

"I believe him," Melody said, as though she were handing down a ruling.

"Yes," Ziza said, "I believe you would."

"I also believe we are getting far afield," Melody said.

"But he *was* murdered," Ziza said. "Probably by someone who is right here in Mansion House."

"Police business," Melody said. "Something for Nick Story to get around to. Now that he's gone, it doesn't really make all that much difference how Mr. Van Schoonhoven died, does it? I'll continue with my plans; Sherman will get us more good press; Andy will finish—and I mean it—his illustrated history. And Ziza will get Naomi aboard. Obviously we are the winning team. We have no bad memories to weigh us down."

"I can add something more," Hagadorn Mills said, raising his hand as though he were waiting for the teacher to call on him and enjoying in advance the stir his carefully delayed announcement was going to make. "The case is closed. The

Mounties got their man. Or should I say woman. Nick Story took Mrs. Van Schoonhoven away with him just before I caught sight of you heading upstairs. In fact, I followed you because I thought you had the inside story." He smiled sympathetically. "Guess not."

"Arrested?" Ziza asked.

"Not in handcuffs, no, but led away by authorities. They put her in the back seat of the police car, and uniformed officers sat on either side. I'm surprised you didn't see it from up here, Ziza."

"There has to be a mistake," Ziza said.

"Well, then," Melody said, "that takes care of that. See, Ziza, there was nothing to fret about after all. Now it's our serve—advantage us."

19

❧

"You must be out of your mind," Naomi said.

She was in Harry Van Schoonhoven's old office, behind the desk, sitting very erect in his oversized swivel chair, her back in no place touching the seductive curves of the molded leather. Charley Butler was on the couch facing her, and Frank sat next to him in his wheelchair. Although she was talking into the telephone, she was looking at them. They nodded their heads in agreement.

"Nick Story says we're misconstruing," she said to the Butlers, not bothering to cover the receiver.

"I was telling the boys," she said into the phone, "that you said we are misconstruing."

"He says," she said toward the couch, "that Gwen is not under arrest but that they had some questions to ask that could only be asked at the substation."

"And what might those be?"

"And what might those be, Mr. Story?" Neither Frank nor Charley took his eyes off Naomi.

"He says he does not discuss official police business with civilians."

"But he is discussing it with Mrs. Van Schoonhoven," Charley said.

"Charley says you are discussing it with Gwen."

"He says, Charley, that they are not discussing anything; he is asking questions."

Frank muttered something.

"Frank says that I should remind you of the laws of habeas corpus."

There was a long silence while Naomi listened. "In effect, Frank, he is saying that he fully understands the state and federal laws on this matter." There was another long silence. "And he says he would like to get back to work."

"He has totally overlooked the drug aspect," Charley said. "Tell him that. Tell him that there's been all sorts of drug-dealer hanky-panky going on around here. Tell him Mr. Van Schoonhoven might have uncovered the secret identity of a big shot, a kingpin, and had to be wiped out."

"The mob," Frank said.

"Frank and Charley think you should look into the possibility of organized crime being behind Harry's murder."

"He thanks you for your advice," Naomi said, "but says that if he doesn't get off this line immediately, the next shift is going to come on and he'll never get Gwen back here before dark."

"Tell him we appreciate his meeting our demands for the immediate release of Mrs. Van Schoonhoven, assuming, of course, that no harm has come her way."

"Charley says that he appreciates . . ." Naomi stared into the telephone receiver. "It seems that Mr. Story has hung up on us."

"Rude," Frank said. "The manners of a policeman."

"I think he has a lot on his plate right now," Naomi said.

"But not too much to ignore the voice of the people, *vox populi*. Thank you, Naomi," Charley said, getting up and reaching for Frank's wheelchair. "I think we've accomplished just what we set out to this afternoon."

"Mrs. Van Schoonhoven will be home by nightfall," Frank said.

"Unfettered," said Charley.

ð   ð   ð

Naomi walked the Butler boys to the Parlor door and then
went out to the front porch and down the steps to the driveway. She had not been back to the mess hall since she moved
into Mansion House after the accident. It was a nice day for
a walk. Her legs were stiff from too much resting. What she
needed was sun and exercise, so she decided to wander over
to the old camp. Something the Butlers had said made her
want to look around.

Her car was now in the junkyard behind Sheen's Garage
(in the front row with several other cars in surprisingly good
condition), and the insurance company had notified her via
computerized letter that it was a complete loss. Totaled, Mr.
Sheen had said, shaking his head with the profound sadness
of a bartender refusing to pour another drink. A check for
the car's secondhand book value (not much) would arrive in
the course of time after the paperwork was cleared up. That
morning she had borrowed a Smyrna pickup truck and gone
to clean out the trunk and glove compartment. The car certainly did not look totaled. Internal trouble, Mr. Sheen said,
bent axles, the sort of thing a woman probably wouldn't
understand.

The bottle of scotch in the trunk *had* broken, and she would
not buy another. She'd had enough of good-luck charms. But
she did throw its screw-on top into the cardboard box of odds
and ends she was bringing back to Smyrna, along with badly
folded road maps, a jumper cable, an unused folding umbrella
she had received for sending money to a listener-sponsored
FM station and an old-fashioned X-shaped tire iron that had
been in every car she had owned. If she were still a reporter
she would have thought strongly about digging into the possibility of insurance investigators' being in cahoots with local
garages for kickbacks.

But now there was something else to look into. Not Harry's
death, not exactly. That was for the Nick Storys of this world.

But she was curious about the talk of a drug connection, of local drug activity. It would be a relief if there were an "outsider" to blame for the trouble. If Tim Jacobsen were at work on the house—and on a day like this he should be—maybe he could shed some light.

Was it prejudiced, Naomi asked herself, to think that just because Tim was young and a dropout of some kind that he would know about drugs? Probably, but for what she had in mind, Tim fit her profile.

When she got to the mess hall, Tim's scaffolding was empty. From the look of it, nothing much had been done since the last time she was there. The same old clapboards were scraped, nothing new. The ladders were still in the same position. Even the old wheelbarrow, with its folded tarp, was where it had been the last time Naomi had noticed it, still holding an inch or so of water from some forgotten rainstorm.

Naomi was not sure which of the old cabins was Tim's. She had not visited the area since she had returned to Smyrna, but she remembered seeing his light shining through the trees the first evening she had arrived and was sure she would have no trouble finding it. They had called the cluster of bunkhouses the Village. One of the oddities of a camp that refused to indulge in baseball and other team sports because they fostered an "unhealthy" spirit of competition was that the entire day-to-day operation of the place was based on rivalry among the cabins of the Village. They all had Indian names: Mohawk, Oneida, Onondaga, Cayuga, Seneca, Tuscarora (which used up all the tribes of the Iroquois confederacy) and Leni-Lenape (an Algonquian tribe that was a favorite of Young Father Quick's because, he claimed, they were especially peace-loving).

All the buildings in the Village were still standing, although with their jerry-built additions and inept attempts at winterization, Naomi would have recognized none of them if they had not still displayed—safely out of reach over the doorways—their old signboards with the names spelled out in twig letters. Now that the spring growth had begun to shoot up higher every day, the Village looked like an abandoned refugee camp, overgrown and deserted, the cabins nailed shut except for Leni-Lenape. Lenny Le Nape, as the kids had called it. Or just plain Lenny, who sounded like a hard-sweating comedian on the Catskills borscht belt and to Naomi's secret delight nicely undermined the Quicks' rustic intent. She found Tim there, carefully at work on a mountain collage.

"Aunt Nan, I presume?" She stood on the newly repaired front step.

He looked up in surprise and walked across the room toward her, his expression perfectly blank, as though he did not recognize her. She half expected him to close the cabin door in her face, but at the last minute his face broke into a smile. "Come on in," he said. "Maybe you have some opinions on how a sunset should look."

"It's been done."

"What?"

"Catskill sunsets. Every time you look at a picture of these mountains it's a sunset. You would think the sun never rose around here. Do a sunrise, facing toward the river."

He looked at her as though he were seriously considering it. "The old lady wouldn't have done one," he said. "From what I've heard she was strictly a sunset sort of gal."

"I knew her. You're right."

"Have a seat. I can't offer you anything, even the beer's run out. I've lost my pusher."

"Your . . ."

"Mr. Van Schoonhoven. He'd bring beer. I'm going to have to get used to buying it for myself. That's tough."

"I think you'll work it out."

"I suppose." He picked up a scrap of soiled canvas and considered a place to glue it. "We don't actually know each other, you and me." He dropped it back on the pile and picked up a piece of cork.

"I'm—"

"I know that," he said. What I'm saying is that you and me have never talked to each other before."

"No."

"And now you're here talking about sunrise-sunset. You could sing a song about it."

"The police have taken in Gwen. Mrs. Van Schoonhoven."

"Arrested?" he asked.

"No, just questioning."

"Weird."

"She's coming back later today."

"Weird." He began cutting the cork into small bits. "When in doubt make more rocks," he said. "These mountains can always take more rocks."

"What do you know about getting drugs around here? Is it hard?"

"I heard you were a drinker, but no one mentioned drugs. You think maybe I can get you stuff?"

For a minute she considered saying yes, just to see what would happen. Undercover work. "No, I'm just curious. The Butler boys think drugs may be behind the killing and all."

"There's a pair for you. Like everyplace else, drugs are around, all over. The high-school kids are smoking, nothing much more than that. You hear about crack. Lots of crack down in Newburgh, New Paltz, maybe, some here I guess. Mostly around here it's beer and pot, ham and eggs, pork and beans. There's been big stashes of pot turning up, room-fuls of it. But who gets killed over pot? This is the eighties, lady, almost nineties, almost the twenty-first century, even in Greene County."

He began gluing the cork fragments to the side of what looked like a bark cliff. He was very intent on what he was doing, careful not to put on so much glue that it spilled out around the edges of the cork. Naomi watched him squinting in concentration and wondered if there were something wrong with his eyes.

"How old are you, Tim?"

"Twenty, a little older."

Still an age at which he did not think that an odd question, she thought. Twenty years, a little more, almost as long as she had been alone. So that, she thought, is what all that time could look like.

"You moved Lew's bones for the Butler boys."

He looked at her quickly and looked away. There definitely was something wrong with his eyes. One of them was slightly off, not quite crossed. "It's not something I want to be talking about."

"You thought it was a good joke?" She did not look at him either.

"No. I was doing a favor."

"For the Butlers?"

"Talk to them about it."

"I can't," she said, surprised to hear herself saying it to this boy. "I can't bear the notion of having to listen to their explanations. But what's yours?" She looked at him again.

"I was being helpful, a good guy."

"Is that why you're making those pictures?"

"This is for the dollars. Cash on delivery from Mr. Benedikt. There was no cash involved in the bones. It was a favor, that's all."

"They asked you."

"They asked me."

"If I asked you to do something, would you do it? As a favor?"

He looked at her as though he were weighing how well he knew her, how much he owed her. "Sure. Why not?"

"OK, be ready. One of these days I just may take you up on that."

❧   ❧   ❧

On her way back to Mansion House (this was turning out to be a tiring day), Naomi saw Ziza coming out of the Gnomes'

House. Ziza noticed that she had been spotted and, to Naomi's way of thinking, began to act as guilty as hell. There was a lot of exaggerated waving, and then she ran to catch up with Naomi. "You caught me snooping," she said.

"Really?"

"Back to the scene of the crime."

"Isn't that what the murderer returns to?" Naomi said, deciding not to be easy on her young friend.

"I was looking for"—she paused to grope for a word—"well, for anything I might find. Down in that cellar."

"It's dark down there," Naomi said, "or at least it used to be. Anything turn up?"

Ziza pulled a small high-intensity flashlight out of her pocket. "I'd like to say I found a matchbook from some local roadhouse where we could go and be told that they had had only one customer in the past month and just happened to have his name and address. But no luck. Nothing. Just a lot of scuffed-up dirt and some cigarette butts that must date from the other night. Marlboros. Kool Lights. Four of the former, two of the latter. One Carlton. No lipstick traces. End of report."

"I'm impressed."

They had come through the woods and were heading into the old box factory parking lot. Ahead of them was the hill that led to the Heart. They walked in silence.

"Melody Horn came to see me this morning," Ziza said and paused for a comment that never came. "She seemed to think we're especially good friends." Another pause; another silence. "She seems to think I can throw my weight around and get you to back her and not the hired guns from Great Bear and Godalmighty."

"I suppose she could be right."

"But I'm not doing that. I hope you understand, throwing my weight around."

"I should hope not."

"So don't tell me whose side you're on. I don't want to be in the position of having information to withhold from Madam Horn."

"It's all too exhausting," Naomi said and stopped in her tracks. "This has been my first really active day since the accident, and I'm not sure I have my sea legs yet." They were just high enough to be able to see the stream as it passed the old swimming pavilion.

"Could I ask you two questions?"

"If you've been crawling around in the dark counting cigarette butts, I suppose you've earned an answer or two."

"It's only one question, really. I know you've said you didn't know you had Llewelyn's stock coming to you."

"Of course I knew. A lot of stock. A lot of stock worth a lot of money. Once a body turned up."

"That wasn't my question, actually, but it's an interesting answer. My question is this: Did you know Mr. Van Schoonhoven was trying to sell off the community?"

"Harry was never very much good at being coy. I thought he was up to something, but I confess that what I thought he was up to was Melody Horn."

"Where were you that afternoon, the day Mr. Van Schoonhoven died?"

"That was another question. Or are we getting into multipart answers, A, B and C? I was at home. Home? I was in the old mess-hall kitchen. And if you want to know the awful truth, I was cleaning mouse droppings off the open shelves. Listen to me"—she laughed—"mouse droppings. I'm getting genteel in my wealthy old age. It was mouse shit, lots of it, and no one had cleaned it up in years. No witnesses. It's the kind of dirty job you do when you're compulsive and alone."

"You didn't see Tim around?"

"No, the phantom housepainter was still a mystery at that point. So I'm afraid you've caught me without an alibi. Now do you take me down to headquarters to share a cell with Gwen?"

"You didn't kill him. That's *not* a question."

"Oh, yes, I'm afraid it is, but I had better reasons to kill him than a lot of stock certificates." With that she started walking and did not say another word until they reached the front steps of Mansion House.

❦ ❦ ❦

At first, Naomi thought a crowd was waiting there for them. But as they got closer, she could see that it was not actually a crowd, just the Butlers and Melody Horn and Sherman Benedikt and Hagadorn Mills and a few community employees. And it was not waiting for them. It surrounded a state police car. As Naomi and Ziza came around the curve of the Heart, Nick Story was getting out of the driver's seat and coming around to open the passenger door for Gwen Van Schoonhoven.

Looking straight ahead, Gwen waited for the door to be opened, and as Nick Story held it for her and reached in to take her arm, she slid out and graciously acknowledged the group with a decidedly royal nod. Her Highness returns from touring the provinces, Naomi thought. The Butler brothers, though nowhere near each other, burst into applause.

"We did it," Charley Butler shouted from behind the car. "It took a phone call to the right place, but we got you out of there."

"Before harm was done," Frank added from his wheelchair at the top of the steps.

Melody Horn gave her a quick kiss on the cheek, softly murmuring something that sounded to Naomi like "Back where you belong."

Nick Story, still holding the door, looked over toward Naomi, and for a moment she thought he was going to tell her to take Gwen's place in the front seat. Instead he simply winked, closed the door and walked back to his own side of the car. Without having said a word, he got in and drove off toward Olde Smyrna Road. Everyone watched until the car disappeared into the pine plantation, and then everyone started talking at once.

Mrs. Van Schoonhoven forgot her regal pose.

"The coffee I've drunk, you wouldn't believe it. Cup after cup. I think it's a trick to make you have to go to the bathroom, if you'll excuse my French. To make you feel uncomfortable. Every time there was a pause in the conversation someone was handing me one of those dreadful Styrofoam cups that burn your hand the second you touch it, instant coffee, powdered milk, no cream."

"What were they asking you?" Melody Horn wanted to know.

"Time questions. Where was I when? Well, I was in the kitchen for a long time that afternoon making the corn soup for our little dinner that night, and then I had a nice lie-down in my room upstairs. Did anyone see me? In the kitchen, yes. In my room, I damn well hope not, thank you. Had I seen Mr. Van Schoonhoven? Not since lunchtime, no. Was I sure he knew about the dinner party? Of course I was sure. We had a plan. Who *had* I seen that afternoon? You, Melody, briefly, I believe. Naomi, no. Ziza, no. Mr. Benedikt, no. Andy, I don't think so. Tim, good Lord no. And on and on. Money. Personal questions about Mr. Van Schoonhoven. Questions about the community they had no business asking."

"Such as?" Hagadorn Mills asked.

"Questions *no* one has any business asking." A flash of the old regal quality there, Naomi thought.

"What it sounds like you need," Ziza said, moving past Sherman Benedikt and taking Mrs. Van Schoonhoven's arm, "is a good drink." She moved her up the stairs and across the porch. "And consider that professional advice."

"A delightful idea," Mrs. Van Schoonhoven said, and calling behind her as they walked down the cobblestone hall toward her husband's old office and the liquor cabinet, she said, "Naomi, you come along, too."

Surprised by Gwen's request—their get-togethers, especially the last one with the Great Bear representatives, had never been especially friendly—and puzzled about what Ziza was up to, Naomi at first hesitated. Had she been invited or summoned, the way a pet dog was called in for its bath? Curiosity won out, and she followed them up the steps, sensing but ignoring the glances exchanged by Melody Horn and Sherman Benedikt, Charley and Frank Butler. Hagadorn Mills, with no one to look meaningfully at and feeling put in his place for asking an improper question, headed back alone to the Children's House and his tables of photographs. He had to revise the final chapter of the community history, making the future of the company a bit more vague. And he had a telephone call to make.

By the time Naomi reached the office, ice was already in three glasses, and two of them also contained what looked like scotch. "Naomi," Ziza asked, "tonic or stronger?"

Stronger would have been nice, but her answer was "Tonic."

"A big sip now," Ziza said, a mother telling her child to take her medicine, "and then tell us what *really* happened."

Mrs. Van Schoonhoven took a much longer sip than any mother would have expected, leaned back on the couch, took another sip, rattled her ice as though hoping for an early refill and began to talk. Naomi was on the couch with her, Ziza in a leather chair facing her across a coffee table covered with Smyrna ring catalogs.

The stories about what had happened were, of course, inaccurate. She had not been taken away in the back seat of the squad car with a policeman on either side of her. She rode in the front with Nick Story, and they did not go directly to the state police substation in Leeds. He had taken the winding back roads by way of Catskill. And they had talked as though they were old friends, at first about nothing much at all. They stopped at the drive-through window at McDonald's and ordered milk shakes and two large fries and ate them in the car under the trees down at the old boat yard.

"In Catskill, just before the creek runs into the Hudson," Gwen said. "*You* must remember the spot, Naomi." Naomi did, although she did not respond. "It used to be a popular parking spot for kids. They've built a condominium there now."

"Sounds like a high-school date," Ziza said.

"Well, yes, it was, that part."

"Before they made you drink all that coffee," Naomi said.

"Such a polite man, Mr. Story. He told me about his house up on the mountain and all the work he's done on it over the years and about being a policeman down in New York. But the more he talked the more he wanted to talk about Harry. And he asked a lot of personal questions about Harry's drinking. When he got too personal I told him so, and that's when we went on to the police station."

"And the coffee."

"Forget the coffee, Naomi," Gwen said, some of her old hostility surfacing.

"He kept asking you about Mr. Van Schoonhoven's drinking," Ziza said, guiding the conversation back to where she wanted it.

Which reminded Gwen that her glass was empty. "I'll have the other half of my drink now," she said with a coquettish smile, and Ziza gave her a refill, topping off her own as well. "That was something Harry would always say for his second drink. 'I'll have the other half now.' Sometimes that other half would keep coming all night long. But he wasn't a bad drinker. He knew how to put it away, and he knew how to handle it. So he always said."

"That's what Nick Story wanted to hear about," Ziza prompted.

"Yes, but more about if Harry ever tried to stop drinking, if he had seen a doctor about it. I told him Harry could stop any time he wanted to and every now and then would. 'I won't drink for a fortnight,' he'd say about once a year or so.

It was always a fortnight. I think he thought it sounded classy. 'Not a drop. Not even a beer.' And he wouldn't, which proved to him that he wasn't an alcoholic."

She took another long sip of scotch, inhaling it as much as drinking it. "Which is why I wanted you to come along, Naomi." Her smile was not a friendly one as she peered over the top of her glass. "I'd like to make some use of your expertise. Pick your brain, as it were. Tell me about Antabuse. Mr. Story kept saying that that's what killed Harry, and he wanted to know if there was any chance Harry might have been experimenting with it. You take it, don't you?"

"Years ago, briefly. But how did you know?"

"I have my ways."

"Oh, Gwen, just tell me."

The smile again and another slow sip. Ziza almost said something but kept quiet and watched. "You told that A.A. meeting in Catskill you took it," Gwen said.

"And someone there told you? I can't believe it." Nick Story was the only one it could have been, and she did not believe he would betray her anonymity like that. "Who was it?"

"It wasn't a little bird that told me. I heard you myself."

"You?"

"I don't belong, of course." She took another sip to prove it. "But Harry got this notion, because I refused to join him on his fortnights, that I might have what he called a problem."

"And he sent you to a meeting?"

"Took me, and waited down on Main Street in the car. We ran into you and Mr. Story afterward, if you remember. That was a surprise, seeing Nick Story. I hadn't realized he was there."

"But I didn't see you at the meeting, and I can't see how I could have missed you."

"I came late, looked in the door and saw you up front with that brown paper bag—a bottle, obviously—talking about the days when you were a drunk. Frankly, from what I had been hearing I hadn't realized you stopped. But I decided not to intrude and stayed in the hall listening. I left before you finished. It made me realize it wasn't a place for me."

"No?"

"No."

"Antabuse," said Ziza, the prompter.

"Mr. Story said Harry was given some, or took some, and that it killed him, gave him a heart attack when he took a drink. He was trying to figure out if Harry might have done it on purpose. God, no, I said. His head was full of nothing but plans. Or who could have been around to give it to him."

"Or who," Ziza said, "knew enough about it to use it."

"That, too," said Gwen, "or who had some." The pause was longer than it needed to be. "Naomi, what about you, do you still have any, what is it? Powder?"

"It's a little white pill with a line down the middle so you can break it in half," Naomi said. "I might still have a few on the bottom of an old plastic container in my medicine chest back in the city. It's possible, I suppose. Who ever throws away old medicine? But I have none up here."

"Just how common is an Antabuse heart attack?" Ziza asked.

"I'm not an expert," Naomi said, "but it must be rare. The point of Antabuse is that it makes you feel terrible, deathly sick, when it's mixed with alcohol. The patient willingly swallows a ticking bomb, knowing that all it takes to trigger it is one little drink. But for someone to bank on it triggering a heart attack, to be so sure she—or maybe he—would use it to murder, well it seems to me that someone would have to be very familiar with the health of the victim. Very. He—or maybe she—would have to be very sure the victim was a walking heart attack ready to happen."

"And that he was bound to take a drink," Ziza said.

"Yes," Naomi said. "But that was something the murderer could make a pretty safe bet on. Right, Gwen?"

"Assuming he wasn't in the middle of one of those damn fortnights."

20

❦

The police car pulled over at the path leading from the cemetery.

"Want a lift?"

Ziza stooped down to see who was behind the wheel. "Are you a strange man?" she asked.

"Not that I've noticed," Nick Story said.

"OK, then," she said. "My mother told me never to accept rides from strange men."

He unlocked the passenger door, and she hopped in. He did not make the turn into Olde Smyrna. "It's a nice day for a ride, don't you think?"

It was about eight o'clock in the morning, and Ziza was in her running clothes. Perhaps because Nick Story was a policeman she seemed to think she had to explain what she was doing. She had just finished her usual five-mile loop, she said, and, again as usual, had cooled off in the shade of the old Dutch Reformed Church cemetery. "Ever been there?" she asked. She interpreted the vague movement he made with his shoulders to mean no. "It's an interesting place. Lots of Dutch inscriptions and more nasty-looking angels than can dance on the head of a pin."

"They say graveyards are restful," he said. "Lots of folks are certainly dying to get in."

"This morning I noticed that there was a whole family of

Vanden Bogarts. I wonder if they were ancestors of Humphrey."

"Everyone's got to have ancestors somewhere."

"You're very deep this morning, Mr. Story. Next thing you'll be telling me that there are more dead people now than ever before in history."

"That sounds about right." He turned off onto a small blacktop road that cut diagonally across a freshly plowed field. They seemed to be headed toward Catskill. "Lots of people say fall's the prettiest time of the year up here," he said. "But I'll take just about now in the spring. The mud's gone. The leaves are fresh. The old apple trees up at my place in East Jewett have just dropped their blossoms. The apples they produce don't amount to much unless you're into worms, but the blossoms are something to see."

"You've got to spray the trees every year if you want decent apples."

"That's what they say."

At the end of the field the road crossed a small WPA-era bridge and made a sharp right turn in a totally new direction. "Am I going to be questioned?" she asked. "Is that what's happening here?"

"Talk is all. You mentioned the Vanden Bogarts, maybe I'll get around to mentioning the Van Schoonhovens. It probably won't come to much."

"Could it possibly have been suicide?"

"Who?"

"Come on, Mr. Story, let's just have this out without being coy."

"No, it was murder. Call me Nick."

Ziza did not mention her 3 × 5 cards. In fact, she herself had not yet added the new information she had picked up yesterday. "I'll tell you what I think is a key point," she said. "No glass." She waited for a reaction.

"I don't get it."

"No drinking glass in the Gnomes' House cellar. The killer

either brought Mr. Van Schoonhoven there after he died or he took the glasses and the bottle of whatever they were drinking with him when he left."

"It sounds as though you picture this as some sort of murderous wine-tasting party."

"No . . ."

"So, it's not what I'd call a key point. Worth noting, to be sure, but hardly key, although I appreciate your interest."

Story shifted noisily into a lower gear. They were now headed down a steep grade, straight downhill without the usual turns back and forth, obviously headed toward the river, and the closer they got the dustier it became. The new green leaves had already taken on a coating of pale gray. They had moved into range of the gritty fallout of the cement plant. At the bottom of the hill, the trees had died out entirely, and Ziza could see clouds of gray powder spilling from a tall smokestack as colorless as the heaping desert of dust that surrounded it.

"The lordly Hudson," Nick Story said. "A couple of years ago the City of New York suggested this as the site of an atomic-power plant to run the subway system. They claimed that since it was already an environmental nightmare, one thing more wouldn't make any difference. But it never happened."

They turned north on the river road, although the river itself was hidden by gray mounds.

"No," he continued, "I think the key point is Mr. Van Schoonhoven's heart condition."

"He looked—"

"He looked as though he would pop off if he ran up a decent flight of stairs. But who *knew*? Melody Horn did. His health records spelled the whole thing out and they were in the company files. His wife—"

"She said she knew about a mild condition."

"Sure, that's what she said, mild. She probably knew more than that. The Butlers? I doubt if there's anything about

Smyrna those old maids don't know. And Naomi? I'd love to know what that woman *really* knows about anything. You seem to be her best friend around here. . . ."

"So people keep telling me."

They had passed a sign saying WELCOME TO CATSKILL and pulled into the first fast-food place they came to, a McDonald's. "How do you take your coffee?" he asked, and when they pulled up to the drive-through window ordered two large regulars and two hot apple pies. He passed the steamy paper bag over to Ziza. "Hold this for a minute. I'll find a cool place to park."

Ziza considered suggesting the old boat yard down on the creek but had a feeling that was where they were headed anyway. "Access to Antabuse," she said. "Another key point."

"Exactly," he said. Just before they got to the bridge over the creek, he turned right and threaded his way around the potholes until he came to a grove of tall maples. He parked in the shade, next to a sign that said space was still available in the condominium behind them, the Rip Van Winkle.

"Rip's everywhere around here," Ziza said.

"Bridges, motels, golf courses, liquor stores, go-cart raceways, you name it. It's not a bad old town, though." He handed her a coffee, a hot aluminum-foil envelope and an inch-thick pile of napkins. "President Van Buren was married in the living room of a house just back there. Thomas Cole, the landscape painter, lived here. Now it's more famous for training boxers. Floyd Patterson a few years ago, Mike Tyson." He had angled himself into a corner of the front seat so he could watch her. "Open the foil around the apple pie to cool it off, but don't bite into it for a while. You'll burn the roof off your mouth."

She took a similar position in her corner but pulled up her knees so her feet were on the edge of the front seat.

"I've just about decided you're not a suspect," he said. "You're someone who just happened to be here, right?"

"Right."

"Someone who turns out to be very curious about what is going on and just can't help asking questions. I'd probably decide all the way if I knew where you were that afternoon." No need to say which afternoon.

"Around. Walking around."

"Around the camp?"

"Some."

"And you saw?"

"Nobody."

"And nobody saw you?"

"Probably."

"Probably. This is my first case like this, you know. After all these years, a real murder to solve. So I'm trying to solve it by making up stories, murder stories. Such as one about a woman from some sort-of-famous, sort-of-wealthy old family who's married to a guy who is where he is because he married her. She's sick of him and finds he is about to get rid of the family company, her family's company. She's figured out a tricky way to kill him that the dumb local cops would never even notice. So she does kill him, late in the afternoon of a day when she has scheduled a big dinner party as a cover. That's one story."

"And I suppose," Ziza said, "another is about a sharp-as-a-tack businesswoman who has soft-soaped some hick-town businessman into letting her take over his company, and when she finds he is stabbing her in the back, she does him in. On the evening of that same dinner party."

"Close," he said, "very close. I'd add the fact that she had made some financial commitments on the side that she could not get out of. And then there is the wild card, another woman, a widow of the man who would have been running the company if he hadn't died when he was young. She comes back to claim his inheritance. The fact that the head of the company is trying to sell the place out doesn't faze her a bit. Once the body of her husband turns up—very conveniently, perhaps a subplot there—she knows she has enough stock to block any sale, so her reason for killing—shall we mention his name?—Mr. Van Schoonhoven isn't money.

"It's revenge. Maybe she has a pretty good reason to think her husband's death all those years ago wasn't an accident, maybe he was killed by a man who saw his way—he had married the boss's daughter, after all—to move from second fiddle to first chair. She knew he had a heart condition. She had personal knowledge of Antabuse and even had some. So she got her revenge."

"I don't believe it," Ziza said.

"I suppose I don't, either," he said. "I took a weekend course once at the FBI, and they said, reading between the lines, when in doubt suspect the spouse. That sounds like blue-chip advice to me."

"Is that all the stories you've been working on?"

He was watching her closely, his pale-blue eyes not leaving her face, a slight smile on his aging farmer-boy face. She was aware, without looking, that he was idly untying the laces on one of her running shoes. She did not move her legs or glance down.

Well, there's another story I can't quite pull together. There's no motive that I can find. About a young graduate student. Maybe from a divinity school or a place like that, who claims to be writing a paper no one has seen her actually working on, who spends her time asking more questions than seem necessary, who always happens to be popping up when no one really wants to talk with her. What can I make of that? Where was she that afternoon? Had she, maybe, opened one door too many?"

She would call his bluff. She could feel the second of the double knots on her laces being undone. "What," she asked, "if she were standing at the top of a flight of stairs, listening?" She looked at him as intently and as dispassionately as he looked at her. "What if she knew someone was at the bottom of those stairs listening to her? What if she left the house and then hid outside to watch and see if someone came out of that supposedly empty building after she left?"

He had either finished untying the knot or he had stopped. "If she saw something, that would be an important clue. It's not something she should be hiding from her friend the police detective. What, actually, did she see?"

She ignored his question and asked, "What about this as another possible story. What if there was a policeman assigned to a fairly boring territory who made his life more interesting by working with the local underworld? What if they made it worth his while to ignore the sizable drug stashes they were depositing in his jurisdiction? What if the head of a respected local company who had a weakness for dropping off at the local watering holes stumbled on to what was going on? Maybe he even discovered his own property was involved, his employees, all this at a time when he was trying to swing a deal with a very respectable bunch of Wall Street types. Maybe the man—shall we use his name?—maybe Mr. Van Schoonhoven made threats. Maybe the policeman, who could well have had some personal knowledge of Antabuse and certainly recognized a potential heart patient when he saw one, acted. Maybe he was even standing in the shadows of the bottom of the stairs, the body of his victim at his feet. Maybe he stood there and listened to someone at the top of the stairs listening to him."

She felt the pressure of his hand on her ankle and then a constricting sensation as the laces on her running shoes were tightened. He looked down as he tied the laces in an expert double knot. He must, she thought, have been a runner himself.

"Making up stories is not going to get us anywhere. Facts are all we have to work with. Anyway"—he laughed, and it sounded to Ziza like an honest laugh—"I've heard that the suicide rate among novelists is dreadful. Worse than for policemen." He slapped the sole of her shoe lightly, as impersonal as a clerk in a shoe store. "Your hot apple pie should be cool enough by now. Eat up. I've got to get you home and then do something about catching a murderer."

21

❧

The last trip Naomi had made to Catskill with the Butler boys had ended in an accident. This time they came in Nick Story's unmarked police car. She sat in the front seat with Nick. Frank and Charley shared the back seat with, of all people, Gwen Van Schoonhoven. Frank's wheelchair was folded up neatly in the trunk. They were on their way to town for a meeting, an outing—it was the only word Naomi could think of that fit the bill—organized by Nick Story, and Lord only knew what he had said to get Gwen to come.

It was an uneasy trip without much chitchat. The only time conversation picked up was as they approached the accident site, and both Frank and Charley vied for being the first to point out the exact spot Naomi's car had skidded off the road. (Forced off the road, Naomi thought, but she kept her thoughts to herself.) And they asked Nick if he could slow down so they could get a better look, even though it was almost dark. Story had, but just barely.

He was to be chairman of the meeting, apparently the first time he had ever been asked, although Naomi suspected he might have volunteered. She was not quite sure what he was up to, but he seemed to be up to something. He had asked them all to come with him, he said, because he needed their moral support and help. Naomi would have liked to believe those were the only reasons.

Once they arrived at the empty, low-ceilinged social hall in the church basement, everyone was given something to do. Charley set up three long rows of folding chairs (supervised by Frank, who knew exactly how they were to be arranged), and Gwen was supposed to make coffee, but she asked so many questions that Nick ended up doing it himself. Naomi's job was to write the topic of the evening's meeting on the blackboard. It was to be a Step Meeting, as it was every other week, which meant that instead of general discussion, the group would be talking about one or two of the Twelve Steps, the dozen principles on which Alcoholics Anonymous was based. Step One was an acknowledgment of being powerless over alcohol, and when, weeks later, they reached Step Twelve (a commitment to carry the message to other alcoholics), they would go back to Step One and start discussing the whole thing all over again.

This week, since they went so well together, the topic was both Steps Eight and Nine. Naomi printed (Had she written on a blackboard since doing long division in Mrs. Pelton's fourth-grade class? Could she do it without making that terrible squeaking sound?) in large capital letters: *Made a list of all persons we had harmed, and became willing to make amends to them all.* And then: *Made direct amends to such people wherever possible, except when to do so would injure them or others.*

By the time she finished and turned around to face the room (she had not squeaked once) many of the chairs had been filled. Paul from the liquor store was there. He waved, called her by name, said it was good to see her back, good to see that she had been put to work. She waved back, hoped she smiled, but resisted his salesman-of-the-year good spirits. Rather than joining either friendly Paul or the Smyrna clique (a Butler sat on either side of Gwen Van Schoonhoven, as though they were afraid she might make a break for the door), she picked up a cup of coffee (it gave her something to do with her hands) and sat by herself. Right away she was sorry she had not taken one of the pamphlets that Nick had put out next to the coffeepot. It would have kept her occupied until things got under way.

So she counted the house. Twenty-six so far, including the Smyrna faction, and more coming in, a far bigger turnout than last time, and there were more younger people, teenagers, kids in their early twenties who filled up the last row of chairs and said not a word to one another. In the car Nick had mentioned that there was a new judge in town who was giving suspended sentences on run-of-the-mill drinking and drug cases if the defendants promised to attend a month of AA meetings. It was changing the complexion of the meetings, he had said, more sullen people there against their will.

And what did they think, Naomi wondered, seeing the man who might have arrested them, maybe slammed them against the sides of their cars, handcuffed them, read them their rights so fast they couldn't have understood a word even if their heads had been clear, seeing him up there in front of the meeting in a shabby preacher-blue suit? Did they wonder if he was secretly taking attendance, making mental notes on who was there, taking names, maybe even making notes for the judge about what was said? At their age, she would have wondered. She did wonder about his real agenda.

"It's time," said Paul, who kept track of such things, and Nick called the meeting to order. The old, familiar, comforting pattern was about to begin, grumpy teenagers or not (the notion that they were all wolfish members of Tim Jacobsen's Cub Scout pack amused Naomi). She leaned back in her chair, closed her eyes, breathed deeply and relaxed. She needed this meeting, she thought.

But something went wrong right away. As Nick launched into the usual preamble about how Alcoholics Anonymous was a fellowship of recovering alcoholics that took no political positions and was financially self-supporting, a flurry of coughing broke out from the Butler boys and was picked up by Paul, who began signaling wildly to Nick Story. He stopped speaking, stared at them and finally got the message.

"Sorry," he said. "I forgot the most important point. I'm Nick, and I'm an alcoholic."

"Hi, Nick," came the answer, and the familiar pattern was established.

Story's approach as chairman was not personal. He did not tell horrifying drunk stories about himself or entertainingly self-effacing anecdotes of raucous adventures on the bar trail. He simply started the problem for discussion: Who have we harmed? How are we to make amends? And instead of asking for a show of hands, he said they would begin at the far end of the first row and move around the room, giving everyone a chance to speak. After some muttered "Fuck that"s from the back row, he added, "If you aren't ready to make any comments, just give your first name and say 'Pass' when your turn comes."

No one in the first row, all regulars, said "Pass," not until it became Gwen Van Schoonhoven's turn. The catalog of those harmed was familiar enough—wives, husbands, children, employers, employees, friends, strangers in a bar, strangers in the front seat of a car rammed head-on. The lists were easy enough to make. The speakers had a harder time telling about making amends. Paul, as usual, talked about working in a liquor store, both drunk and sober, and the group tittered at his reminiscences, much, Naomi thought, the way a congregation would react to a priest's telling a smutty story, shocked but vaguely excited. There was almost a hint of sexual excitement about it, an alcoholic behind the counter, surrounded by all those forbidden bottles, taking money to give to others what he himself could have no longer.

As Paul talked, the door at the back of the room opened and the sound of high heels clicking across the linoleum floor caused every head in the room to turn. It was Melody Horn in a red silk pants suit. She paused behind the last row and turned as though she might leave. Paul stopped talking in the middle of a story about how, drunk himself, he had no trouble at all shortchanging even drunker customers.

"Have a seat, please," Nick said. "This is an open meeting. Everyone is welcome."

"I was invited," she said.

"Of course."

"By you."

"Yes."

"You didn't say . . ."

"We are in the middle of things. Why don't you just have a seat for now."

After a moment, every eye in the room on her, she came over to the second row and sat down next to Naomi. Naomi nodded a hello. Melody leaned toward her. "Some kind of cops-and-robbers thing?" she whispered, raising one carefully shaped eyebrow.

"I think," Naomi said, "you may be right."

"There's another thing to consider when we are thinking about accountability," Nick said, perhaps trying to expand the discussion. "And that's that drunks bring out the worst in everyone they deal with. How responsible are we for that? How much that went wrong around us was really our fault? How responsible are we for the evil we trigger in others?"

Paul ignored the interruption. The way to fleece a drunk, he said, was in making change. A few times—back in those old days when he did such things—he tried jacking up the price, charging, say, the code number on the label rather than the real price. But that usually backfired. "Drunks know to the penny what a bottle costs. What they're weak on is change, sometimes even on whether it was a ten or a twenty they gave you. They don't count anything, just scoop up the change, and into the pocket it goes, small bills and all. They just want to get that brown paper bag and make it out the door. Sayonara." That got an appreciative chuckle from the group, and he sat down. He had said nothing at all about amends.

Next it was Charley Butler's turn. It was his first meeting since the confession, and he had a lot to cover. He began in detail about that chilly morning when he found Llewelyn's body washed up next to the canoe rack, more details than before, the color of the canoes, the condition of the sky, the clouds, the wind, what camp activities had been planned for the day.

Naomi could not stand hearing another word about it and was relieved when Melody Horn tapped her on the arm. "I had been told this was going to be some kind of community-action meeting," she whispered. "By Nick Story, himself. He told Sherman Benedikt and me that it would be worth Olde Smyrna's while to have some sort of representation there. Here."

Naomi suspected that Melody was trying to be kind by diverting her attention from what Charley was raking over. It surprised her. It was not the sort of thing she expected from Melody Horn, and she appreciated it. "I think he is trying to be provocative, hoping to stir things up so someone gives something away."

"Not a very fresh tactic, if you remember that absurd poem the Reverend Ziza read at the memorial service. And what did she learn from that?"

"I think," Naomi said, "this is more along the lines of 'What's a nice murderer like you doing in a dump like this?'"

"Do you think he actually expects you or me or Mrs. Van Schoonhoven to raise a hand, jump up and say, 'It was me. I'm the one that killed that fat, red-faced bastard'?"

"If you did, he'd probably give you a kiss on both cheeks."

The two of them giggled like schoolgirls in study hall, and Frank Butler shot them a sour look.

Charley had mentioned the word "Guardian" several times, and even though she had tried to listen only to Melody, Naomi heard again about wrapping the body in clean canvas like a sailor dead at sea and storing it in the root cellar under the Gnomes' House until the "right time" had come. But now Charley was off on a new tack, hangovers. The more he went on, the more the back row emptied out as the kids, in twos and threes, headed quietly toward the door. Dead bodies might have caught their attention, but an old fart's hangovers were the pits.

"The hangover that morning," Charley said, "the morning I found poor Llewelyn, is not one I'd soon forget. Most mornings then were hangover mornings." This surprised Naomi. "We would never have a drop during the day or while the campers were awake. But after taps my brother and I would usually have a drop or two, discreetly, of course. We were not rowdies. But that night was the last big campfire of the season. The campers were running wild, playing tricks on each other and their counselors. We were up later than usual, and I suspect we went far beyond the usual limit. We had become worried about the personal lives of some of the people we cared for." Frank turned again in his wheelchair and gave Naomi another look, this time a kinder one.

"And I think," Charley continued, "we might have taken it out on a bottle. So that hangover was fierce, the kind that makes decisions, everything, even the light, seem sharp and clear, the kind of hangover that makes you swear that you've been a damn fool and will never drink again." (A knowing chuckle from the front row for that.) "So that was our state of mind, and I wonder if we would have acted differently had it been otherwise. I now wonder if we might have harmed an innocent bystander and if there's a name we should have added to our amends list." His voice trailed off, and he paused for a moment, gathered force and continued, "But I believe our role as Guardians was good and correct and nothing to apologize for. And I also seriously wonder—I've wondered this for years—if besides an amends list there should also be a revenge list to help put things in the past right." He crossed his arms, as though in punctuation, and sat down.

"The point of the Eighth Step," Nick said, "is not to make a hit list. The word's 'amends,' not 'avenge.' "

As Nick spoke, Gwen Van Schoonhoven stood and, remaining crouched over as though she were afraid of blocking someone's view, slipped past Frank and moved back to the second row, where she sat down on the other side of Naomi. "I'm not even giving my name to this bunch," she said.

So it was Frank's turn to speak. Since he couldn't stand, he spun his wheelchair around to face the group. "I'm Frank," he said, and while everyone else was saying "Hi, Frank," he said, "I'm an alcoholic." He gripped the armrests as though he were about to stand up and said, "I just want to say that I don't think all alcoholic decisions are bad ones. Just because you're drunk or hung over doesn't automatically make what you do wrong." He stared at Charley for a moment. "And, Lord knows, there are enough dumb sober decisions."

The front row liked that, Naomi noticed. She also noticed that the back row was now completely empty.

Then Frank launched into a disorganized cluster of comments about the old days at Smyrna and the small discussion circles ("not unlike what happens in these rooms") dominated by Young Father Quick. He brought up Aunt Nan's famous story to the newspaper reporter about having to give up her doll because she showed it "special affection," and launched into a story about a lamb.

"Worthy," Charley interrupted.

"That was his name," Frank said.

" 'Worthy is the Lamb,' " Charley said. "Revelation 5:12."

" 'Worthy is the Lamb that was slain, to receive power, and riches, and wisdom, and strength, and honor, and glory, and blessing.' Revelation 5:12. Another of Young Father's favorite passages. So that is what we named one of the lambs one spring, and Young Father had a fit."

"He sold it," Charley added.

"To a butcher in Catskill," Frank said. "Smyrna never sold any of its livestock, but he sold that one. Again, special affection, just like Old Father and those dolls twenty years before. We had to be taught a lesson, but we never complained to any newspaper about it. Unlike some. I have never done the Eighth Step. I've not made any amends." And he spun his wheelchair back into place.

When it came to Melody Horn's turn she simply said, "I'm a guest" ("So am I," echoed Gwen Van Schoonhoven), and then Naomi, who was the last to speak, said, "I would like to make amends, but, like Frank, I don't think I ever have. I just remember what I can. I don't believe in revenge. Since Aunt Nan has been mentioned, I'll defer to her. She told me once, years ago, just after my husband disappeared, that people shouldn't try to get even. Human beings are just too bad at it. They never get it right. They do too much or too little and botch it all. Revenge is something best left to God."

The meeting ended with everyone holding hands, staring at the floor and saying the Serenity Prayer: "God grant me the serenity to accept the things we cannot change, courage to change the things we can, and the wisdom to know the difference."

"Keep coming back," Paul added.

Some of the regulars surrounded Charley and Frank ("Long time no see!"); Melody Horn rushed up to Nick Story to set a few things straight; Gwen and Naomi remained in their seats. Gwen was holding on to Naomi's arm. "All this talk of revenge makes me sick," she said. "But as a conciliatory gesture—think of it as an olive branch—I have to make amends with you about something."

"Me?"

"Your accident, with the Butler boys? I did that." Gwen kept facing forward, not looking at Naomi, as though they were not to be seen speaking to one another.

"You?"

Nick Story was talking to Melody, but he was watching them, and listening.

"Well, Timmy, Timmy Jacobsen. I loaned him the truck and gave him a few dollars. He was supposed to scare you is all. Send you on your way. But he did too much. Don't let on to the Butlers that I've said any of this. No one was supposed to get hurt." She sounded relieved, as though everything were now all right.

"You just wanted me to go away. That's all?"

"You aren't Smyrna."

"I was Lew's wife."

"Llewelyn," Gwen corrected.

"Lew." It was not a challenge, but a simple, quiet statement.

"No one was *supposed* to get hurt." Irritation was creeping into Gwen's voice. "Timmy didn't even know the Butler boys were in the car."

"So it was Tim who screwed up."

"Timmy's a good boy, but careless. Doesn't always think things through."

"And what about with Harry, were you careless about that, too?"

"What?" She looked at Naomi for the first time.

"What was supposed to happen with Harry? What was the plan? Just scare him? Shake him up? What?"

Naomi could feel Gwen's fingers digging into her arm.

"You are a terrible, terrible woman," Gwen said, fighting for breath. "I offer you an olive branch, and then you say that to me? Terrible. You never belonged here. Never."

22

❧

Ziza and Tim had been wandering around the main floor of Mansion House turning the lights on and off as they went. They had poked around Mr. Van Schoonhoven's old office (already stripped bare), looked into Sherman Benedikt's carefully arranged desk drawers ("Ghost town," Tim said) and were totally baffled by the endless accordions of computer printouts stacked on Melody Horn's desk. "There's either too little or too much," Ziza said. Then they raided the kitchen refrigerator for cheese and cold cuts and a six-pack of Bud that someone had tucked behind the lettuce.

They had their picnic surrounded by the display of Aunt Nan's collages in the Parlor.

"Cat's away," Tim said. "It gets creepy for the mice. Where is everyone?"

"Meetings, mostly," Ziza said. "There's a meeting in Catskill, some sort of community-action thing." She didn't mention that Nick Story had promised to see that Mansion House would be empty. "Sherman and Andy went to the drive-in movie, something called *Bucket of Blood* in a horror-show triple feature."

"Grown men don't go to drive-ins."

"I think it was their way of avoiding whatever it was the others went to."

"They could have just refused. 'Just say no,' right?"

"With Melody I think it's easier to have other plans."

Tim popped the top of another can, took a long sip and as an afterthought offered it to Ziza. She shook the Bud in her hand to show that she still had some.

"This is like baby-sitting," she said.

"Thanks," he said, "I like that."

"No, I mean being alone in someone else's house. I used to love baby-sitting, snooping around, taking food from the fridge, looking in bedroom drawers, medicine cabinets, that sort of thing."

"Inviting a boyfriend over."

"Never."

"Take much?"

"It wasn't for stealing, just looking. I was actually a good sitter, good with kids, played games, read stories, didn't just stick them in front of the TV. As a kid, though, I think I was pretty rotten to sit for. I remember once one of my sitters had her boyfriend come over after my parents were gone, and she thought I was asleep. I suppose I didn't know much, but I knew he wasn't supposed to be there, so I snuck out, took his shoes—he had taken them off in the course of things—and hid them in the oven. All sorts of hell broke out later. It was a snowy night, so he couldn't just take off in his socks. They were still searching when my mother and father got home, and when my parents couldn't find them either, they had to wake me up. Years later my father would tell that as one of his funny Ziza stories, but it wasn't so funny at the time. I never had that sitter again."

"Lousy kid."

"You know how it was. Kids don't like their folks going away and leaving them, so they cause mischief."

"I never had a baby-sitter."

"And I never had a pony," she said.

"That doesn't make sense."

"Jokes don't always."

"With a joke you're supposed to be able to say, 'I get it.' " He drained his beer and twisted another from the plastic container. This time Ziza joined him.

"It's just that you sounded so mournful when you said 'I never had one' that I was trying to sound just as deprived."

"My mom taught me to be able to take care of myself," he said, defending his mother. "Anyway, I had an older brother who was sometimes around."

Ziza sensed that they were slipping off her secret agenda. She had promised Nick Story that if he emptied the house, she'd do some scouting around. "So," she said, "if we're baby-sitting this old barn, why don't we get back to snooping the way baby-sitters should. What do you say, shall we hit the Van Schoonhovens' suite next?"

"I'll try to keep my shoes on."

"Just bring the beer," she said.

The Van Schoonhovens' apartment was on the second floor, on the opposite end of the building from the Butlers'. They raced there and paused while Ziza knocked, just to make sure.

"The doors at Smyrna are never locked," Tim intoned— pulling off a recognizable impersonation of Mr. Van Schoonhoven's official addressing-the-staff voice—and then tried to turn the knob.

It was locked. To Ziza's surprise, he pulled out an American Express card and slipped it between the lock and the jamb. The door swung open.

"Never leave home without it," he said, using the same voice.

"You're not a member?"

"It was the Schooner's—expired, of course. He was tossing it out, so I took it. It comes in handy."

They paused at the threshold. The room in front of them was dark except for the faded blur of distant moonlight. "Have you been here before?" she asked.

"Was never asked. No one ever is."

"Let's not let that stop us now," she said and reached in to snap on the ceiling light. It was a larger room than she had expected, filled with more furniture than was sensible: Gothic marble-topped tables, heavy Victorian chairs and sofas, too many mahogany curves and brass finials. On the floor were several layers of Oriental rugs with the designs of buried carpets peeking through the holes in the ones on top. On the walls were dark, oversized portraits of very serious old men. It was not dusty, although at first it seemed as though it should be, but everything about the room proclaimed Ancestors and Inheritance.

"Christ, my mom's trailer has more floor space than this," Tim said. "It looks like the Salvation Army warehouse."

"This must be every bit of Quick family furniture Gwen could get her hands on," Ziza said. She crossed the room and looked into the bedroom beyond. There was a huge bed whose tall, multiarched headboard would have been at home behind the altar of a village church in Tuscany. In a wide but shallow bay window were two identical Morris chairs and two identical brass floor lamps whose faded parchment shades looked as though they might have been decorated years ago by a young Aunt Nan.

"What do we look for?" asked Tim.

"Anything that turns up," Ziza said. "Just open drawers and see if anything catches your attention." She added, hoping it was not necessary, "We're just looking, though. Leave everything where you find it."

"She'll never guess we've been here."

Ziza went into the bathroom and could hear Tim opening and closing drawers at a terrific rate. The medicine cabinet was crowded with prescription bottles from the same Catskill pharmacy. Most of the typed labels gave only the patient's name (more for Mr. Van Schoonhoven than for Mrs.) and instructions (three times a day after meals, daily at bedtime). Ziza looked for ones reading "Disulfiram, half tablet daily before breakfast" and finally found one in—of course—the very back. She wrestled with the childproof top and eventually opened it. Inside, under the cotton wad, was an almost full bottle of small white pills, smaller than aspirins, with a line down the middle. She took a sample, carefully wrapping it in a Kleenex, and put it in her pocket. Oddly enough, although the pharmacy was the same, the patient's name listed was neither Mr. nor Mrs. Van Schoonhoven but a Mrs. G. Jacobsen.

She took a quick look through the rest of the room. With its pastel-blue walls, it looked fresh and new, as though it had been redecorated within the past year. Everything was spotless. A small cabinet was carefully stacked with perfectly folded towels, arranged by size with the darker colors on the bottom, the lighter on top. A toothpaste tube, cap on, lay on the sink. In the toothbrush holder above it there was only one toothbrush, red and well rinsed, with no paste caked into the bristles.

"Want to know something funny?" Tim said, coming through the door. "Most of the drawers are empty. One closet is empty. And all the clothes are Mrs. Van Schoonhoven's. She's already cleaned out everything that belonged to the Schooner. It doesn't even seem to be in boxes anywhere."

On the way out, Ziza ducked into the bay window to see if the book on the marble-topped table between the two Morris chairs was what it seemed to be. And it was. Idris Quick's old history of Smyrna. She turned to the "Well On With The Work" chapter. Gwen Van Schoonhoven had an uncut edition of her father's book.

Tucked inside was a dust-stained photograph of the Camp Smyrna staff, or at least a part of one. It had been cut down to include only two people, a smiling Llewelyn (not a "Say cheese" smile but a real one) and a laughing Gwen who was looking at him and not the camera. But because the group was standing so close together, bits of elbows and shoulders of the people who stood on either side of them were still there, a small woman in white shorts next to Lew (Naomi,

probably; her hand seemed to be on his arm), a beefy, tight
T-shirt next to Gwen. No doubt it was Harry.

"Where to next?" Tim asked.

"How about Melody Horn, since we're in the neighborhood?"

"Why not? Since we're in the neighborhood and she's not."

Her apartment was directly across the hall, and—true to
the Smyrna tradition—it was unlocked. Ziza snapped on the
light.

"Jesus," Tim said. "She's a fuckin' slob." He sounded personally offended.

Ziza did not say anything, but she agreed with him. The
room was a mess. The place seemed to be furnished with
whatever was at hand—more care had gone into outfitting
Tim's cabin, Ziza thought—and every surface was littered
with discarded clothes. Everything about it was smaller than
the Van Schoonhovens' apartment, smaller rooms, smaller
windows. The ceiling even seemed lower, although Ziza knew
that was impossible. The bedroom, except for the litter, was
curiously empty. A double-size futon lay along one wall. On
its left side was a Noguchi floor lamp with a torn paper shade
and a pile of paperbacks. Tom Clancy. Washington Irving's
collected tales (maybe she was reading up on local color,
looking for some tourist angle for Olde Smyrna), the Great
Bear and Highfield annual report, a copy open and facedown
of *Frankenstein* (she had made it to page 28). The clearest
space in the room, almost a center of calm, was one of the
old camp mess-hall tables. It held a Leading Edge computer
and a square red plastic box (for floppy disks, probably) but
no papers. An astonishingly new-looking secretarial chair was
aligned directly in front of the keyboard.

"I don't think there are any drawers here to check out,"
Tim said, carefully moving a pile of silky beige underwear
with his foot.

"Do you have any idea how to see what might be in that
computer?"

Tim looked around as though searching for the person Ziza was talking to. "Me?"

"We probably couldn't have understood it anyway," Ziza said.

She looked into the bathroom. Unlike the Van Schoonhovens', it had not been remodeled in years. There was no medicine cabinet, only a huge white-framed mirror hanging over the sink. Next to it a pine washstand held a selection of shampoos and conditioners that would have been the pride of any drugstore north of Manhattan. There was also a tray of birth-control pills, not the method Ziza would have expected from Melody. No other medicine of any kind was in sight.

"Nothing in the closet but dresses and shoes," Tim said. "Lots of them."

Ziza looked anyway. There were a lot of them, all right. On the top shelf, under a pile of unopened packages of pantyhose, was something, a picture, probably, or a record album, wrapped in brown paper. She slipped it out and carefully unstuck the masking tape. It was one of the collages, Mansion House, full of detail, every brick accounted for. It was smaller than most of the "recently discovered" works, showing the old house in fall, when the leaves were at their most colorful, and, of course, at sunset. In front of the house, and standing all out of proportion to it, was a smiling young man in khaki shorts. He was wearing heavy boots and a white T-shirt emblazoned with a golden crown.

"One of yours?" Ziza asked.

"No, of course not," he said. Then he looked again, more carefully. "No, it's not. That's a real one," he said, his voice full of admiration. "A beauty, isn't it?"

"One of the best. I wonder why it isn't with the others downstairs?" she said.

"It's the only one I've ever seen with a person in it," he said.

"Maybe it's Melody Horn's ace in the hole," she said. She

didn't say that out of the two apartments they had looked into so far they had uncovered two pictures of poor Llewelyn Quick.

"I'm really getting into this," Tim said as Ziza carefully rewrapped the picture and replaced it on the shelf. "Who's next?"

"How about Hagadorn Mills? He's someone we tend to forget about."

To get back to the other side of the building, where his room was, they cut through the open balcony above the Meeting Room.

"You know what was great about the old Schooner's memorial service?" Tim said. "Seeing this place full of people. And not just the usual people."

"You're getting tired of the usual people?"

"Wouldn't you? I've been thinking of maybe going to Alaska. That's where you can make money. Or Australia, if there was some way to get there."

"Pioneering?"

"Something like that."

"Running?"

"From what?"

Mills's door was locked, but Tim put his plastic to work again and they were soon inside. It was a small room, almost identical to the one Aunt Nan had. A single bed meticulously made up with tight military corners stood along one wall. A floor lamp had been pulled up next to the pillow. On an end table within reach were a clock radio and a well-thumbed copy of *Silver Trumpets in the Valley*, by Hagadorn Mills. Stuck to the jacket was a huge gold-foil star proclaiming WINNER OF THE PULITZER PRIZE FOR HISTORY. Some of the star's points had been worn off. Or perhaps picked away by the fingers of a restless reader.

"Our friend Andy has an interesting way of putting himself to sleep," Ziza said.

There was no sign anywhere of the research Mills was doing

on Smyrna. All that, Ziza supposed, was down in the Children's House. He was obviously a man who did not bring his work home with him.

"This place is one big zip," Tim said. The closet contained three lightweight suits, one tan, one dark blue, one herringbone. There were also a tweed jacket, twelve—Tim counted them—identical blue button-down oxford cloth shirts, all hanging in the same direction, and two pairs of sharply pressed khaki pants. Arranged under the suits were three pairs of shoes (two of them with shoe trees inside) and a brand-new pair of rubber fisherman's boots. A bamboo fly rod was tucked into the back corner. The shelf held a rubberized rain hat and a plastic bait box. Tim looked inside. There were a half dozen flies, all still sealed in plastic bags, and an unopened envelope of filament leaders.

Ziza took a quick look. "It seems Andy has a new hobby that he hasn't quite gotten around to taking up," she said.

"It's all crap," Tim said, "some sporting-goods store's idea of what to pawn off on an idiot. This guy is even more pathetic than I thought."

The desktop was bare, the drawer all but empty. Some stationery—thick and expensive-looking—was piled on one side. There were several books of twenty-five-cent stamps (Jack London commemoratives), all full. No correspondence addressed to Mills. In the other corner was a thin packet of bank statements held together by a rubber band and a butterfly paper clip full of check receipt stubs. Most of them were from Olde Smyrna Community, Mills's monthly salary, and he was pulling down far more than Ziza would have guessed. Toward the bottom—they were arranged in strict chronological order, of course, the oldest stubs appearing first—intermixed with the Smyrna receipts were ones marked Consultation Fee from Great Bear and Highfield. The most recent one was dated two weeks ago. Without thinking, she whistled soundlessly.

"Find something?" Tim asked, looking up with obvious disgust from the unused reel mounted on the pristine bamboo rod.

"More crap," Ziza said. "Just crap." Each receipt stub, and there were five of them, had been for $2,500. "We should probably be moving on."

She took a quick look at the bank statements, which were about as revealing as the rest of the room. Each month he wrote the same number of checks: one for cash to get him though the month, a mortgage payment to a bank in Middletown, Connecticut, for his house near the Wesleyan campus, some utility bills. On the deposit side, the balance steadily built up.

Tim stuck the rod back into the closet (Ziza hoped he had put it in the right corner), and she arranged the drawer as it had been. They were out in the hallway and she had just finished checking the door to make sure it had locked behind them, when Mills came around the corner.

Ziza knew she was armed with dangerous new knowledge, but suddenly she felt like a guilty Halloween trick-or-treater confronting a responsible adult.

"Hi, kids," Mills said brightly, as though it were the first day of class, but he looked puzzled. There was no reason for them to be on his corridor.

"Andy," Tim said, making a vague gesture toward his brow, something between a salute and the tugging of a forelock.

"Professor Mills," Ziza said. The danger, she thought, was not that Mills would guess where they had been but that Tim would start giggling. She knew this was serious business, that they weren't trick-or-treaters, but what about Tim? "The movie's over so soon?"

"We were misinformed," he said. "It wasn't a horror triple feature at all but a *Rocky* marathon, all of them, one after the other. So we just had a pizza and came back." He looked as though he expected Ziza to say what she was up to.

She did not oblige him. "I hope," she said, not daring to look at Tim, "you found the only place in town with decent pizza, Tony's."

"I'm very much afraid we didn't," he said, with rising indignation. "Tomato paste straight from the can with melted Velveeta cheese over nearly raw dough with burned edges."

"They're *all* named Tony's," Tim said. "Tony's, Original Tony's, Unique Tony's." Then he burst out laughing. "They're cousins. Tony, Tony and Tony. They hate each other."

She couldn't help it, murder or not, she started laughing, too. Mills looked confused. Ziza herself felt confused; maybe it was simply a reaction to having almost been caught. Then, to show that he was a good sport, Hagadorn Mills squeezed out a chuckle or two and walked around them toward his room.

The click of the automatic lock as the door closed suddenly sobered them. Ziza imagined Mills seeing what they had just seen. The bed, the desk, the closet door. Had Tim closed it all the way? Or had Mills himself left it ajar? Would he open his drawer? This was not a joke. They were not pranksters on the trail of a good time. They were tracking down a killer.

"I suppose checking out Sherman Benedikt's room is now out of the question," Tim said as they headed down the hall and turned the corner toward the stairs.

"Let's duck into the Butlers' for a minute," she said.

"I don't know. It's getting late. . . ."

"Just for a minute."

"You go in if you want to," Tim said. "I'll watch the door, play chickie-the-cops in case they turn up."

Since the Butlers' room was in the front of the house, Ziza hesitated before turning on the light. Anyone turning into the driveway could see it. But what the hell, she thought, and threw the switch. She knew there would be nothing to find there. The air had that oddly sweet, vaguely dusty smell she associated with old people's homes, with kisses on soft, deeply wrinkled cheeks. She had looked over everything in plain sight when she had been in the room before.

This time she looked in the bureau drawers and the closet. Socks, shirts, underwear. Except for the top one, each drawer was divided down the middle by a cardboard partition. The top drawer held a dozen shiny black Smyrna banks. The closet turned out to be surprisingly large, a walk-in almost the size of a small room. The light was on a pull cord made from an old boondoggle lanyard, something from the camp craft shop. There were few clothes on the one long pipe rack. Most of the space was taken up with old, battered footlockers, stacked like children's coffins in one of those standard newspaper photographs of the aftermath of a giant flood or an earthquake.

The trunks were not locked. Ziza opened one on the top. It seemed to be full of junk, odds and ends. The next one was the same, and the next. There were mismatched socks by the dozen, boys' T-shirts (some of them with sewn-in name tags), half a pair of swim flippers, a single sneaker, another, another. There were old paperback books, a Howard Pease sea adventure, a Bill Stern anthology of baseball anecdotes had been left out in the rain, a copy of *I the Jury* with a lot of pages torn out. There were plastic soap containers still holding soap, toothpaste-smeared toothbrush holders, dented canteens, baseball caps whose bills had been folded so they could fit into back pockets, sunglasses, torn bathing suits, brand-new bathing suits, shower clogs, unfinished homemade leather wallets and key cases, combs with missing teeth. There was no order to the jumble in each footlocker, no effort to fold anything or to keep the clothes separate from the other articles.

Then Ziza noticed the dates. Each trunk had a strip of masking tape on top with a date written on it: 1955, 1956, 1957 . . . The leftover trash of each summer was what it looked like. The lost-and-founds, she thought. Every year, at the end of the summer, Frank and Charley had packed up what was left behind in the lost-and-found and saved it. Were they waiting for the owners to come back and claim it? Unlikely. Could they not bear to throw away anything from the camp? Yes, she thought, they had not even been able to see a body buried.

"Anything?" Tim asked when she came back out to the hallway.

"What you would expect," she said, "maybe a little more."

"Funny old guys," he said.

"Yes." She felt very tired. She had not enough answers, but she felt as though she knew more than she had ever wanted to.

"We should stop pushing our luck," Tim said. "Let's go up to your place."

"No," she said. "Let's go in here for a minute." She pushed open the door to Aunt Nan's room. Naomi was still staying there. She walked through it without turning on the light and went into the small anteroom where Tim had left Llewelyn's bones, where she had found them. She turned on the light. All the pictures looked down on them, all that captured sunlight from so long ago. "Sit," she said, motioning toward the cot. They both sat.

She held her breath a moment and dared herself to say what she had to say, knowing that once she said it the fun would be over, afraid of what might happen next. "I think," she said, "we both know how Mr. Van Schoonhoven died."

23

He did not say anything. He did not even look at her. The only sign that he had heard what she said was that he began to fold in on himself. He clutched his left bicep with his right hand and curled his left ankle behind his right heel, and then he bent over at the waist as though he had a serious stomachache. These must, Ziza thought, be very like the contortions Mr. Van Schoonhoven went through before he died.

Tim held himself like that a moment and then sprang back into shape and beyond, stretching his arms back as far as they could go and shooting his legs forward, a parody of someone waking up, eager to face a new day. He looked at her, smiled and said, "You, maybe. Maybe you know how the old Schooner got it, but you better spell it out for me."

She waited for a change of expression. There was none, just the blank, almost happy look of someone expecting a clever punch line.

"Stop it, Tim. Just stop it."

His eyes widened. The smile remained the same, Tommy on the old TV show eagerly waiting for Mr. Wizard to explain what the scientific experiment proved.

"For Christ's sake, Tim, you killed that man. Your old pal. He came by your place as usual and had his beers, and you slipped in a couple of pills. It couldn't have been hard. 'Another brewskie, Mr. Van S.?' Then you pop the top and drop in the Antabuse and keep up the snappy patter until he's rolling on the floor."

"Me? *Me!*" The smile was gone.

"What I can't understand is how, once the heart attack began, how you could have just sat there and watched him die. The plan must have sounded like a neat trick. The fatal glass of beer, right? But when the dying began, it must have turned real. The joke was over. Someone you knew was gasping for breath. Maybe even asking for help. And you just watched?"

He ran his hand slowly along the inseam of his right thigh, so slowly and carefully he might have been checking for broken threads. He began to reach out toward Ziza but stopped himself and let his hand fall. It lay, half-open, unclenched between them, as though inviting her to pick it up.

She ignored the hand, or pretended to. "You were at the bottom of the stairs in the Gnomes' House. You heard me up there and you waited me out. I told Nick Story I watched from the woods to see who left after I did."

"But you didn't."

She held her breath.

"You ran home," he said.

"Yes," she said, exhaling. It was all over. "You were watching from the window."

"And you saw me there?" The sound he made was more of a cough than a laugh. "Forget about it."

"You were there."

"Proof, little lady, proof."

"Helpful Tim, always there when you need him. Move some bones, there's Tim. Need to force a woman's car off the road, shake her up a bit, there's Tim. I'm guessing, but that was you, wasn't it? Need to search someone's room in a real obvious way so she'll know it's been searched? Tim again. Need a bit of old-time art forgery? Tim's your man. Need to do in an old guy with a weak ticker . . ."

"That sounds like proof to you? You better get back to school."

"Who seems to have been the last person to see Mr. Van Schoonhoven alive? You, when he dropped by for his afternoon beer. You've admitted that. Who was in the right place at the right time to get the job done? You. Who, of all the possible killers, had the strength to get him into that cellar? You. Who had access to Antabuse? You, a prescription made out to your mother."

"And motive, how about that? From where I sit I'm just about the only person around here who didn't have a reason to want the old guy dead. You said so yourself, he was my meal ticket."

"The motive was someone else's. You were just the murder weapon."

"Tell me about it." This time the laugh sounded almost real.

"What I can't get over," Ziza said, getting back to what she thought was Tim's weak spot, "is the thought of him gasping for breath and you just watching. He was your friend. You wouldn't do that with a dog."

"I'd put a dog out of its misery."

"Of course you would."

"If he had been in misery, the dog." His outstretched hand clenched into a fist. "A friend? I guess. You know, he once told me that if Smyrna had been run the way it was supposed to in the old days, he could have picked me as the next boss of the place. Some joke. Each boss was supposed to pick out his own heir, but he couldn't be related. That was the way it was supposed to be. But it never was, he said. It was always rigged. He would have been picked as the heir for sure, he said, if Llewelyn hadn't been the old lady artist's son."

"Aunt Nan's?"

"I guess."

"Her son?"

"So he said. He said when the old lady was in her early forties she had this baby, all hushed up, of course, who had to be passed off as someone else's. And the kid later got to be picked as the heir instead of the Schooner, who wasn't related to anyone."

Ziza was stunned. This explained so much, all the pictures Aunt Nan had so carefully arranged on the walls around them, the portrait in Melody's closet.

"Who was the father?"

"A brave pilot killed in the Korean War, if you can believe it. The Schooner didn't."

"He just told you all this out of the blue."

"He'd had a couple of drinks. He almost always had a couple of drinks, and he got talking about the way things were supposed to be."

The hand relaxed again. Ziza waited. "But it wasn't the way you described it, his death. It wasn't like that at all. It was all very fast. He took a drink. He'd had a couple cans by then, since I gave him the stuff. He seemed OK except that he was sweating a lot. Then, boom, he went down. I thought of mouth-to-mouth. I asked myself if I could suck on that old, fat face, and I could have if I had to. I really could. But he went right away. It was like someone punched him or something. He said 'Oh, no' or 'Shit' or something like that, and then he just fell forward and he was dead. No suffering, none of that stuff you were saying. No begging."

"No goodbye?"

"If he had suffered I would have helped."

"Sure?"

"Am I supposed to say, 'Cross my heart and hope to die'?"

"Die? There's no death penalty in New York State."

"So?"

"So you better start thinking about prison."

"You're telling Dick Tracy about all this?" He sounded honestly surprised, even offended.

"Tim, you've killed someone. It's called murder, and I don't think I'm going to have to tell Nick Story anything. He'll get there on his own. He's probably waiting for you up at your cabin right now."

Neither of them spoke for a few minutes. Ziza tried to think of a way of asking the next question, the hard question. Tim moved sideways on the cot so he could get a better look at her.

"You're mad at me," he said. "Redheads can hold grudges."

She opened her mouth to say something, but nothing came out.

"I was at the bottom of the stairs," he said, "but I was so quiet no one could have heard me. We hadn't met yet, you know. I had seen you running, but I don't think you had seen me."

"No."

"I'd brought the Schooner down in a wheelbarrow I used to build the scaffolding behind the mess hall. I put a tarp over him, and that got his face and hair all dirty. So at the Gnomes' House I used water from the sink in the kitchen to clean him up, and then I carried him downstairs, down to where Frank and Charley had sent me to find the bones. I just got to the bottom of the stairs when I heard you walking across the floor. I'm glad you stopped and didn't come down."

"What would you have done?"

"Something stupid."

"Would you?"

"And then we never would have gotten to know each other."

She thought about what he was trying to say. "Was he heavy, getting him down the stairs?" For the first time since they'd sat down on the cot, she looked at him.

"Naw, not for me, for a big guy he seemed amazingly light. I've lifted heavier. I guess he was all hot air."

"It must have been kind of scary down there, in the dark with a dead body, alone and all."

"I hadn't begun to think of him as dead yet."

"You cleaned him up. That was nice. I remember hearing the water dripping in the sink when I came into the house."

"I was more afraid of you. I didn't know who was up there."

How calm they were, Ziza thought, how matter-of-fact. How perfectly normal this conversation about murder seemed, this conversation with a murderer.

"You called me the murder weapon," Tim said, sounding suddenly indignant, as though the meaning of what she said had just registered.

"Yes," she said. She would ask the next question by simply asking it, friend talking calmly and normally to friend. "Who sent you to kill Mr. Van Schoonhoven? Who told you what to do?" She kept her eyes on him.

"I'm not getting into that," he said.

"You'll have to."

"No," he said. He turned away from her, folded his arms across his chest and slid back on the cot so that his head rested against the wainscoting. Directly above him was a dusty photograph of Llewelyn urging a group of nervous campers up a steep rock outcropping.

"While I was waiting for you to leave I found more of poor Llewelyn's bones"—his voice sounded almost drowsy—"little ones I must have missed the last time around. I put them in an old coffee can on the shelf and left them there. Forgot them, I guess. Do you think Story thought that was a clue? Like the game? Mr. Black in the cellar with a can of bones?"

"The time's coming when you're going to have to tell someone."

"I don't see why."

They were still sitting like that, not speaking, when the others returned from Catskill: Ziza on the edge of the cot, both feet on the floor, eyes steadily focused on some spot closer than the far wall, Tim slumped, his eyes closed in what looked like belligerent sleep.

She heard them coming up the stairs. Frank hopped along noisily on his one good leg, assisted by Naomi, who seemed to think it made things easier if she called out encouragingly, step by step, how far he had to go to reach the top. "Eight steps more," Ziza could hear her saying. "Now it's only seven." Someone else, Charley probably, dragged the empty wheelchair, bouncing it on every tread.

Her first reaction was to hide, but of course she had nothing to hide from. Tim remained motionless. Maybe he really was asleep, an escape right out of the psych textbooks. Naomi found them when she came into her room. "Well, look who's here," she called out, although Tim was the one she seemed to be talking to. Charley rolled Frank into the room.

"My, my," Frank said.

"I think Nick Story just drove up to your cabin looking for you," Charley said, ignoring Ziza.

Tim sat up, rubbed his eyes with the palms of his hands and smiled. "Who brought the beer?"

"We've been having a talk," Ziza said.

"She convinced me that I'm the one who offed the Schooner," Tim said, "but she can't seem to tell me why."

"Good Lord," Frank said, "you better start thinking about what you're saying."

Naomi carried in two chairs from Aunt Nan's bedroom, gave one to Charley and sat down. "We should get Gwen Van Schoonhoven up here," she said.

"She seemed distinctly out of sorts on the ride back," Charley said.

"Something Naomi said to her, was my impression," Frank said.

"Went to her room without saying boo," Charley said.

"Didn't even thank Nick Story for the ride," Frank said.

"She put a quarter in the parking meter, though, paid for the parking," Charley said.

"Really?" Frank said. "That was nice of her. Although that was before Naomi said whatever she said to rile her."

"Policemen probably don't have to pay parking tickets anyway," Charley said.

Naomi interrupted. "You've admitted it, Tim?"

"Why not?" Tim said.

"But you were only the helper," Naomi said. "We've got to get Gwen in on this. Ziza, you go find her."

"I'll go," Tim said.

Everyone, even Frank and Charley, said, "No."

There was a commotion out in the hall, and Gwen Van Schoonhoven burst through the darkened bedroom into the light.

"Speak of the devil," Naomi said.

"They're in here," Gwen shouted toward the hall, "the whole bunch of them." Melody Horn trailed along behind her, followed by Hagadorn Mills and—after a long pause— Sherman Benedikt, who, as usual, carried his metal clipboard.

"Who's been going through our rooms?" Gwen asked. Before anyone could answer, she said, "As a plot it's pretty clear. We get lured to that dumb-ass meeting, and then the Reverend Ziza and her flunky go to work back here."

"Look," said Ziza.

"No, you look at this," Gwen said. She pulled a plastic prescription container from her pocket. "Do I look like a Mrs. G. Jacobsen? What was this doing in my medicine cabinet? Who planted it there?"

"Nice try," Naomi said. Her voice was flat, toneless and not the least bit angry. "But it's not going to fool anyone. If that bottle's there, it's because you left it there. Everybody knows you keep your place locked up tight as a drum."

"Andy," Gwen said, prompting her next witness.

He produced a bent-in-half can of Bud. "It was in my wastebasket."

It was very hard for Ziza not to look at Tim. The kid, she thought, had a knack for forgetting things.

"We need more chairs," Melody Horn said. "Sherman, see what you can rustle up." She sat down between Tim and Ziza, made an elaborate show of looking at both of them and, with a flick of her head, tossed her hair into place. "Our rooms *were* searched. Mine. Mrs. Van Schoonhoven's. Andy's. Maybe more. Andy noticed it first. He's not a Bud kind of guy."

"He came to me, and I sounded the alarm," Mrs. Van Schoonhoven said, staring at Tim until he got up and gave her his place.

"So let's put it on the line," Melody said. "Was it you guys or Nick Story's boys?"

"Don't look at me," said Tim, who was now sitting on the floor, his legs splayed out into the center of the tiny room. "Mrs. Van S. says I'm just a flunky."

"It was us," Ziza said, "and we learned a lot."

"The Reverend Nancy Drew, and what was the name of that dimwit boyfriend of hers?" asked Hagadorn Mills, flipping the beer can to Tim, who caught it one-handed.

"You'll have to check your own collection," Ziza said. "I didn't know she had a boyfriend."

Sherman Benedikt came back with two old dining-room chairs from the Butlers' room. Without thinking about it, the group was now sitting in a circle, with Tim still on the floor.

"Just like one of Young Father Quick's Conscience Circles," Charley said.

"He always had the answers," Frank said.

"Whether you wanted them or not," Charley said.

"I want to hear what Ziza learned snooping around," Melody said.

"Well, I learned that you've salted away what may well be Aunt Nan's most valuable picture. I learned that Mrs. Van Schoonhoven has what seems to be a supply of Antabuse...."

"Because you planted it there," Gwen said.

"And I learned, most surprising of all, that Andy, here, was on the Great Bear and Highfield payroll."

"I knew it!" Melody said, bursting out laughing. "I just knew it. Cloak-and-dagger right here in River City. Sherman," she said with mock seriousness, "you fucked up good and went and hired us a blue-ribbon spy. You should have checked his résumé better. He must have gone to Cambridge like all those fancy British spies."

"I was *not* on the payroll," Mills said. He held his head high. "I was a consultant, and I gave them nothing of value."

"That's something to be proud of, Andy," Melody said. "Of course you didn't give them anything of value. You didn't know anything of value. All you did was muddy up their cash flow. I love it. Love it. Remember, I said we were going to have fun."

Mills ignored her good humor. "And why, may I ask, have you stolen a valuable piece—if Miss Todd is to be believed—of Smyrna's artistic heritage?"

"Wrapped in brown paper and put on a top shelf isn't stolen, old boy. It's strategy. When the art crowd down in Manhattan decides Aunt Nan is the new Grandma Moses, we produce the zinger."

"I would like to get back to Gwen," Naomi said, "and those pills Ziza found."

"I'll just bet you would," Gwen said. "I'll just bet you're the brains behind this whole thing."

"No," Ziza said, "that wouldn't make much sense at all. What reason would Naomi have to kill Mr. Van Schoonhoven? She has control of the stock. The whole show here at Smyrna is as good as hers anytime she wants it."

"I'm sick of stock talk," Charley said.

"So am I," Ziza said. "I don't think stock and money have anything to do with this. It's all a matter of memory and the past."

All of them looked at her. More of them than she expected looked frightened. The crowded room, the unnatural silence, three on a bed, Tim on the floor, the snapshots on the wall, the single window with its crooked shade, the dusty institutional smell—it all seemed to Ziza like a bizarre college dormitory bull session.

"All around us in this room are pictures of Llewelyn

Quick," she said. "You can't look anywhere without seeing him. A lot of people loved Llewelyn. Some of them are here. At least one person hated Harry Van Schoonhoven, and he's dead. It's all connected, isn't it?"

"I was called back here," Naomi said, "because some people knew his bones were going to be discovered." She looked over at the Butler boys. "I don't think they expected me to walk into a murder. I think that's where Gwen upset the applecart."

"After all these years?" Ziza asked.

"That's when things happen," Naomi said.

"I am a real Quick," Gwen Van Schoonhoven said. "Old Father Quick was my grandfather. My *real* grandfather. It's all in my father's book, although that was the sort of thing the community wanted hushed up. My father was Young Father's real brother, his only brother, and Aunt Nan was his baby sister. He never became a community leader because he told the truth about his father and his brother. I know my role in this community. I know who I am. I knew what I was getting into when I married Harry Van Schoonhoven years ago. And at this stage of the game I don't take up murder." Each time she used the word "I" or "my," it was as if she were striking a hammer.

"Did Mr. Van Schoonhoven know who Llewelyn's father was?" Ziza asked. "In those long talks, Tim, after all those beers, did he tell you, swearing you to silence, never to tell a soul?"

"I'm not getting into this," Tim said.

"Or maybe," Ziza said, "he told it like a joke, a good locker-room story. 'Who do you think poor Llewelyn's mother really was, Timmy? And if you think that's funny, you'll never believe the father.' Did it go something like that, Tim?"

"I'm not," he said. "I'm not getting into this."

"You're in it," Ziza said. "We all are."

"What about the story of the jet pilot shot down over Korea

and the woman who wasn't cut out for life in the community?" Naomi asked. "That's who Lew believed were his parents."

"Maybe," Gwen said, "that's what he told you, dear."

"You knew?" Naomi asked.

"I knew his mother was Aunt Nan," Gwen said, "and so did Llewelyn."

"No," said Frank Butler, "you're talking smut now."

"Tim," Ziza asked, "did you go to someone and tell him what Mr. Van Schoonhoven told you?"

Tim stared straight ahead.

"Or tell her?" Naomi asked. "I know it was Gwen who got you to force me off the road and do other little chores such as searching Ziza's room. Maybe you told her."

"Well," Melody Horn said, "I hope you're taking notes on all this, Sherman. Andy can use it to fill in the gaps in his history and maybe sell off a few lines to Great Bear as well."

"This is not a joke," Frank said.

"I think," Ziza said, "that Tim went to Charley and told him what Mr. Van Schoonhoven said about Charley being Llewelyn's father. That's when the plan began."

"No," Frank said, "no, it wasn't like that at all."

"Not at all," said Charley.

"It was to protect the community," Frank said.

"No, Frank," said Charley.

"Yes, Charley. We had been Guardians for Naomi, and now it was time to weed things out, prune the garden."

"No, Frank, don't."

"Charley, did Mr. Van Schoonhoven threaten to tell Frank?" Ziza asked.

"It was nothing like that," Frank said. He was becoming frantic. "No smut. No dirty gossip. Harry had started some sort of secret dealings."

"No secret about that now," Charley said quietly, almost comfortingly.

"And we thought he was up to something funny with the community," Frank said.

"That's why we sent for Naomi. So she could claim her stock."

"But then we had to do more," Frank said. "He was going to ruin everything. He even made cheap remarks about the Smyrna banks, cheap lies."

Ziza was going to ask again about the real reason Charley Butler wanted to see Harry Van Schoonhoven dead, about threats to tell Frank the whole story, but she kept quiet and watched Charley calm his brother's fears.

"We knew where Harry was vulnerable," Charley said.

"He was a drinker."

"Worse than we ever were."

"Or as bad."

"We knew that was the way to get to him."

"And at an AA meeting, someone—"

"It was Paul."

"Someone who should be kept nameless talked about how he once almost killed himself trying to sneak brandies while taking Antabuse."

"Triggered his heart condition."

"We've never ourselves needed crutches to keep ourselves dry."

"Not that we criticize anyone else's way. But that rang a bell with us, the Antabuse heart attack."

"Tim's mother once tried Antabuse. She had been to a few meetings."

"The crutch didn't work for her. She had been to a few meetings but never really got with the program."

"So we asked Tim for help."

"He was our supplier."

"His mother's medicine chest."

"So we gave it a try."

"Tim was a big help."

"Tim got the pills from her medicine chest, and later got rid of them for us. He took care of everything."

They had hurried to the end, playing their sentences back

and forth as always, Charley rushing as though he thought by speeding Frank along they could avoid ever talking about Ziza's terrible suggestion.

"Yes, Tim was a wonderful help," Frank said. "We never could have done it without him. Correct, Charley?"

"Correct, Frank."

In the silence that followed, Frank looked first at his brother and then at Tim as though trying to catch the thoughts they were exchanging.

No one had noticed Nick Story come in through Aunt Nan's still-darkened bedroom. When he said, "Hi," most of them jumped. When he said, "I suppose you wonder why I called you together tonight," no one laughed. When he said, "I've come for three people," Tim stood up. He was still holding the crumpled beer can. Charley took the back of Frank's wheelchair. Frank turned to look at him as though he were going to ask a question, but he did not. There was nothing his brother could tell him that he wanted to hear.

"Tim," Naomi said, "remember when you said you would do me a favor one day?" He nodded. He kept from looking at Ziza. "Do it now." He waited. "Tell me why."

"They said they needed me."

Naomi waited for more.

Ziza prayed for something worth saying but came up with nothing.

"It was the best offer I had," Tim said.

24

Ziza was coming back from her last run at Smyrna when she saw Naomi in the Dutch Reformed cemetery. It was a cool, clear morning, more October than May, as though the year had skipped from spring to fall, not bothering with summer.

"They told me I could claim Lew's remains—that's what they called them—any time I want them," Naomi said. "I'll have them cremated, I suppose, and scatter the ashes over the creek."

"Like his mother," Ziza said.

"I had always somehow imagined that we would both be buried here, you know. But the more I see these terrible angels, the less funny they seem. I think maybe you have to be young and in love to believe 'Think on Death' is a great hoot."

"He never told you about Aunt Nan?"

"He never didn't tell me, never actually lied about her. He was always closer to her than to any of the other old people. She played the piano at our wedding and made quite a show of it. Lew thought that was very funny. He never talked about having a mother. Maybe he didn't even know."

"And a father."

"I think he believed that jet pilot story. Or at least wanted to. He certainly never said anything special about Charley. Like everyone else he never said the name Charley without linking him up with Frank. Frank and Charley. Charley and Frank. The Butler boys."

"And Frank never knew."

"Never wanted to believe it, I suppose. Still doesn't."

"I see it as one wild and silly night."

"Silly? No, romantic, more romantic than either of them could ever have imagined."

"Charley must have been in his early twenties, Aunt Nan in her forties."

"He was still drinking then," Naomi said.

"If there had been a long romance, people would have noticed."

"We'll never know."

"And that story of Old Father taking her doll away," Ziza said. "I suppose when she told that she was thinking of more than a doll."

They walked through the cemetery as they talked. Every now and then Naomi would reach down and pull especially tall weeds from the front of the gravestones.

"The thing about mysteries," Naomi said, "is that they are never really solved. It's all a matter of memory and forget-fulness and secrets that best stay that way. That's why detectives in novels are such fools. They actually seem to think they know what happened. There are always the bits and pieces we can never really know."

About what happened, Ziza thought, about all that really happened the night Llewelyn died. About Gwen's real rela-tionship with Llewelyn, who, after all, was some kind of a cousin. About what Naomi really thought about Harry Van Schoonhoven. About, come to think of it, what she really thought about Tim.

"You said goodbye to Tim?" Naomi asked.

"We did some very solemn waving. Before he got into the police car he shouted something about sending me a postcard. Maybe I can visit him sometime. I'm going back to Rochester, to write my paper, find a job with a church, get on with my life. You're staying here."

"I think Melody Horn and I can make quite a go of this place."

"Without Gwen Van Schoonhoven?"

"The last of the genuine Quicks? We'll never see the last of her. I could have sworn she killed her husband, would have sworn on a stack of Bibles. But, God knows, there will always be room for her here. There's that damn Smyrna tradition, after all."

They were standing in front of an especially well-preserved stone. The angel's hateful eyes burned out at them. Her hair was as wild as Medusa's. Her mouth was frozen into a terrible smirk. The carving on the inscription was sharp and deep.

"That's actually an absurd thing to put on a gravestone," Ziza said. "There's no way you can think on death. Thinking has nothing to do with it."

"No," Naomi said, reaching out and tweaking the angel's nose. "Lew goes into the creek. But I'll scatter him below the Falls. No one should have to go over that thing twice."

AUTHOR'S NOTE

There is a Greene County, and there is a Kaaterskill Creek, with its dozens of waterfalls stepping from the northern Catskills down toward the Hudson River. There is no Smyrna Falls, and the Smyrna Community is, of course, fictitious. Although some aspects of its history and folklore may seem similar to some actual nineteenth-century American utopias, it is not based on any particular community. Most of Young Father Quick's theories are strictly his own. While over the years several children's summer camps have come and gone along the banks of the Kaaterskill, none of them should be confused with Camp Smyrna.

FOR THE BEST IN PAPERBACKS, LOOK FOR THE

In every corner of the world, on every subject under the sun, Penguin represents quality and variety—the very best in publishing today.

For complete information about books available from Penguin—including Pelicans, Puffins, Peregrines, and Penguin Classics—and how to order them, write to us at the appropriate address below. Please note that for copyright reasons the selection of books varies from country to country.

In the United Kingdom: For a complete list of books available from Penguin in the U.K., please write to *Dept E.P., Penguin Books Ltd, Harmondsworth, Middlesex, UB7 0DA.*

In the United States: For a complete list of books available from Penguin in the U.S., please write to *Dept BA, Penguin*, Box 120, Bergenfield, New Jersey 07621-0120.

In Canada: For a complete list of books available from Penguin in Canada, please write to *Penguin Books Canada Ltd, 10 Alcorn Avenue, Suite 300, Toronto, Ontario, Canada M4V 3B2.*

In Australia: For a complete list of books available from Penguin in Australia, please write to the *Marketing Department, Penguin Books Ltd, P.O. Box 257, Ringwood, Victoria 3134.*

In New Zealand: For a complete list of books available from Penguin in New Zealand, please write to the *Marketing Department, Penguin Books (NZ) Ltd, Private Bag, Takapuna, Auckland 9.*

In India: For a complete list of books available from Penguin, please write to *Penguin Overseas Ltd, 706 Eros Apartments, 56 Nehru Place, New Delhi, 110019.*

In Holland: For a complete list of books available from Penguin in Holland, please write to *Penguin Books Nederland B.V., Postbus 195, NL-1380AD Weesp, Netherlands.*

In Germany: For a complete list of books available from Penguin, please write to *Penguin Books Ltd, Friedrichstrasse 10-12, D-6000 Frankfurt Main I, Federal Republic of Germany.*

In Spain: For a complete list of books available from Penguin in Spain, please write to *Longman, Penguin España, Calle San Nicolas 15, E-28013 Madrid, Spain.*

In Japan: For a complete list of books available from Penguin in Japan, please write to *Longman Penguin Japan Co Ltd, Yamaguchi Building, 2-12-9 Kanda Jimbocho, Chiyoda-Ku, Tokyo 101, Japan.*